D0964252

indall, Brian,
elivering Virtue /
015]
3305233938681
a   12/19/16

DELIVERING VIRTUE

Brian Kindall

Delivering Virtue
Copyright © 2015 Brian Kindall
ISBN: 978-0-9909328-6-4
LCCN: 2015914658
Cover Design by Kristin Eames
All Rights Reserved.
Diving Boy Books
McCall, Idaho

For more information visit: www.briankindall.com

DELIVERING VIRTUE

Stainless as the newborn child,
Strays the wanderer through the wild;
Day by day, and year by year,
Must the pilgrim wander there;
Through the mountain's rocky pile,
Through the ocean, through the isle,
Through the sunshine, through the snow,
Still in weariness, and wo;
Pacing still the world's huge round,
Till the mystic Fount is found.

- From SADAK THE WANDERER, by Percy Bysshe Shelley

INDEPENDENCE, MISSOURI - 1854

PART ONE

VIRTUE

FITTINGLY, AND WITH THE suspect irony of a prank fabricated by one of the more mischievous gods on their mountaintop, I first met Virtue after an epic bout of debauchery.

It was morning, although that I did not know. For I was still loitering in my dream, where it was an insufferably hot afternoon. I sat on the bank of a deep muddy river, soaking my feet, watching a tall bearded man in a robe paddle slowly across the current in an Indian canoe. Somewhere, someone was pounding a fist against wood, but otherwise there was no sound besides the sizzle of the sun and the easy lap of water.

The man drew up in his primitive craft. "Shall I take you across?" he asked.

I squinted over the river. There were no trees over there, no cool relief of shade, and nothing much to recommend that yonder shore beyond the one where I already was.

But I have learned that hope dies hard, and curiosity urged me that perhaps there was something pleasant awaiting me on the other side.

"Sure," I told the man. "Just hold on."

But when I brought my feet up out of the water, I was dismayed to discover they were not the two appendages I had expected. Hooves! Cloven and dripping. Like something off a billy goat. There was no way in hell they were ever going to fit properly into my boots. I was stricken with the revelation that no matter where I roamed again, people would discern, from the wobble in my gait, that I was not truly a man.

The fist pounding on wood sound grew ever louder as I stood there on that riverbank beneath the burning sun, pondering my future, while growing accustomed to my new hooves.

Then I heard a voice.

"Rain!" it called, very far away, as if from out of the sky. "Rain, you there? Answer me, Rain."

As I tipped my face to the blue heavens, I inadvertently stirred myself awake, leaving that man waiting for me in his canoe.

As far as I know, he is waiting there still.

"Rain!"

The pounding continued, like some club-headed woodpecker having go at a hollow log. I had a bad taste in my mouth, a bad feeling in my gut, and a grimace in my persona. I was in no shape to enter into the waking world. But at that particular moment, I would have done anything – even something so Herculean as rise up out of bed – to stop that incessant pounding. I stumbled to the door, opening it a crack.

"Yes?" I said, in a voice even more scratched and dry than I expected.

"Rain!"

Distantly, I recognized my go-between, the man who found the tasks that I would then perform. "Cedric Dallon," I said. "How are you?"

"I'm put out, that's how I am."

I could tell by his mien that what he said was true.

"We had an appointment to meet our client this morning. He's been waiting, but I'm sure I don't know for how much longer."

"I thought our meeting was for Tuesday."

"This *is* Tuesday!"

I scratched, and rocked back into the room, as if consulting my calendar. Then I stuck my head back out into the hallway. "So it is," I said. "My apologies, friend. I seem to have misplaced a day."

Dallon turned a color that brought to my mind the line, "My love is a red, red rose..." There was spittle on his mustache.

"Doggone it, Rain! This job is big. And I'm stretched so thin I can't afford to let it go! These people are prepared to pay us more money than you and I have seen in all our other jobs lumped together."

"Well."

"Can you get yourself in shape?"

"Of course. I only need a minute."

I commenced to close the door, but Dallon stopped it with his foot. "Rain," he whispered loudly. "Impress him. You know, in that way you have. Let the man know you speak French and such."

I nodded. "Sure, Dallon." And then I closed the door.

The room was unfamiliar. It smelled like a stable. The curtain was drawn and a blade of sharp white light cut in around its edges. An empty bottle stood upright on the floor in the corner and a woman was curled up asleep beside it. She was naked, as was I, and it did not take Pythagoras to put two and two together in order to calculate the sum of our relationship. It seemed unbecoming of a gentleman to leave her in such an undignified position, and so with no small cumbersome effort I hefted up her fleshy bulk and dropped it onto the bed.

She did not wake.

I pulled back the licorice tendrils of her loosened hair. Someone's little angel, I thought, albeit, after she had taken a dubious turn. She might have been quite pretty, had she not been so god-awful homely. Even in sleep, she wore her difficult existence like a mask, and although I did not recall her face, I was relatively certain that given the proper illumination, and from the proper angle, I might. I found two dollars in my trousers pocket.

"One for ink and paper," I said. "And one for you."

I curled the coin into the girl's fist.

"Well, dear," I said. "I hope we had a fine time."

Then in a fit of romantic delusion, I was compelled to lean over and kiss her cheek. "Happy dreams," I whispered.

She snored quietly while I dressed.

All in all, our farewell had been highly unsatisfactory.

WHEN I CAME INTO the café, I found Dallon sitting with a man whose back was turned. The man wore a black suit of clothes and was strumming the tabletop with long fingers. Even from afar I could see that his knuckles were unusually hairy.

Dallon stood, smiling wildly. "Here we are, Rain." He waved me over. "Here!"

The other man remained seated as I arrived. He did not so much as turn to see. I stepped around to face him, and what a face it was – even hairier than his knuckles, and sour as a green persimmon. It did not take much to infer that he was either a politician, a lunatic, or some member of a start-up cult that deemed such cut of a beard to be a mark of holiness.

I smiled, but it was not easy to do.

Dallon grasped my arm, as if fearing I might bolt. "Mister Thurman," he said, "let me introduce my business partner, Mister Didier Rain."

I offered my hand to the man. "*Enchanté*," I said, and surmised straight away that it was the wrong *pied* on which to start out.

The man just scowled at me, my lonely hand hovering like a cloud without purpose in the air before him. A trickle of sweat dripped down my backbone. I tried again.

"It is a pleasure to meet you, Mister Thurman." I dropped my hand to my side. "May I sit?"

Thurman glared at me a long while, until my smile began to fatigue. I feared the muscles in my countenance were about to spasm when he gave me a nod and opened his great simian paw in a gesture for me to pull up a chair.

Dallon and I sat opposite this man Thurman. He examined my eyes, stirring in me a nausea, and it was all I could do not to look away. Mercifully, a waiter came up just then and asked if there was anything he could get me from the kitchen. I figured the other men had eaten their breakfasts some time earlier, and were already building a hunger for lunch.

"Just bring me a glass of water," I told the waiter. "As tall and cold a one as you can find."

Then Thurman spoke.

"Mister Dallon here has been singing your praises, Mister Rain, whilst listing your many aptitudes, of which, I have learned personally, punctuality is not premier."

I fidgeted in my chair. "Well, I humbly apologize for the confusion on my schedule. It seems my secretary had me down for another day."

Dallon tensed beside me.

Thurman let his gaze drift toward the ceiling. "Will thou darest tarry, oh sinner, for thine own redemption?"

His voice was solemn and deep and I could not tell if he was asking me directly, or rather some shadow he saw floating above my head.

"Mister Thurman is an elder in the church of a new religion," said Dallon. "His people have settled in the Territories, near The City of Rocks."

"Well, that is the beauty of an open country," I said. "It gives us the opportunity to form new beliefs."

"The Church of the Restructured Truth is not new," said Thurman. "It was merely quiet for some centuries, pending the call of Jehovah. We have only been awaiting a leader worthy of receiving its Holy Writ."

Uh huh, I thought. Mormons.

"But make no mistake, Mister Rain. We are not Mormons. At least not Mormons as you might imagine."

"Explain yourself, if you like." (I have learned that men like Thurman generally appreciate an opportunity to bear witness.)

"The prophet Joseph Smith was granted only the first portion of the Almighty's Restored Word. And now, in his martyrdom, Brigham Young has become his successor, as you probably know. He and his people have settled in the land south of us, on the shores of the Great Salt Lake. We hope always to remain in harmony with his tribe, as we are in league on many counts. But *our* prophet, a true leader of pilgrims, was granted further direction from heaven, a more thorough and ancient instruction that goes beyond the simple teachings in The Book of Mormon."

"An epilogue," I offered. "A divine afterthought, so to speak."

Thurman did not appear to appreciate my lay definition for his most sacred text. He clenched his fist into a furry ball that resembled a palsied opossum trying to tunnel up his sleeve. "You are not a believer," he asked, "in any faith?"

A baboon could see that I was sabotaging the interview. And honestly, with my stomach roiling so tempestuously at that moment, it was hard to care. But I thought for Dallon's sake, I should put forth greater effort.

"Do not misunderstand me, Mister Thurman. I mean no disrespect. But let us say that I personally am still gathering information on the subject, in hopes of someday forming an opinion that will serve my soul's salvation."

He smirked knowingly through his whiskers, and said, "Pagan."

I smiled back. "If you say so."

"I suppose it makes no difference in the errand at hand," he said. "Gentiles are often very useful as servants to the righteous."

"Well then, how may I serve you?"

Dallon spoke up. "Mister Thurman's people have asked us to make a delivery to the City of Rocks."

"Do you know the place?" asked Thurman.

"I have seen your promised land on the horizon more than once. It is a true geological anomaly, a natural Jericho. Although I confess to never having ridden through its center, as my deliveries have always taken me by way of routes north, or south."

"And what kind of deliveries do you primarily undertake?"

"Anything," I said. "I have delivered stained-glass windows, a brood mare, porcelain dolls, and even a family Bible that some settlers, in the chaos of their departure, accidentally left behind."

"And what of human cargo?"

"Oh, yes," said Dallon. "Rain here took a lawyer as far as Fort Boise just last season. And the summer before that he escorted a government surveyor to the Divide."

Thurman seemed unimpressed. "I think you will find our shipment to be of a more delicate and precious nature than anything you have delivered thus far, Mister Rain. And as for myself, considering the bloodshot marbling of your eyes, and the reek of drunken indiscretion that seems to emanate from your every pore, I do not consider you fit as the supplier of our needs. As The Prophet so wisely sayeth, Never an ass trust with its tail at both ends."

At that point, with my wits at their lowest ebb, I guessed that the delivery was of blasting powder, or some other such substance of an equally explosive nature. I imagined myself leading a string of donkeys with bombs strapped to their backs. What else could the good citizens of the City of Rocks so desperately need? I was quite prepared to pass on the mission in lieu of being blown to kingdom come. I was quite eager, to be honest, to find a place to lie down. A nastiness was gnawing at my insides, and was seeking a route by which to escape.

"Rain speaks all sorts of languages," said Dallon. My partner always considered that an impressive point in my credentials, and one he readily interjected whenever he sensed the client was losing interest. "Tell him, Rain."

I nodded modestly. "It is true. I have a propensity for foreign tongues, that of the Indians, as well as the Old World Romance languages, with a modicum of Greek besides."

At that point in the interrogation, it was customary for me to recite a bit of Homer or Dante, but it was obvious, by the disinterested manner of Mister Thurman, that such an oration was ill advised.

Thurman stood. "May I confer with you alone, Mister Dallon?"

The two schemers left me for some privacy across the room just as the waiter brought me my glass of water. I thanked him, and stared into the beaker, considering it, and water in general.

There is a certain place I had been in the Sawtooth Mountains – a secret dominion, one could easily imagine, of pixies and nymphs. Water always made me think of it. I had visited it only once, upon completing a delivery to the Territories, and then wandering well off the beaten path. I have traveled many lands, all around this big world, but never was I anywhere that seemed more the stuff of a dream. I felt as though I were moving through a fanciful painting. Those peaks swept up like buttressed cathedrals into the cloud-cluttered sky. The snow-capped summits were peopled with silent white goats – guardians watching down on me as I wandered aimlessly through their labyrinth. After some time, I happened upon a small glade – a narrow band of orange and purple flowers festooning a stream tumbling over boulders into a wide pool. I dropped to my knees and took suck of that sparkling water.

Cold it was!

And pure.

No wine compared.

No kiss.

I drank my fill, and then, happy as a lamb, I stretched beside that burbling brook and fell into restful, oblivious slumber.

I have contemplated that simple experience many times, weighing it against the tawdriness of my typical day, and have concluded that there are few enough times in a life when we are granted such a brush with paradise. Mostly life is hard, and harder still. It is a struggle, an endless thirst which one never seems to slake. But I carry that memory with me like a memento from heaven, a little reminder that it is quite possibly worth my while to carry on. And I have often wondered if, before I die, I will ever again have the opportunity to partake of anything so utterly sublime.

I could hear pieces of what Thurman and Dallon were saying, although it was obvious that I was not meant to. They seemed to be playing some sort of heated parlor game, one in which the first player offers a word, and then the next player tries to come up with another word that is the first word's opposite.

"A Miscreant," said Thurman.

"Cultured," parried Dallon.

"Charlatan."

"Dependable."

"Heathen."

"Poet."

And so on, and so forth.

I was considerably impressed with the breadth of their individual lexicons. They swapped antonyms for what seemed like hours, building a minor plethora of oxymorons, and it did not take much stretch to guess they were each in turn offering their contrasting opinions of my character. I had given up caring who would win the battle.

I took a big swallow of my water. It was warm as piss and tasted, if one ever cared to make the experiment, like licking the underside of a dog.

That was all it took to trigger in me a revulsion, a profound distaste for civilization and its septic waters.

I heaved.

Thurman and Dallon came over to watch.

Now there is perhaps no more compromising position than the one in which a man finds himself on all fours, uncontrollably barfing up, while trying to explain himself in dignified prose. Convulsions make such an endeavor most challenging. All the poison from my recent depravity seemed to be flushing at once, by way of my gullet and nostrils. I fear I made quite a mess of the floor.

When I was finished, I felt greatly improved, although somewhat sheepish. I stood and wiped my mouth on my sleeve.

The waiter had appeared, and was assessing the disaster with sadness.

Dallon stood beside Thurman, not speaking, but revealing what was on his mind by the hopeless slump in his posture.

"Pardon me," I said.

Thurman spoke. "Regrettably," he said to Dallon, "the final decision is not mine to make."

He gestured for me and Dallon to follow him.

I handed my last dollar to the waiter. "For your troubles," I said. But I could tell he did not think it compensation enough for the task that I had left him.

OUTSIDE, THE SWOLLEN BLISTER of the sun washed everything with jaundiced light. It pained my eyes. People were coming and going on foot and in wagons, dodging and zagging, as if they were all savvy to some sort of design in the confusion. Thurman, too, seemed to know right where he was heading. He led Dallon and me through the melee until we came to a big catalpa tree off the main street. The tree was in late bloom, hanging heavy with tired white blossoms and filling the air with its musky perfume. There was a bench in the shade, and upon it sat two women and a man. The man looked to be Thurman's twin – same wrap-around muttonchops, and dressed like a crow – only born about twenty years after his brother. One of the women appeared to be the mother who had endured the arduous and protracted labor of their birth. She was old and wrung like a rag. But the second woman, although she wore the startled expression of a doe about to take a bullet, was young and inordinately pretty. They all stood when we approached. The pretty one hugged a bundle to her chest.

Thurman gestured for Dallon and me to wait just outside the perimeter of the shade. The sun pounded down upon us. Then he went to talk to the trio at the bench.

I could not make out what they were saying. They seemed to be discussing business in a private glossolalia. They kept glancing over at us. Dallon muttered out of the corner of his mouth. "Just keep smiling, Rain. I'm not sure how we managed, after your little show, but I don't think we've lost this hand just yet."

I peered into the sky, hot and pale blue. A few swallows were darting about, snatching little moths on the wing. I wondered what it might be like to fly.

"Mister Rain," called Thurman.

I stepped into the shade with Dallon right behind me. The haggard woman and the other man came forward to meet us, but the pretty girl stayed back.

"This is Brother Benjamin," said Thurman. "He deals with our contracts and legalities."

Dallon and I shook the man's hand and uttered the obligatory niceties.

"And this is Sister Sarah."

The woman had a parched smile, like a bend in a desert river. "Bless thee," she hissed, and squeezed my hand.

"You will follow all parameters of the prophecy," said Thurman, "of which Brother Benjamin will now read, so as both parties might be in undisputed accord."

Benjamin stepped forward and read from an official looking paper.

"Thou shalt bear no arms," he said, "neither for protection, nor for hunting. Trust in the Lord, for He shall afford you food and safe passage.

"Thou shalt eat no meat.

"Neither inebriants nor stimulators are to be consumed." He looked at me, and clarified. "No liquor, coffee, or tobacco, or any variety of other Indian potions you might find on your travels."

I nodded like a good boy, but I still was not clear as to what I was agreeing.

"Thou shalt partake in none of the carnal pleasures." Benjamin blushed through his beard when he said that part. He kept his eyes on the paper. "Such misdeeds shall be punishable by God, and ye shall surely suffer for your transgressions. For he who fraternizes with evil shall surely be subject to it in the end himself."

That was when it occurred to me that maybe I was being asked to transport the pretty girl to the City of Rocks. To say the least, I became intrigued.

"As the instrument for the prophecy, you shall convey the bride, with her virtue intact, to one Prophet Nehi, who will then pay to you, in earthly currency, the balance of thirty thousand dollars."

That, too, caught my attention. An unreasonably large sum. I was used to far less.

Brother Benjamin then put away the paper, and Thurman stepped forward and asked, "Are you clear on the guidelines for the prophecy?"

Dallon nodded eagerly, wiggling like a retriever who is about to be thrown a stick. "We are." He glanced at me. "Rain is."

I might have nodded too. I do not remember. I was looking past Thurman at the pretty girl. I was thinking that my share of that thirty thousand dollars would allow me to get back to the project that had been haunting me for so long.

"There is just one more point," said Thurman.

Behind him, the girl was handing her bundle to the old woman.

"Our young sister has had a vision," said Thurman. "In it, she was vouchsafed an immaculate experience by the Spirit of God. She will now determine if you are the True Deliverer, Mister Rain, or merely an interloper."

He summoned the girl, who then walked forward with her hands held demurely at her sides. She stood before Thurman, listening to his direction. "You must be absolutely positive," he told her.

Something in the way he said that caused me to squirm.

Thurman turned and leveled an accusing finger straight at me. Then, in that holy booming voice, he asked the girl, "Is it he?"

She just stood there for a time, looking me over, while I looked back at her. I will not lie. Even under scrutiny, with all eyes trained upon me, I was unable to help myself. Some animal part raised up inside of me and took me over. In my mind I was imagining what the girl looked like beneath that dowdy Mormon dress. I was already wandering the feminine wilderness of her body, roaming along the slope of her shoulders, through the peaceful valley of her bosom, and down and down the milk white plain of her beautiful belly. And although it may only have been my own narcissistic conjecture, I am almost certain that she was performing a similar appraisal of my own secret person.

Then she stepped close to me. She was somewhat diminutive, and when she tipped back her head, it was as if she were offering me her throat. I looked into her eyes – two cool blue pools into which I suddenly longed to plunge. The girl raised her hand and laid it against my cheek. Her touch was eerily familiar, as if from some half-remembered dream, or some other life I had lived in a sweeter time. Her lips were red and full and damp, even in the heat of that arid midday. Lovely little beads of sweat glistened like dewdrops on her brow.

Finally, she unbuttoned my shirt, opening it so my chest was bare to her breath. It was all I could do to stand. She placed a single finger over my heart, lightly tracing a shape on my skin.

I closed my eyes.

I could not have said accurately which way was up.

I was ready, right there in plain view of everyone, to offer that girl every ounce of my world-weary self. I was most assuredly prepared to sink away to her most ardent and oblivious depths.

"Rain." She whispered my name. "Rain."

WHEN I OPENED MY eyes, the girl was walking away, leaving me in an embarrassing state of undress and near rapture.

The thunder of Thurman's voice shook me from my reverie.

"You have a large raindrop, Mister Rain, tattooed upon your chest."

I peered down awkwardly at my tattoo, trying to focus. "Yes," I said. "I do."

"What does it mean?"

I tried to remember. It was not something I thought about most of the time. "Oh," I said. "My mother had it put there when I was a child, as a mark of birthright, so that I might someday receive my legacy without question of who I am."

Thurman nodded. Then he turned to the girl who stood beside him. I heard him say, "Are you certain?"

The girl gazed back at me over her shoulder. Those translucent blue eyes. Then she nodded.

"The raindrop," said Thurman, "is the final proof of the prophecy. It seems your birthright, Mister Rain, is more miracle than you might have expected."

I bobbed my head. "Well," I said, "some people would not recognize a miracle if she were to step right up and kiss them." It was, of course, an imprudent thing to say, and I regretted it directly.

After shooting me through with one last disapproving look, Thurman led Dallon and Benjamin to the side to fill out paperwork. I buttoned up my shirt and put my disheveled and shaken self back together. I stole a glance at the girl, but even after our intimate interaction, she did not return my attention. She seemed done with me. I know it sounds puerile, but I felt slighted somehow, jilted, as if I had been used up and cast-off all in one swoop.

No matter, I told myself, we will get to know each other over the long course of our journey.

Old Sarah and the girl (I still had no name by which to call her) were fussing over the bundle, and that is when it occurred to me that their actions were somewhat peculiar. The old lady gently bounced the package a couple of times, rocking it back and forth. And then, weirdly, the girl bent into the bundle with her face, kissing whatever was inside. She had tears on her cheeks. I had seen religious rites where a believer laid her lips upon a relic, or talisman. Such devotions often move the devout to a passion. And so I assumed perhaps that that was what I was witnessing now. Then Sarah came to me with the bundle.

"You two need to get acquainted," she said. And then she carefully placed the bundle in my arms. "This," she told me, "is our little Virtue."

Of course, it had been a baby all along. I should have known by the way they cooed and worried over it, but I had spent no time with infants, and so I beg excuse for my stupidity.

I gazed down into my arms, bedazzled. I had never held a babe. The child, one could clearly see, was a girl, small and light. She seemed made of feathers. She sucked her tiny fist and stared up at me with a pair of freshet blue eyes. I already knew those eyes. They were the young woman's eyes in miniature. They seemed to peer directly into my deepest regions. They seemed to know me better than I knew myself. From nowhere, a fathomless sadness washed inside of me, a wave of inexplicable nostalgia and loss. Followed by a flood of joy. I do not know how to explain it entirely. It was such a push and pull. I have since tried to understand, have gazed into the moon and struggled to write it down, but have yet to find the appropriate string of words to express that ineffable moment. No poetry, it seems, will serve.

"Have you ever changed a soiled diaper?" asked Sarah.

I stared at her, not quite sure I was hearing her right. "No," I mumbled dumbly.

"Well." She smiled, and patted my hand with her wrinkled fingers. "It is high time you learned how."

NOW IN ORDER TO convey a sense of my impression of what happened next, it is necessary for me to erect a conceit as baroque, confused, and absurd as the situation in which I found myself. Let us say, in keeping with my earlier dream, that I was now partly a goat, endeavoring to piece together a nonsensical puzzle – one made up of baby parts and whiskered faces – while somnambulating through the fog of a goat's worried hallucination.

While the other men discussed logistics, Old Sarah gave me instruction in the finer points of a baby's toilet. This alone was a small and disquieting nightmare, and I surmised more from the crone's hominid gestures and tone than from actually comprehending a single word she was telling me. The old lady tutored me at length about the various powders and ointments and degrees of freshness required for a baby's sanitary contentment. But while working within the parameters of my horny, ruminant brain, I must have come across as somewhat dimwitted. At one point, I understood I was to fold over a corner on the diaper so that I might learn to fashion a special style of flattened knot that would be more comfortable against the child's sensitive abdomen. But as I was all hooves, I royally botched this simple undertaking.

"Never you mind," Sarah assured me. "You will learn."

And while I vaguely grasped her words, I greatly doubted their truth.

Virtue remained patient through it all. And I must say, I was impressed with her from the git-go, both with her ability to produce such a robustly pungent mess, and with her placidity throughout my bumbling efforts of dealing with it. She already seemed separate from the ignoble world into which she had been born – a tolerant tiny demi-goddess suffering the ineptitudes of we mere mortals. Her blue eyes remained fixed upon me as I took instruction on the proper approach to swabbing and powdering her nether regions.

I glanced about for the nameless doe of a girl who had earlier been nuzzling the bundle of Virtue, the one who had so deeply touched me, but she seemed to have vanished into the sultry air.

"Would it not be more prudent," I asked Sarah, "to have the child's mother do the changing?"

She gave me a long-suffering smile. "Indeed it would, Mister Rain. But the Lord asks us to endure the most unlikely trials as proof of our faith. We must remember the examples of Noah and the Flood, or of Abraham and Isaac."

I recalled that Biblical tale in which God asked Abraham, as confirmation of his devotion, to take a knife to the throat of his only legitimate son. And although, to my knowledge, I have never been a father, it did not take much to imagine the tortured anguish Abraham must have suffered as he prepared to lay open his son's jugular.

But then – Ha-ha!

At the last second, God stopped Abraham's arm just prior to plunging the blade. A sort of holy joke, not dissimilar, it always seemed to me, from the variety contrived by Yahweh's more Olympian counterpart, Zeus. I tried to think now which role I was playing in such a reenactment of that scenario, and felt a chill when I then remembered the fatted ram God had provided as a sacrifice in Isaac's stead.

"And now for the feeding," said Sarah. She showed me a bottle full of milk upon which was attached a vulcanized rubber teat. "Above all," she inculcated, "you must be striving for cleanliness."

I nodded, as if I knew what she meant.

She instructed me in exacting detail on how best to boil the glassware and nipples for sterilization, and how then to warm the milk and test its heat so that it might mimic the very stuff tapped from a mother's breast. "Not too hot," she warned, and dribbled a drop of the milk onto her under wrist. "Like so."

The day was so warm, she told me, that the milk was nearly already at the correct temperature. "But be careful you don't go and let it spoil."

I nodded again, but I could not have been more lost had she been explaining an algorithm in some lost dialect of Mesopotamian.

She then had me hold Virtue in the crook of my arm, while she got the child started at the nipple. I took over, holding the bottle gently tipped so that a steady supply would drain into the child's puckered mouth. It was an odd sensation when it all came together. A tad tense, but not at all unpleasant. And for the first time in my life I felt I knew just a little bit of what it might be like to be a mother.

Virtue continued watching me, approvingly, I imagined.

"Well, Mister Rain," I heard Thurman say. "You seem to have a natural talent."

I felt myself blush as the others came close to where I was administering to the babe. "Yes," I said in my best manly tenor. "But it is not something I would want to do every day."

Thurman nodded sympathetically. "And yet," he said, "it is established. For the foreseeable future, at least, that is exactly what you *will* be doing."

I laughed, and then looked to Dallon, my intermediary, to translate from Affiliate Mormon to Goat. My partner grinned surreptitiously, and looked away, inciting in me a slight anxiety.

"But the child's mother will surely be tending to all her needs," I said. "I am only to protect and lead them through the perils of the journey."

No one responded verbally, and I saw a troubled expression play out on Thurman's whiskered façade.

"Correct?" I said.

Thurman cleared his throat, and then recited from some invisible text he had etched in his mind. "And the mother shall part ways with her child. And The Blessed Deliverer shall then accompany the bride through the wilderness, conveying her into the waiting arms of the Prophet."

I was scrambling in my skull, adding up all the information I had so far gleaned, putting together as many pieces of this abstract mystery as I could. I drew the most obvious conclusion and voiced it to the dark-suited man before me. "So why am I learning so much about infant care," I asked, "if the mother is to leave the child behind?"

Thurman looked at Dallon, who chewed his mustache and hunched his shoulders. Then Thurman turned back to me. "I thought it was clear, Mister Rain."

I shook my head and smiled feebly, feeling the rhythmic throb in my wrist as little Virtue continued to pump on the bottle.

"Well, Mister Rain. It is not the mother who is to leave the child behind..." He parted his hairy hands before him, as if drawing a curtain to let in some light. "...it is the child who will leave behind the mother."

I gazed down at Virtue, sucking away, and watching me.

I was deeply confused.

Then, like a chump punch to the gut, it struck me.

"*Virtue* is the *bride* to whom you refer?"

"Yes, Mister Rain. As the prophecy so decrees."

I involuntarily stamped a hoof. "Baaah!" I replied, or something equally as inane.

"Ours, Mister Rain, is not to reason why."

Admittedly, I did not know piddledy-poo about baby humans, but I deduced that this one I held in my arms was relatively new. She could not have been more than a few weeks old. She seemed ages away from ever donning a white dress and strolling down the matrimonial aisle into the arms of anyone – prophet, or otherwise. She was too perfect and pure and small. A protective instinct stirred inexplicably in my solar plexus. But then I told myself, Rain, it is not your place to meddle.

"Well," I muttered, and peered directly at a catalpa blossom that had fallen to the ground. "You people certainly do think ahead."

WISDOM IS A CURIOUS commodity, and bashful, too; it so often flees the scene in the moment of its greatest need.

A wiser man would have laughed at this good Mormonesque joke presented so strategically by Thurman and his dreary brethren. He would have handed over the babe, tipped his hat, turned on his heel, and walked as quickly as he could to the nearest saloon for a tall glass of stupor. A wiser man might have stopped to weigh the practicalities of the situation. Maybe it was the effect of the heat, but somehow those selfsame practicalities got all twisted and reversed and turned updown sideways in the void of my wisdom-washed brain. Or maybe it was Virtue's eyes watching me that did it. She possessed a subtle power that was already entangling my heart. My deepest most motherly parts were unwilling to give her up to just any Thomas, Richard, or Nehi. Not that my reputation was so spotless in such matters, but whom else, besides myself, could I trust with her fragile purity? Honestly, I could not say clearly what I was thinking. My good sense seemed muddied with a hearty dash of brazen foolishness.

All that aside, I ultimately told myself, Rain, you are most surely bust, and without much to recommend you otherwise. Thirty thousand dollars is an opportunity not to be taken lightly.

Besides, I had an obligation to Dallon. I knew he was courting a young lady in St. Louis, and needed every asset he could muster to impress her. I have always felt irrationally obliged to do my part for the cause of love, although, undeniably, it did seem my partner had not been forthcoming on the somewhat irregular details of this particular assignment. But mostly, as Solomon once so wisely warned all men, it was finally and indisputably vanity that was to be my undoing. Vanity, vanity, sayeth the preacher – that great submerger of acumen.

I had become increasingly disillusioned with life in the last few years, poured out and empty, and not much given to the magic of my existence. I was growing old before my time to grow old had arrived, inhabiting, one might say, those bare ruined choirs, where late the sweet birds sang. And so when Thurman and his flock suggested that I might be integral in some sort of cosmic prophecy, I eagerly and shamelessly licked his hairy hand while awaiting his next command. For who does not secretly feel that he is destined for greatness, if only greatness will take the bother to seek him out?

"You are asking me," I said to Thurman and company, "to carry a glass of water for a thousand miles across rough ground."

Thurman nodded. "Indeed we are."

"The chances are great – are, in fact, likely – that spillage will occur."

My cunning wordplay did not appear to faze their resolve. Such is the marvel of a collective blind faith.

"In the likelihood of the child's death," I persisted, "what are the compensations for everyone involved?"

"Mister Rain," said Thurman, shaking his head. "You are thinking wrongly of the enterprise before you. What you do not understand is that this venture is preordained by God. The One and Only. All of your needs will be anticipated. You should feel honored to be the vehicle of His will."

I do not know how I might have appeared to him when he said that. It is quite possible that I inadvertently swelled my chest and glowed. I fear I might have revealed a somewhat preposterous hobbledehoy superciliousness.

"The child has a destiny, Mister Rain. And as with a powerful stream into which you have found yourself flung and are unexpectedly floundering, you can fight against it, or you can go with its flow. Either way, you will end up where you are inevitably being carried."

I was not accustomed to being metaphorically outmaneuvered, and I could only guess that Thurman had been given a bit of help from some divine and invisible wordsmith. Perhaps I *was* involved in something big here.

Little Virtue finished off the bottle right then, and turned her head so the nipple pulled free from her mouth with a soft slucking pop. She batted at it with her pink knuckles, a bubble of white foam forming between her parted lips. As I said, I was a childcare neophyte, and so it was as much a surprise to me as it could have been to anyone watching when I then lifted the girl gently, and lay her facing backward over my shoulder. Someway, I knew just what to do. Maybe, I considered, some instinct remembered how my mother had performed the same motion with me when I was quite small. I patted

Virtue's back with my palm, and gave her a little bounce, swaying, in that way mothers do.

Everyone – Benjamin, Dallon, Sarah, and even Thurman – was grinning favorably as I demonstrated my inherent maternal expertise.

"God bless thee!" croaked Sarah, with a fairly disarming enthusiasm.

And then everyone repeated in chorus. "God bless thee!"

I just stood there, puffing with motherly pride, while Virtue voiced her own blessing in my ear by way of a whispery, milk-scented burp.

AND SO IT CAME to pass in a fortnight that a baby girl, two geldings, a she-goat, and one so-called Deliverer set off on the long and onerous journey to the City of Rocks.

It was a relief to leave Independence behind. Even under these quixotic circumstances. It always felt good to part ways with streets and buildings and vile humanity in trade for open and unsullied country. A sense of opportunity came with such an action. A world of magic awaited. I was a poet again, and a ream of pure white paper lay rolled out before me. Now it was left only to my muse to urge me toward a heroic epic of the most lasting poesy. Surely mine was not dissimilar to the optimism that infected every pilgrim soul who ever took those first steps westward into the Wonders of Nature. They tossed their common sense. They all shared a refusal to abandon their most improbable hope. They all sought the end of that elusive and mythical rainbow arching over the elysian fields of their most childish dreams.

Of course, all those folks were perfect fools.

Every last one of them.

Myself, most indubitably, included.

PART TWO

PERILS

THE HORSES PROVIDED FOR our journey were quite handsome – a cross between trail-savvy Indian ponies, and broad-chested farm animals. One was glossy black with white knee socks on all but his right foreleg. This gave him an eccentric and lopsided appearance, which seemed a deliberate decision on his part. One imagined him choosing to leave off wearing a sock on that foot, like some ornery youth, or trend-setting dandy, and the rest of us could learn to like it, adopt it for our own fashionable purposes, or lump it. I dubbed him Puck for his spirited and amusing temperament.

His counterpart was a steadfast sorrel with a suggestion of appaloosa showing itself in a constellation of dark spots dotting his left rump cheek. He was graced with an uncanny *legerdemain* of the four-hoofed variety. I never knew him to so much as stub his toe, or miss a step, even by close of the longest day over the roughest terrain. Although he most decidedly deserved a name to match his noble character, I came to affectionately call him Brownie. If a horse could be kindhearted, Brownie was. When I removed his bridle at eventide, he would often nuzzle my shoulder in a show of gratitude. I found he had a gentle and rolling gait, and so of the two animals I tended to ride Brownie more often, as he made it easy on the buttocks after long hours in the saddle. Puck was relegated to packhorse, but he did not seem to mind his lowly station. He carried twin trunks slung over either side of his sawbuck, filled as they were with our kitchen kit, baby paraphernalia, an assortment of girl clothes, and, of all humorous curiosities, a full size wedding dress to be delivered along with the child.

Both horses got to be good friends with me, and although I tended to spend more time on two legs than they did, there was an air of equality among us as we set about in teamwork to perform our common cross-country commission.

The goat, I argued with Thurman, would only be a hindrance. How would she ever keep up? But as he so vividly illustrated, she was a necessary member of the caravan.

"The child will need milk," he admonished. "And Mister Rain, unless you have developed an ability beyond the typical male of your species, I suggest you take her along."

I soon learned my worries were unfounded. The long-legged gal turned out to be an intrepid traveler. She jogged right along with the horses, tirelessly, her bulging milk bag swinging in cadence to mark her steady pace. I had never seen her breed before, but I guessed she was of some variety cultivated in the Arabian Desert, or some other locale geographically severe and wide on the map. She was completely the color of sand, right down to her eyeballs and horns. For all I know, she might have been part dromedary. She came to me nameless, and nameless, I am ashamed to admit, she remained. For she was, after all, an invaluable member of our band, and I have often regretted not treating her in a more kindly manner.

But the truth is she bore an uncanny resemblance to Old Sarah, all the way down to the wiry hairs on her chin. It was as if the hag had slipped a part of her own soul into the creature's skin so she could keep a close watch on me. This put me off in more ways than one, but never did it bother me more than when we had to make a stop so that I might fill a pail on Virtue's behalf. At such times, kneeling beneath the nanny, and tugging away at her dusty udders, I would sometimes see Sarah's dehydrated face floating before me. She nodded approvingly at my work, and I had to force myself to think of other things less revolting.

"Come with me and be my love," I quipped. "And we will all the pleasures prove..."

But Sarah only smiled more broadly. "Bless thee!" she bleated. "Bless thee!"

This unnerved me to no end.

I carried Virtue in a type of sling that held her high against my chest. This ingenious contraption allowed my arms to remain free underneath so that I might work the reins and steer my horse. It was reasonably comfortable, although my neck did ache something fierce by day's end. The little girl proved an admirable traveling companion, not too much trouble except for those horrendous, odoriferous diapers, and her endless thirst for milk.

To put it casually, Virtue was unusual in many ways, and would prove herself even more glaringly extraordinary as our journey progressed. I have no doubt that any other youngster would have been screaming and fussing the whole time, driving a sane man over the edge of his patience. Most children I had observed generally acted in such a manner. But Virtue possessed a sagacity that belied her age. She seemed astute enough to understand that no matter how uncomfortable she might be – no matter how sunburned, bug bit, or in need of a stretch – it was not going to serve her to complain. Any time I looked down at her, she was looking back up at me, patient and calm, her eyes reflecting the cloudless blue sky, as if in meditative contemplation of her rightful place in the world. I had heard the term Old Soul used to describe certain characters in novels and in poems, but until meeting Virtue, I had never encountered anyone to whom such a moniker so aptly applied. Was I in charge of an angel?

Still, I was used to a more galloping pace when making my deliveries. And although it was now high summer, and toastier than a raging inferno, I already feared falling short of the City of Rocks before first snow. The space between us and there was great, with many perils strewn between, and having to stop all the time to boil bottles, drink milk, and rinse laundry was a major detriment to our forward locomotion.

WE TRAVELED NORTHWEST ACROSS country until we reached the muddy Platte. It was late in the season, and most of the settlers and gold seekers heading west to Oregon and the honeyed hills of California had already left some three months prior, in hopes, as it were, of crossing the mountains before the passes were closed with winter. As a result, we had the road mostly to ourselves in the early stages of our journey. There were only a few tradespeople along the waterway moving freight between the upstart towns that were sprouting like weeds on the shore. I was so occupied with my charge, and earnest in my duties, that I do not think it fully registered with me what an oddball troupe we appeared to be. We solicited more than a few sardonic and quizzical stares, but generally, at first, I hardly noticed.

Then a man pulled up next to us in his buckboard. We rolled along side by side on the rutted road. He looked over, and then, dumbstruck, and nearly tumbling from his cart, he looked again. He even stood up, balancing precariously on his seat, so he could get a clearer view.

"Is that there what I think it is?" he hollered over the rattle of his team.

"That depends."

His cheek was abulge with tobacco, and he spat a quantity of sickly brown liquid into the road at my goat's feet. He wiped his chin on his sodden sleeve. "Depends on what?"

I did not answer, as he appeared bereft of intellect, and not worth the trouble of the breath I would need to draw in order to form the words to make an answer. But he persisted.

"Is it a runt person?"

The heat made it difficult to be cordial. "It is a gift from God," I informed him. "An angel sent to light our darkened way."

He sat back down and scratched the stubble on his throat. "Say," he said with a grin. "Are you the mama?"

He *was* a dolt, but his question irked me. "No, friend," I replied with mock good nature. "I am merely the wet nurse."

He thought this was tremendously humorous, and started in on a fit of laughter that caused tobacco juice to squirt from his nose. "Well, mister," he cackled. "You sure are one ugly woman!"

Generally, except in extreme situations, I am not quick to temper, but if I had not had a baby hanging from my neck right then, I might have jumped over and punched that man senseless. Clenching the reins in my fist, I fantasized briefly about that very act. But then again, had I not had a baby hanging from my neck, I suppose there would have been no need. As it was, I just kicked Brownie in the ribs, urging him to a trot, and leaving the man to gag on his own maniacal mirth.

"Sorry, Brownie." I stroked the horse's neck. I felt ashamed for taking my frustration out on such a gallant beast.

I peered down at Virtue, and shrugged an apology to her as well. "That there was a duck of the variety most commonly referred to as a *crétin*," I said. "Dumb as a rock, and not worth the space he takes up on the planet."

Virtue smiled.

I had to smile too.

There was no denying that we were joined in a most comedic situation.

From then on that is how it went for a while. Every time we encountered people on our route they felt it necessary to make comment on the peculiarity of our procession, and, specifically, on my position as the baby-toting leader. Traveling sideshows got less freakish attention than we did. It was as if these people had never seen a baby, a man, two horses, and a goat all in one place at the same time. Most amazing! They seemed to think I had given birth to the child myself, and now they wanted to chide me for my aberrant accomplishment.

"Howdy, ma'am," they heckled me.

And, "Is this your first? Why, darling, your hips don't seem near wide enough to pass such a healthy child!"

And, "What a pretty little thing! You just let me know if you ever need a man to help you make another one just like it."

After a time, I must confess, these jibes began to wear on my patience and self worth, not to mention the subtle harm it was inflicting upon my masculinity. "Remain calm, Rain," I told myself, trying to shrug it off with a smile. "Stay the course."

It proved good that I did not have a gun, as I might have filled more than one of my tormentors with holes. I found myself tensing my jaw, riding in a state of relentless apprehension.

Until, at last, we drew near to Delight's.

THE PLATTE, IT IS popular to say, is a mile wide, and an inch deep. But this is not strictly factual. Especially in the lower reaches, where, particularly with the springtide, channels and whirlpools can run deep and treacherous. To get from one side to the other it is necessary to hire a ferryboat, and a few men have made small fortunes hauling across the *fleuve*.

One such man was Avin Tuttles. He had set up shop on the perfect site for such an enterprise. The seasonal tide of the river here was comparatively predictable and manageable, the banks gradually sloping into the flow, and he had rigged a crossing line on large mechanical spools that could be reeled in, or let out, adjusting to the fluctuating water level. Whereas all other ferry crossings had drowned passengers at one time or another, Tuttles and his sturdy barge had proffered no sacrifices to the ever-ravenous river gods. He had become renowned in the region for his success ratio. A man of reputation. Still, everyone called him Boob. Boob Tuttles. A somewhat derisive appellation, considering his stature, but one he did not appear to grudge. He reckoned such a name could only arise from other men's envy, and so he bore it proudly. He was a contented and successful businessman, forever donning a veneer of complete placidity. Nothing, it seemed, could shake his unwavering equipoise.

But there was one thing the ferryman did not know about himself, one more claim to his fame of which he was unaware, and the true reason behind his nickname. Boob Tuttles was the blissfully ignorant cuckold of the most vivacious and hardworking prostitute a man could ever have wed.

Delight Tuttles.

Flaming hair and lips of velvet.

Ample of rump and bosom.

Skilled and limber and willing to bend over backwards – quite literally – at the drop of a hat.

DELIVERING VIRTUE

In their little corner of Eden, Delight was the apple of Boob's eye. He worshipped her like a goddess. As tokens of his devotion, he ordered her combs and dresses from East Coast catalogues. He bought her scented lotions and a pink parasol to protect her delicate facial skin from the demon sun. In an ultimate expression of his love, he even named his crossing after her. And from all corners of the plain, like tributaries coming together at a confluence, men would travel for miles to line up and wait their turn at Delight's Landing.

In the time it took Boob to pull his boat across the river, unload, and then return to dock for another round, Delight, having streamlined her own homegrown trade, could transport a man from the edge of animal lust to that far shore of a pleasurable and spasmodic offloading of his virile burden. And all for a dollar. At such a bargain, even if he had no real need of riding Boob's ferryboat, how could a man pass up a stop at Delight's?

I, for one, never could.

Now, even under the questionable circumstances, I felt a growing need to pay a visit. It only got worse the closer we drew to the landing, until at last, we arrived.

"We will only be stopping here for a respite," I told Virtue. "Then we will be on our way."

I will not say that her expression was censorious, as that may only have been a coloring from my own conscience, but she did not seem for one instant to buy my subterfuge. As I have said, little Virtue was astute. Her steady gaze gave me to know she was not one to be hoodwinked by a simpleton like myself.

"Didier!"

Delight stepped from her house and strode forward, twirling a parasol over her shoulder as if it were an enormous rose. It was good to see her. I felt an anticipatory trembling in my most sequestered regions, and a fondness in my heart. For Delight Tuttles was many things to me, but she was second of all a friend.

Boob was down at the shore with his barge, lashing a wagon's wheels to the deck, and securing a pair of oxen for the next crossing. Upon hearing his wife's enthusiastic warble, he stood up.

"Look, Avin. It's our dear friend, Mister Rain."

I tipped my hat to Tuttles, and, in taciturn fashion, he returned the gesture before squatting down and continuing with his task. He said nothing. Tuttles was a man of limited verbosity.

Carefully, so as not to bump Virtue on the saddle horn, I climbed down off of Brownie. When Delight came near, her mouth dropped open. "Why!" she gasped. She glanced at me, then the goat, then, reaching out, she laid her fingers on Virtue's tummy, and laughed. "Why, Didier! I didn't even know you were expecting!"

"Hardy-har," I sighed. "It is to laugh."

"What on earth?"

"A delivery," I said. "And one I fear, in my current condition, I am unable to explain sufficiently without a stammer."

She flashed me a whore's knowing smile, and turned to Boob. "Avin, Darling," she called. "Mister Rain has offered to give me another quick lesson in Latin. Do you need me to do anything else for a while?"

This ruse was one Delight and I had devised over the course of our relationship, a clever amusement between us. And Tuttles, with his pride out-wresting his brainpower, considered these so called Latin lessons yet another gift of highbrowed culture to bestow upon his lovely wife. He even went so far as to pay me a dollar for my services, which I, in turn, would slip to Delight before riding away into the happy sunset.

Boob raised a calloused hand, waving his approval at our scholastic endeavors. A freight man waiting on the barge behind him was rigorously stroking the neck of an ox and wearing a grin as wide and stupid as his face was able to contain. He seemed ready to burst with his want to spoil our secret joke by giving away the punch line. I suppose that should have put me on my guard, but then I was not thinking only with my brain.

Delight dropped her pink sunshade to the ground and relieved me of Virtue while I tied the horses and the goat.

"She surely is a seraph," said Delight. Her come-hither smile melted to one more wistful and strange. She held Virtue pressed to her heart. "I never could have one myself, you know." Delight peered at me with sorrowful eyes and patted her own midriff. "Barren," she whispered sadly.

This put me off a bit, I must confess, as my mind was not on Delight's deficiencies, but rather her soft-cornered bounties. I did not know how to respond. She appeared to be truly remorseful, so I endeavored to readjust my attitude accordingly. "Oh, Delight," I said. "I am sorry. I was ignorant of your misfortune."

Delight rocked Virtue in her arms, her neck bending in that awkward sideways-style one so often sees in old paintings of the Madonna and Child.

"However," I said, as consolation, "at least that makes it easier for you to ply your trade."

Delight stared at me, her green eyes blinking vacuously.

"I mean, not having to worry about the consequences." I shifted from one foot to the other. "I simply mean, not having always to be concerned about begetting a child, especially one that does not look like Boob's." I swallowed. "I mean Avin's."

She nodded slowly, as if she were hearing my minced and burbling words from under three feet of water, and I felt it necessary to change the subject before it got any more personal and unwieldy.

Tuttles was just leaving the shore, heaving on a cable, and pulling his well-loaded ferryboat out into the river. The entire craft creaked under the strain of its burden. A man and woman sat with their wagon and a pair of sway-backed mules, awaiting the ferry's return so that they might take their turn to cross to the other side. The boy accompanying them was languidly tossing green apples into the water. An old man with a skinny white dog sat in the shade of the apple tree, sucking on a pipe. A sweet and sulfurous suggestion of smoke could be detected on the sallow air.

I turned to Delight. "Latin?" I suggested.

Delight handed me her parasol and cuddled Virtue. She forced a smile, as if she were switching masks. But alas, although she led me willingly into her domicile, I could not help but sense that our stolen adjournment into the pleasurable throes of transitory amorousness had been slightly compromised by this passing conversation on the subject of her fruitless womb.

THE VISITOR'S ROOM, AS it was so aptly called, smelled, predictably, of mannish exudate and bottled lilacs. A warren of a variety of which I was all too familiar. Such quarters, be they kept in hotels or houses or tents or caves or barns, all issue forth the same telltale redolence belying their bawdy purpose. I can only surmise that Avin Tuttles had never visited such a room, as a regular to these chambers could mistake it for nothing else. That he unwittingly sheltered such a boudoir under his own roof beam was proof enough that Tuttles was an innocent, and a passing visitor almost felt a big brotherly affection for him and his naïveté.

I have often contemplated my own ignorance of the corresponding fragrance permeating the connubial quarters occupied solely by a man and his faithful, tender wife. Surely such a monogamous idyll is perfumed with the breath of paradise.

I imagine the patter of a small rain on the roof.

I imagine a cool, damp breeze wafting through the curtains of the western window.

But then paradise is such a well-hidden part of this world in which we reside, and so I have come to conclude that such couches of bliss are only for fairytales and lonely midnight dreams.

Thus the need for consolatory accommodations.

Delight was more interested in Virtue than in me. A fact for which I struggled not to begrudge her. But the Platte was running low, and Boob would be returning soon, so our time was fast ticking away. Business, after all, was business.

"May I help you out of that dress?"

"Oh," said Delight, and she glanced back at me from where she was mooning over Virtue on the foot of the bed. "Sure you can."

I stepped behind her, unlatching the clasp at her neck, and peeled the dress from her creamy shoulders. My breath left me at first view of her alabaster flesh.

She slipped the dress off the rest of the way and let it drop to the floor, stepping out of it and then hooking it expertly with a toe and kicking it to the side while I tended to the subject of my own disrobing. Delight then removed her lace undergarments, without ever turning away from Virtue the whole time.

I was soon naked myself, except for my socks, my member already at attention and poised for its spelunkulatory adventures.

Delight bent with her back to me – a pure delight to behold. "Let there be delight," I murmured. But I must say, at that particular moment, I felt more like I was viewing a marble statue in a museum than an actual woman I was about to embrace. She was only a few feet across the floor, but she seemed much farther away, in another world and time entirely, playing pata-cake with little Virtue.

As a gentle reminder that she had company to attend to, I cleared my throat.

Delight spun around with a look of glee flushing her face, and I stepped one step forward, anticipating our encounter. But then she surprised me by saying, "I think the little doll needs a fresh diaper."

"Truly?"

"I'll just change it quick."

I shrugged. "Can it not wait?"

"I don't think so."

"But," I whined, "I will have to don my clothes and go get her kit from the horses – an enterprise most consumptive of our valuable and fleeting time."

Delight brightened. "Don't worry," she said. "I have just what we need in my other room. You look after the child while I go and get it. I'll be back in a snap. We don't want the little thing to be uncomfortable."

Uncomfortable was the fulcrum word here. I was. Delight swept out of the room, leaving Virtue on the bed, and me in my condition of pending resolution. I suppose it would have been a funny picture to see. I felt a sudden embarrassment as Virtue gazed upon me in my undress. My hands involuntarily moved to cover myself.

"Oh, Virtue," I said. "Will we never cease to find ourselves in these comic charades?"

She giggled at my question, and then kicked her legs. I had to laugh, too.

The little girl was stretching out fast, growing like a flower who was getting plenty of water and sunshine. I had not noticed her yellow hair when we first met, but already it was growing long and lovely and

I thought to myself that I should take up the habit of combing it at end of day so that it would not get tangled. A paternal thought which greatly surprised me. I found myself for the first time in my life wondering about the rate of a child's growth pattern. Fawns are born and can walk all in the same day. Ducklings swim as soon as they break out of the egg. I knew humans generally took a little more time to mature. They are born, one might say, underdone. But Virtue seemed to be developing extra quickly, and I gave myself credit for taking such good care and keeping her well fed from the no-name goat's rich supply of nourishing milk.

"You are a natural, Rain," I muttered to myself. "A born guardian and deliverer."

"What?" Delight came back into the room.

"Oh," I said. "Virtue and I were just discussing the bewildering dilemma of Oedipus."

"Virtue? Is that her name?"

"Yes," I said. "It is."

This pleased Delight enormously as she set about changing the little girl's diaper. "You just sit down and rest yourself," she told me. "This won't take long."

Inelegantly, I sat in the room's only chair. It was brushed velvet and felt peculiar to my backside, as if I were making contact with the plush fur of some strange breed of exotic beast. I leaned back, waiting my turn for Delight's attentions. But although *I* sat, my phallus, blessed as it was with a mind of its own, preferred to remain standing.

"Little Virtue," cooed Delight. "Good to meet you, darling. I'm Dee. I'm going to be your friend."

As I waited, I marveled at the slim difference between the parlance used by a mother to sooth a baby as compared to the same used by a whore to stimulate a customer. To my mind, at that moment at least, there really seemed no difference at all. This epiphany made me at once discomfited and further excited. I felt like a boy lost somewhere in the wilderness limbo between babyhood and manhood. But as yet, that wilderness is where I would remain, as Delight was occupied with caring for Virtue, and singing her a lullaby.

> Little birdy up so high,
> What keeps you up there in the sky?
> Little birdy on the ground,
> Where is blue heaven to be found?

DELIVERING VIRTUE

As she sang, a weird tremor crept through my being, and I recalled my own mother singing that selfsame cradlesong to me when I was very small. I had not thought of that for many years, and it was very like finding an old dream hidden away in the dusty attic of the brain. *Petit Oiseau,* she sang, for she was French, and knew very little English. In the next instant, a sadness leapt up and gripped my heart – a confusing mix of nostalgia and regret. I peered down at the raindrop tattooed on my chest. I found myself wondering if my mother was still alive, and if so, would I ever see her again before I left this earthly life? It was a most mystifying moment. And one that might have been prolonged, and plunged me ever deeper into melancholic introspection, had it not been for the primal yawp that right then ushered forth from the river's shore.

"Dheeeee!"

Vaguely, although it was greatly twisted with anguish and fury, I recognized the booming and foreboding voice of none other than Boob Tuttles.

MY ERECTION WILTED IN a wink and plopped over onto my belly like a dead daisy.

Instantaneous panic, it turns out, has that effect.

I jumped up and lurched to the window, parting the curtain with a thumb so that I might peek out clandestinely and understand what was the trouble.

I did not like what I saw.

The barge was at the near bank of the river, cocked sideways and abandoned, unmoored. A single terrified ox was tugging fiercely at the tether securing it to a post on the deck. The other ox was just climbing out onto the far shore; even with the distance the animal displayed an attitude of distress that was unambiguous. The wagon that had been strapped to the barge was now cut loose and floating downstream in the middle of the river, surrounded by the bobbing flotsam of a dozen crates and barrels. Atop that sinking ship was the freight man, cowering and holding on for his life as he swept away into the torrents of his uncertain fate.

"Damn!" I said.

It did not take much to comprehend that the bastard had told all to Tuttles. I should have suspected it of him from the start. The lout! He just could not keep his yap shut. And Tuttles, with what must have been a revelation burdened with the sum of all of Delight's suspicious activities over the years, reacted in pure animal fashion.

This, he must have understood, with no small measure of shame, is why they call me Boob!

And now the man was stalking straight toward the house, fists swinging at his sides, rage boiling over inside of him like a pan of milk left a smidge too long on the flame.

"Dheeeeee!"

What a horrible voice!

And what a beast of a man!

A life of pulling a weighted ferry back and forth across the river had developed Tuttles to a state of muscular abnormality. He looked to be carved from a hickory stump. No one – especially gunless – stood a chance in a fight with the ferryman.

I spun back to the room, scrambling for a suitable action. Delight had scooped Virtue up into her arms, and was squeezing the little girl to her breast. This seemed inappropriate considering the circumstances. The woman's dress and underthings were strewn asunder. I picked up a shoe and handed it to her.

"Get your clothes on!"

But she only held tighter to the little girl, as if she felt somehow her salvation depended upon it.

Virtue remained unnervingly calm.

I instinctively pulled on both of my boots, but realized, upon peering down at each of my bare knees, that my trousers would then have to go on over my head. Not possible!

The old man's white dog was barking in the distance.

The distressed ox was bucking and lowing on the barge.

Tuttles was close now; I could feel his stomping steps through the floorboards as he drew up to the front door.

I glimpsed a premonition of the most embarrassing case of righteous manslaughter ever to splash the front covers of the St. Louis newspapers, one in which a naked trespasser – myself – is throttled by an enraged cuckold in a room with a baby, a whore, and a grimy diaper. It would be an inglorious end. But then, searching frantically for escape, I came upon a desperate plan of action. I gathered up my clothes in a bundle, and attempted to pry Virtue from Delight's hold.

"Give her to me," I whispered forcefully. "Virtue and I will hide in the wardrobe."

Delight was hesitant. She peered into Virtue's blue eyes like a mother unwilling to sacrifice her child to some arcane rite. Tears glistened in her own bright green eyes. But then, resolute, she nodded once, and handed over the babe.

Virtue and I stepped into the closet and had just pulled the door closed behind us when Tuttles fairly exploded into the room.

"Avin!" said Delight. "What on earth!"

It was dark in the wardrobe, with only the slightest sliver of light leaking in along the door, but I detected the huffing, infuriated bulk of Tuttles only an arm's length away. He surveyed the room, seeking me out. I tensed my legs, preparing to spring upon him and pummel him with my fists if he should open the door, but then I realized that I had a child in my arms. Foremost, I must secure Virtue's safety. Only then could I defend myself. Although I suspected that such a delay in my slim advantage of surprise would most certainly spell my doom. It was a quandary of a most vexing variation.

But apparently it did not even occur to Tuttles to investigate the wardrobe. I imagine he thought that such a hiding place was just too obvious and silly and unbefitting of even the most lowly excuse for a man to ever be considered, so he stepped across to the window, ripping the curtain from the rod. He seemed to think I had escaped by way of that open portal. Would that I had!

"Avin!" cried Delight. "Heaven's sakes!"

Tuttles audibly gritted his teeth.

"I spilled some soup on my dress" said Delight. "I was just changing it when..."

"Say something," growled Boob, "in Latin."

Delight laughed, but I detected a fearful tremor in her voice as she so did. "Why, darling!"

"Say something."

"But..."

"I want to hear some words of Latin come from your lips."

"You're upset. This doesn't seem the time for..."

"Say some Latin!"

Surely, I thought, the woman must know at least *some* old Roman phrase or incantation she could utter to appease her husband. But I guess if she did it was lost to Delight in the face of her pressing conundrum.

"Avin," she said, and in those two syllables I heard her voice turn to the silky, cooing tone she had so often used as prelude to our many past encounters. "Avin, you're upset. We can work this out. Let me sooth your anger. Tell me what's the trouble."

I could not see, but I imagined her stepping toward the man, perhaps laying her fingers on his heaving chest and leaning in for a kiss. Was I going to have to remain in this closet the whole time they were making love? But no. Tuttles would have none of it. He seized his wife, much in the manner of a grizzly bear springing upon a doe.

Delight screamed.

And then Tuttles dragged her from the room.

When I heard the front door bang, I slinked out of the closet. I was not particularly proud of myself in that moment, and it did not help to have Virtue gazing at me so serenely and with what appeared to be an infantile smirk of indignation.

"What?" I asked her, as I laid her on the bed. I quick removed my boots and pulled on my pants. "Monogamy is a gambler's game. Tuttles should have been on his guard." I held up my palms. "What else am I to do?"

The little girl startled me then when she rolled onto her belly and crawled away over the covers. I lunged for her, but there really was no need. She was merely moving to a more comfortable place away from me, near the headboard. I did not need to fear her tumbling off onto the rug.

Outside, Delight's cries were ringing in the humid air.

The ox kept bellowing; the dog continued its yapping.

I slipped on my shirt just as there issued forth a wild splashing and thrashing in the edge of the river. I leaned to the window and took a peek.

Tuttles had his naked wife dangling by her red head of hair, and he dunked her under the water, holding her there for a time, until he finally pulled her up coughing and screaming and looking a mess. There was mud all down her front, and her arms were covered in greenish waterweeds.

"Jesus!" I said, and grabbed up a boot.

Tuttles kept up this punishment while I hurriedly finished dressing.

Virtue sat on the pillows at the head of the bed, waiting, her tiny hands folded in her lap.

Delight's screams gave way to an alarming sequence of coughing and heaving up river water from her lungs. It was horrible to hear.

I slapped my hat onto my head, gathered up Virtue, and made for the door. "All right," I said. I was determined to help Delight someway, but as yet, I had no clear idea how.

The couple with the boy was standing a ways to the side when I came out of the house. Their mules were whinnying with agitation, rearing up in their braces, and the man was trying to keep them calm. "Whoa, girls," he said. "Whoa up."

The old man stood at the water's edge and was pointing at the river with his pipe as Tuttles continued to baptize Delight.

"Son," said the old man. "Son, you're gonna drown 'er if you don't let up."

Tuttles submerged Delight for the longest time. He was shaking with a lunatic's ire. Everyone seemed to hold a breath together, as if we all hoped it might somehow help Delight hold onto hers. But it was no good. At last, Tuttles lifted her up by her hair, holding her at arm's length, like a fisherman pulling a pike from a trap. She hung limp. She did not so much as flop or quiver. There was no mistaking the droop of lifelessness that had inundated her body.

The woman at the shore screamed.

Tuttles seemed at that moment to snap from his dream of vengeance, only to plunge directly into a nightmare of remorse. He tossed his dead wife away from him, as if he were repulsed, as if he could not stand to touch her. He stood thigh deep in the river, madly rubbing his hands on his shirt as Delight's flaccid body bobbed and sank and turned over just beneath the silty water sweeping her downstream. Her red hair bloomed and wilted at once like a short-lived rose. It was eerily beautiful, macabre. Her white skin flashed and flashed and sank away.

"D," whispered Virtue. "D."

Tuttles waded to the bank and dropped to his knees in the mud. He slumped with his head bowed, holding his hands over his face. Then he began to weep.

Great lamentations that seemed to issue from the very pits of his personal hell.

A man wallowing in the woeful ruins of his own paradise lost.

Delight's pink parasol rested broken and soiled in the yard. It looked so out of place, like a gut-shot flamingo, and I found myself wondering how it had come to be there when I so distinctly remembered collapsing it and standing it inside the door just a short time earlier. Such, I suppose, are the incongruent and hackneyed ramblings of a mind suffering shock.

The air was sullen.

The people and animals all held themselves still and silent, as if observing a moment of stunned and collective reverence.

A man might have felt he was viewing a bucolic daguerreotype – an instant of time held apart and separated from all the myriad other instants of time – had it not been for the drift of smoke lifting from the old man's pipe, and the restless surge and churn of the river that was background to it all. One almost sensed Delight's spirit hovering for a last glimpse at this tiresome world before lifting away. But then, I suppose that was likely just a hopeful speculation.

I walked quietly to my horses and goat. They seemed knowledgeable of the events forthwith transpired, even those unsavory happenings occurring behind closed doors, and I found myself unable to meet their eyes. I lifted Virtue's sling from where it hung on Brownie's saddle, and then awkwardly pulled it over my neck, nearly knocking my hat into the dirt. I was fumbling, jittery. The sling seemed suddenly inadequate now to carry the child, as she had grown so much, but I was in no place to fashion another at this particular time, so stuffing her into the little hammock as best I could, we made do.

Tuttles did not look up as I awkwardly mounted my horse. The spunk and anger were all drained out of him. I felt he knew I was there, but it had gone past mattering to the man. I, he must have realized, was just one of the multitude who had trafficked his wife's treacherous byways.

"Tck! Tck!" I urged Brownie and Puck and the nameless nanny to move away. "Let us go," I said softly.

Delight's Landing receded as we journeyed forth into the fiery evening sunshine. Virtue traveled with her typical, admirable aplomb, a living pendant hanging weightily from my neck.

Bilious shadows reached over the landscape. Bullbats took wing over the water. Invisible insects started up their choir of humming and clicking and buzzing in the riverweeds. I was filled with confusion and gloom.

"*Et fecit Deus firmamentum,*" I mumbled, "*divistique aquas, quae errant sub firmament, ab his quae errant super firmamentum.*"

"And God made the firmament, and divided the waters which were under the firmament from the waters which were above the firmament."

It was perhaps among the very first lines I had ever heard said in Latin. It came to me now on the water-voice of the river. A fitting eulogy for Delight. One I had learned long ago, back at the commencement of my own life's road, when I was but a boy.

WE JOURNEYED INTO THE night, a gibbous piece of moon hovering over us like a watchful eye. I was inspired to cover some ground during these cooler hours. In truth, I was eager to put some miles between myself and Delight's Landing.

Our blue shadows stretched before us.

But for the clopping of hooves, and the wet whisper and plash of the river, everything was quiet. Even the bugs and toads had gone to bed.

Puck and Brownie plodded thoughtfully onward.

The goat was occupied in some sort of esoteric rumination to which only she was savvy.

Virtue, watching me from her cramped sling, remained tolerant, cherubic, wise.

I seemed to be the only one on edge. My thinker was awhirl. Bits and pieces of the day were now mixing inextricably with the tatters of old forgotten dreams and limericks and memories from my past. I was having difficulty deciding where to place the line between what was real in this world and what was merely a fanciful fiction. We seemed to have crossed over said line, into a world of whimsical horrors. The moonlight washed everything all the same. It made me drunk with bewilderment. I worried that my sins had led me into hell.

Delight's demise became surreal to me now. Her gurgling screams. Her startled eyes. Her lovely white corpse lapsing into the murky stream. Had that truly occurred? I pondered her fate. One instant she was here, and in the next instant she was not. But then, in the end, I suppose that is how it is to be for us all. I considered her as a being among the millions with whom I share this planet. Delight had been a good sort. Not a harlot in the strictest and most disparaging sense. Surely she was just misunderstood.

"But then," I said aloud, "we are all just a race of misunderstoods."

DELIVERING VIRTUE

None of my companions commented on my inspired blurt of insight, agreeing with me, or otherwise, by way of so much as a whinny or bleat, and so, in embarrassment, I held my tongue to any further revelations. And yet I could not help but wax philosophical, if only in my secret thoughts.

Delight was merely overflowing with love, I decided. So much so that she had to give some away. She only wanted to nurture, due to some force intrinsic to her sex. And granted no child by the gods, she turned her attentions instead to the childish sides of men.

I nodded at my own shrewd assessment and muttered, "Misunderstood."

Virtue squirmed in her sling.

Then, as was my habit in times of boredom and torment, in an effort to sooth myself, I began a free and rambling recitation from whatever fragments of poems issued forth from my troubled heart and lips.

"My heart aches," I began, "and... little birdy... a drowsy numbness pains my sense as though of hemlock I had drunk, Or emptied some dull opiate to the drains, One minute past, and Lethe-wards sunk... ker-splunkety – plunk... If a Clod bee washed away by the sea... into the dead salt sea I hear lapping from afar... like a star... as you are... my own true love... you are so far... where is blue heaven... where is blue-eyed heaven to be found?"

And so on, and so forth, beneath the tranquilizing light of the moon.

DAWN FOUND US STILL on the go, albeit rather more somnambulistically than when we had, so many hours prior, absconded chez Tuttles.

My eyes were drooping.

"We will carry on a ways farther," I told my cohorts. "This time of day is more temperate and pleasing and good for travel. But then when the sun becomes too fierce, we will find ourselves a grassy plot on which to recline in the shade for some hours of slumber."

No one audibly balked, which I took as signal enough that we were all in agreement.

The Platte churned and boiled on our right. I had become increasingly suspicious of its covert agenda. Always in the past it had appeared so benign. But the river looked unkind to me now, populated with underwater bugbears and hobgoblins of a most rascally and ruinous nature. Although it may only have been a childish superstition arising from my troubled nocturnal musings, I felt the river was watching us as we ambulated upstream along its bank. In that early light, it slipped along like some dirt-brown snake awaiting an opportunity to bind us in its suffocating coils and drag us down and down.

It hissed among the bull rushes.

It seemed comprised of venom.

I tried not to let my imagination overpower me, but still, I watched that serpentine watercourse sidelong, ever wary of its true intentions.

By and by, the morning passed.

The sun grew predictably hotter.

I was just about to pull up and stop when I spied something ahead that moved me to wonderment.

"What on earth!"

Now the American Frontier is most undeniably a breeding ground for curiosities. No one familiar with it would deny such a profundity. In my many crisscrosses over the Territories, I had encountered more than one combination of parts joining together to form an amusing and bastardized collaboration. And I suppose at that moment I had become so accustomed to being one of those very anomalies myself, that I felt it a relief to be exceeded in my own ludicrousness.

"Someone out here is weirder than we."

That felt pleasing to my self-regard.

"Let us go see who these eccentric folk are," I suggested. "Perhaps we will be entertained."

They were not moving fast – somewhat like periwinkle snails sliding across a hot skillet – and so they were easily overcome.

The man leading was gaunt and tall and dressed in a ragged black suit that was heavily decorated with red flannel patches at the knees and elbows. He wore a top hat lacking a roof. It strongly resembled a piece of sooty stovepipe crunched down onto his pate. I was surprised to see that he sported a less kempt version of the same telltale beards worn by Thurman and Brother Benjamin. Fleas were fairly visible having an orgy in the deepest forests on his chin. The fellow held a book extended in front of him, attempting to read, while watching his steps at the same time.

"Verily, verily..." I heard him incant. "I say unto you..."

His voice was loud and held that quavering gravity one associates with zealots, disappointed fathers, or morose auctioneers.

He seemed to be reading for the diversion of his dress-wearing companions. They were female, I supposed, but they had had nearly all the more agreeable signs of femininity drubbed out of them.

The man turned when he heard our approach. He held his book toward me, as if it were a loaded pistol.

"Good day," I said.

He returned my cheery salutation with a chilly and distrustful squint.

At this close range, I could see more clearly the personalities accompanying him. What a sorrowing spectacle! They were a dull lot, addled and drained by the heat and their toil. Three girls – or near women – it was hard to tell which. At the very least I understood that they were old enough to endure the rigors of propagation, for each showed a swelling beneath her dress front indicating an impending birth to be fulfilled in the not so distant future. Two of them pushed red wheelbarrows heaped with what must have been the group's worldly possessions. One of them held a filthy toddler resting on her hip like a sunburned, drooling piglet.

"Nice morning for a walk," I said, and, taking a chance, continued, "The Lord has provided us a beautiful day."

The females did not speak, only let their mouths drop open in a pant. But the man grew friendly and bobbed his head.

"Indeed," he said. "The Lord provideth."

"To where, may I inquire, are you bound?"

The man removed his hat. "We're going to Zion."

"And which Zion might that be?"

"The one," he said, "at the City of Rocks."

I nearly fell off Brownie. But I hid my flabbergastment, and did not indicate that that was my same destination.

"What..." I shifted in the saddle. "That is a long ways from here. What takes you there?"

"We mean to join the Prophet Nehi in his kingdom. To help him people the earth with our own kind – the Chosen Ones." The man shot me a suspicious look. "Do you know about the Restructured Truth?"

I did not reply. I did not want to reveal too much to this rag-tag, as I feared we were somehow in cahoots in a way that I did not appreciate, endeavoring, as we were, toward the fulfillment of a common deific dream that we neither one completely understood. I deliberately changed direction in our tête-à-tête.

"What is that you are reading?"

The man glanced at the book in his hand. "Covenants," he said. "Revelations granted to the Prophet and given to his flock for our instruction."

I regarded the pregnant girls. Their dresses were all soaked in sweat under the arms and dusted with dirt from the trail. "Would it not be better to allow the lady-folk to do the reading, and perhaps you yourself push a cart? Such donkeywork does not seem fit for their fair sex."

"Yes," he said. "I know that's true. But I've been cursed with a bad back. Whereas they are strong, and willing. And besides," he grinned, and held up his book. "It is as the Lord hath commandedeth."

Considering his sapped and swollen harem, it did not take much to grasp how this old lecher had acquired his strained back.

"Besides," he said. "They can't none of 'em read."

The girls stood before me, an unsettling and suppressed intensity revealing itself from behind their languid masks. They appeared enthralled by the sling around my neck, and, of course, with Virtue, who was quietly waiting. I tipped my hat to the girls. "Ladies."

They stood motionless. If not for the recurrent blinking of their eyes, one might have thought they were lumpy figurines.

"Let me introduce myself," said the man. "I am Timotheus McDonald. And these are my helpmeets." He held his hat toward the girls. "Shadrach, Meshach, and Abednego." He held his hat toward the pig-child. "And this is my son Neb."

I studied the girls, noting that they all shared the same nose and narrow face. "Sisters?"

"Yes," said the man. "Orphans. Their ma and pa died in a house fire. But the Lord saw fit that they should themselves survive. They were destitute when I came across them at the poorhouse, and all alone, and so, as God instructed me in a vision, I took them under my wing."

Perhaps it was the heat and my need for sleep, but I felt suddenly sick to my stomach. In my more perverse moments, I had had similar visions myself.

"And who might you be, sir?"

"Oh," I said. "I am just a tourist enjoying a holiday."

That was when the girl – Meshach, I think it was – stepped forward and whispered into the man's ear. At this, Timotheus became suddenly agitated. He put on his hat, and then took it off again, stepping toward me.

"Why, beggin' your pardon... But... You're not the Deliverer, are you?"

I was at a loss. As I said, I did not fancy being associated with this miserable lot, but I suspected that I *was* indeed the same Deliverer to whom he referred.

"How many miles do you figure you travel in a day?" I asked.

"Oh, well..." He did not appear to want to change the subject, but said, "Three on average, I suppose. Sometimes as many as five."

By that rate, I summed, they would reach their fabled Zion sometime next century. Not that they would ever last that long. I imagined a pair of vultures chatting over the carcass of one of the girls.

"How's your believer?" asks one vulture of the other.

"Tough," he replies. "And spiced with a little too much indoctrination for my taste."

At the very least, they were doomed to spend a miserable winter in some cave along the way, copulating and birthing and starving. But then, I was reasonably certain that the Good Lord might instruct them to roast an infant or two to get them by.

"God's ways are truly mysterious," I muttered.

I felt Virtue give me an elbow to the ribs, as if signaling that she was ready to move on.

Shadrach then stepped forward, away from her cart. "Please," she said. Her voice was all aquiver. Tears glittered in her eyes. "Please," she repeated. "Is it you? Are you the Blessed Deliverer?" She trained her gaze on Virtue. "Is she the Holy Betrothed?"

An intense discomfort swept through my being. I felt sorely put on the spot. I felt unreasonably responsible for this girl's happiness. How, I marveled, did this ever come to be? She seemed so terribly desperate.

It was against my better sense, and not something I might have done given the leisure to think it out, but I could not let this poor creature take one more step westward without providing her with a bit of hope, no matter how ill-placed it might be. So I smiled at her, using a smile I had once seen in an image of Christ as he was painted on the ceiling of a church. I lifted my hand toward her, beatifically. And then, at the mercy of some foolish force guiding me, like some wooden puppet at the beck of his master, I softly spoke.

"Bless thee, sister."

That was all it took. A grateful, sunny smile spread across the girl's soiled face.

A blackbird trilled in the cattails.

And then, in the next instant, a great gush of amniotic water burst forth from between the girl's legs, splashing in the dust at her feet.

Everyone turned to stare.

Shadrach peered down at her shoes.

"A miracle!" grunted Timotheus.

I took that opportunity to turn my horse and quickly ride away.

I am sure it was irresponsible of me not to stick around and play midwife, but I did not so much as glance back over my shoulder.

We galloped for a ways, until my heebie-jeebies subsided, and then we settled into a more casual pace. I looked down at Virtue and shrugged.

"Sorry," I said to my hoofed friends. "That was not as much fun as I had hoped."

A WELCOMING TRINITY OF poplar trees stood on a hillside in the distance, and I steered our course in their direction.

It turned out to be a veritable oasis – a shady escape from the torrid midday sun.

An artesian spring effervesced from among the trees' roots, forming a small stream that trickled down the slope toward the river. The liquid ushering forth was fresh and deep-earth cool, and although it was not so snowy sweet as the water of my Sawtooth Mountain idyll, it was by far the best thing I had tasted in a good while. The animals and I drank long and hard, and then, after I had relieved the horses of their riggings, I regarded Virtue. She sat on a blanket, waiting.

A bone-deep weariness besieged my body; the trail's hardships had caught up to me all in a blink, and now the prospect of kneeling beneath the goat, filling a bucket, and preparing a sterilized bottle for the little girl seemed an insurmountable chore. But I knew she must be hungry. I yawned. And then, overcome, I yawned again.

I pondered Virtue; wearily, I looked at the goat.

And then, flitting to the fore of my somnolent recollector, I saw an image, the inspired likes of which could only have arisen from the pastoral tale of *Daphnis and Chloe*.

I studied the goat more closely. She was munching leaves, her milk bag heavy and full near to bursting. Turning to Virtue, I asked, "Shall we give it a try?"

She appeared to nod, as if reading my thoughts.

I lifted her into my arms and walked over to the goat. With one hand, I took hold of a horn and led the nanny toward the spring.

"Stand still," I told her.

I cupped my free hand in the water and washed the dust from the goat's teats. Then, kneeling on one knee, and with Virtue sitting on the other, I leaned forward, carefully positioning the child so that she might be directly beneath the goat's udders.

Virtue waited with her face pressed into the nanny goat's bag, and for a moment I worried that my idea was foolish and unbecoming of the Holy Betrothed. But then the little girl grasped one of the long taupe nipples, turning it toward her mouth. She knew just what to do. She wrapped her pink lips around it. Directly, she began to suck.

Unperturbed, the goat acted as if this were the most natural thing in the world. She was obviously relieved just to have the pressure subside. "Baaaa!" she said, and went on munching leaves.

"Eureka!" I enthused. For this discovery would make my life much simpler. "No more bottles."

As Virtue imbibed, I struggled not to topple over. So weary was I. I felt as if I had been drugged, and I looked at the stream distrustfully, wondering if it might be some narcotic offshoot of the Styx.

Finally, I could stand it no more.

"I am sorry," I said to Virtue. "But I cannot go on a minute longer."

I lowered her from the dripping teat and sat her on the ground, milk dribbling down her chin. Then I turned and crawled a ways on my hands and knees. "I just need..." I yawned. "...to take a short rest."

I collapsed face down into the leaves of grass.

And then I remembered no more.

Body and soul, I dropped into a black and dreamless sleep – a little foretaste of death.

I AWOKE GREATLY DISCOMBOBULATED.

Birdsong hailed me from afar.

A shiver of leaves; a blurp of water.

I felt as if I had endured an extended journey – one that carried me out beyond the farthest reach of the stars – and now I was coming back to where I had begun; I felt as if I had taken a tumble into spirit land, Persephone's lair, and now – after being desecrated and harried within the parameters of my own soul – I was being spit back out into the land of the alive.

I lifted my head from the grass. My brain seemed made of rock. I struggled to my hands and knees. A tremendous burden pressed down on me from above, but it proved only to be the weight of the air. My skin prickled. My eyes were blurry. But lo! When I was finally able to focus, I found myself perplexed to be staring directly at what appeared to be a gravestone.

?

I gawked for a while, and then, lifting a finger, I traced the melancholic epithet scratched into the sandstone marker.

"NEVERMOR HER LAFTER WILL BE HERD"

It gradually came clear to me that, of all the places to doze, I had inadvertently chosen to prostrate myself directly over a grave. I peered down at the body print pressed into the grass where I had slept.

Yes.

And yes.

Somewhere down there, on the other side of that thin and worm-ridden blanket of sod, were the moldering bones and sweetbreads of a cadaver. At this dastardly revelation, I found myself palsied with a profound sense of necro-inapropriato.

"Oowuh!" I keened, and spun away.

Panting, with large drops of sweat rolling down my face, I endeavored to gather my bearings.

First I spied the goat. She lay with her legs folded beneath her, blasé, chewing her cud while reposing against the trunk of a tree. Puck was in the distance, out beyond the shade, grazing. When he heard my moan, he looked over, but then went back to his meal.

Virtue's wrinkled blanket was spread on the ground, but the girl was not there.

I jumped to my feet.

"Brownie!"

The horse whinnied softly behind me, and I whirled around to find the animal straddling the streamlet. His expression gave me to know that he had everything under control.

"You need not worry," he seemed to say.

And sure enough. There, beneath the protective arch of his body, was little Virtue. She sat waist deep in a basin-sized pool, her yellow hair matted to her head, her dress soaked. She smiled at me, perfectly pleased, and held out her hand. A blue pebble lay in her dripping palm like a stone teardrop.

"Oh, precious darling!"

I hopped over and snatched her up into my arms, holding her tight. She, in turn, wrapped her arms around my neck.

I could not say what then came over me. Some force strange and unfamiliar. But I did *not* want to let her go. I hugged her to my heart, leaning against Brownie's shoulder for support. "Oh," I said, and began to laugh and laugh – a near maniacal merriment that started small, built up, and then would not cease to flow.

"Ha ha ha!" I laughed. "Har har ha!"

I would have been sorely pressed to explain myself.

"Ha ha! Oh, darling! Ha ha ha!"

On and on like that for a good long while.

When my hilarity at last subsided, I took in the scene around me. It was the same time of day in which I had originally collapsed, and at first I thought my nap might only have lasted for a single minute. But then observing the well-trodden grass, and the plentitude of horse apples and goat pellets littering the ground, I deduced that my torpor had been much more lengthy. At the very least, I had slept a full twenty-four hours, plus a minute, give or take. A complete revolution of the earth.

"I feel a bit like Mister Van Winkle," I told Virtue, as I shucked her from her sopping attire.

Even she seemed to have grown a mite older, a tad bigger than I remembered her being when I had held her beneath the goat just the day before.

I went to the girl clothes kept in one of the trunks and rummaged for a size larger dress. The one I found was pale yellow with blue cornflowers printed all over it, surprisingly flamboyant for Mormon wear, and not proper for the trail, exactly, but I held it up for her to see.

"What do you think of this?"

She nodded, and smiled. I swear she did. And so I closed up the trunk and brought the dress over for her to try.

I kneeled before her as she sat posing in her new outfit. She held her arms out to her sides, palms down, as if modeling for me. I had an odd sensation, another in my continuing series of odd sensations for that day. But as I viewed the little angel before me, I was granted at once a premonition coupled to a nostalgic and long submerged recollection – I saw a vision of Virtue as she would someday appear as a young woman; I saw a vision of Virtue as she had always appeared throughout the ages. I will never be able to explain this entirely, as I have come to learn words express much, but not all. Serve it to say that it was just one more confused and mysterious epiphany granted to me that day in the shade of that enchanted grove.

We spent the rest of the afternoon readying for the journey ahead. I washed diapers. I fashioned a new type of sling in which to carry the child. Wrapping the saddle horn in cloth, I prepared a padded seat for Virtue to sit upon. The new sling would now hold her face out to the approaching world, a soft strap holding her close against my belly and lower chest. Her little legs would now hang on either side of Brownie's neck. This would allow her the amusement of viewing the scenery and tousling Brownie's mane. It was a bit more cumbrous than the original design, as I had to hold my arms wider to work the reins, but it accommodated Virtue's growing person with more ease of movement for her, and she accepted the truss with a girlish alacrity.

The day melted with the heat and the evening approached with the promise of a cooler time for travel. After filling Virtue at the nanny's milkworks, we mounted up and set off. The gloaming would come with a settling breeze, and then the moon would light our way through the night.

As a self-amusing joke, I left Virtue's too-small dress tied by its sleeves to the branch of a tree, suspecting in my mind that the poplar grove might beckon McDonald and his child-wives with its magical offering of shade and clean water. They would surely look upon the dress as a miracle tendered them by their god. Perhaps they would even swaddle their newborn in its folds. I did not figure it mattered if the latest whelp be male or female, as that particular band of wayfarers seemed to suffer anyway from some small measure of gender confusement.

MOST EVERYTHING WAS GOING well. We settled into a routinized march that put the dusty miles behind us while inching us closer to our goal of the Prophet's fabled rock city. Puck and Brownie remained fit. No-name goat traveled fast while eating on the fly, producing prodigious quantities of milk on the thinnest diet of tares. Virtue remained healthy. After a time, the moon rose ever later, waned to a sliver among the stars, and then went dark altogether, forcing us to travel by daylight. Hot work. But everyone met up to the challenge, and I was duly impressed with my team. Embarrassingly, and with no small measure of distress on my part, I turned out to be the weakest knot in the rope.

Since I was a young man, I have suffered a recurring medical condition that, at the times of its utmost severity, makes undistracted productivity quite elusive. It is delicate to discuss, but as it is integral to my burden in this life, I have been forced to deal with it as a lame man might deal with a clubfoot, or a blind man the nonuse of his eyes. Undeniably, I am perhaps placing my malady in the company of the more noble infirmities, the likes of which were so favored for cure at the hands of the Savior himself. For surely nowhere in the King James Version of the Bible will you find a case in which Christ lays his healing touch on my particular affliction. No. I have found but one surefire treatment for my most debilitating disorder, one that can at times be difficult to acquire on these more unpopulated stretches of the frontier.

To make short of the long of it, I had the most intensely engorged membrum virile a man could humanly endure. An ailment that had become re-irritated so many days earlier, at that first delicious premonition of Delight's snow-white skin.

Unfulfilled, it pained me something awful, making my hours in the saddle near to unbearable. My vision swam with the hallucinatory puzzle pieces of the female body. Breasts and lips and derrieres floated all around my hat. My pulse became erratic; I breathed in a huff. And a general numbing dizziness consumed me, a result, I presumed, of my blood evacuating my brain and arms for that more enthusiastic limb of my body. More than once, I nearly pitched off Brownie in a lightheaded faint.

The situation was becoming increasingly dangerous, until at last, I could stand it no more.

"Whoa!"

It was late in the afternoon, but not yet time to call it a day. My comrades found it most surprising that I had chosen to stop where I did. There was but a small willow tree on a stagnant backwater of the river, offering only enough shade for us all if we huddled together. The mosquitoes hummed in the air. Puck shot me through with a smirk of exasperation. He stamped the ground with his hoof.

"I am sorry," I said. "I only need a moment."

Of course, I did not elaborate. Since I was traveling with two females (one only a child) and two geldings, it did not seem their empathy would be easily solicited in this particular situation.

I haphazardly spread Virtue's blanket under the tree, and sat her on it to wait. She looked at me searchingly, but I did not return her gaze.

"Take a rest," I told everyone, and then I walked away briskly, in a rather bow-legged fashion.

The obvious answer to my impediment was to find a bit of privacy in which to relieve myself by way of my own hand. Any normal man would have done just that, and then got on with his day. This was my hopeful intention as I dropped into a low wallow out of sight of the others. I quick pulled my trousers to my knees, preparing to unload my burdensome niggle into the bug-rich mud between my boots.

I gazed down in disgust and wonder. There was my gargoyle, rearing up pink and gnarled in the sunlight, seemingly wearing a grin.

"Hello, Old Lucifer," I said. He so often seemed an ornery entity separate from my person as a whole.

Uncomfortable as I was, I did not commence to strangulate it first thing. Instead, I endeavored to recall an ancient form of mediation I had read about, one devised centuries ago by monks dwelling on the banks of the Ganges, a system designed to clear one's mind of all thought and disturbance.

"Breathe in," I whispered to myself.

Om.

"Now breathe out."

Again - Om.

I practiced this in and out breathing for a few more inhalations, and although I believe I might have achieved some fleeting seconds of lucid mind-wash, I could not completely void my consciousness of the more distracting elements, namely – one must forgive my candor – an apparition of the female organ. It hovered before my mind's eye like a lotus flower to which a man might feel compelled to bow down. But for all the eroticism implied in that vision, I was simultaneously beleaguered by yet another vision that was its nemesis.

As a boy, I attended a parochial school for adolescents. My father had insisted that I do, and my mother, although doubtful of its benefits, had at last complied. As a result, I was placed in the care of priests. Of course, there were many lessons I learned in the Bible and in Latin and Greek – lessons I would carry with me throughout the rest of my life, and which would serve me to a greater and lesser extent accordingly. But the one lesson that I most remembered, the one that took the deepest hold of my young imagination, and has haunted my adulthood, was the one tendered to me by a certain Father Bartholomew who felt compelled to take me aside and instruct me personally in the perils of being a man.

I was delicate in those days; budding poets often are. So much so that my fellows often referred to me as "*le joli garçon*," or "Pretty Boy." No doubt this quality was what worried the good Father. He suspected I was sure to fall victim of the more squalid sides of men, and so he felt compelled to take me under his cloak, instructing me in the arts of avoidance of the more heinous sins.

"I, too, was a sensitive lad," he told me. "I understand what confusions you must be feeling."

Although I did not feel particularly confused at the time, I went along, as I found private tutelage did have its benefits. Namely, the priests often held secret stashes of tasty treats – fruit pastries and candies not allowed to we students otherwise – and so it was ultimately my sweet tooth that betrayed me and led me into Father Bartholomew's private cell.

I prefer not to dwell on the particulars of the encounter that has since so hauntingly consumed my imagination. Suffice it to say that I found myself in close quarters with a naked man. Although the good Father did not lay a hand upon me, I felt myself being used for inspiration as he gazed upon me and masturbated. This was a selfless act on his part, he assured me. He was merely showing me what was not allowed so that I might never be in doubt as to what was "wickedly wicked." He was, in pure soteriological fashion, risking his own salvation for my soul's edification. Although disgusted, I felt obliged to be grateful.

"Do not turn away," he instructed. "You must lay your eyes on the sins of men so that you yourself will not succumb."

The bon-bon he gave me turned sour on my tongue as he reached his convulsive conclusion. Then, weeping like a wretch, he handed me a leather strap.

"Now you must flagellate me," he instructed. "I must pay with mortal pain for my offenses. Self-abuse is a direct ticket to the deepest pits of hell!"

I half-heartedly let the strap fall against his bare backside.

"Harder!" he commanded. "Harder! And harder still!"

I endeavored to placate his unholy need, eventually coming down hard enough so that the strap made a sickeningly satisfying slap, again and again and again, as he elaborated on the details of the fiery black hole of hell.

By end of night, I had raised a multitude of bloody stripes from his skin.

I had as well scarred my own consciousness with the experience.

Alas, this was the doppelgänger that so impinged my mind whenever I prepared to self-serve – the memory of myself before a weeping man coupled to the hellish image of a flaming vagina. So impressive had it been on my young and formative mind. So unshakably tight was its hold on my integrity.

I drew one more deep breath. "Om." And then, peremptorily wiggling my fingers in the air, I took hold of my self.

As I feared, that was all it took.

Brother Bartholomew grimaced from my mind's eye. "*Mon Dieu!*" he moaned.

Directly, my hardness softened, turning to a fleshiful putty in my palm.

"Damn!"

Try as I might, I could not enthuse it back to rigidity, and therefore could not draw forth the venom poisoning my pilgrim's progress.

I stood there over the mud, tugging and rubbing.

"Please," I begged.

But to no avail.

My eyes were watering, and a large lump of dust had settled in behind my Adam's apple. I angrily hitched up my pants, knowing full well what would happen as soon as I did. Sure enough. I had not taken two steps back toward the animals when I felt the rigidity return down below. The ache, if anything, had compounded. I could hardly walk. I could hardly see where to place my steps.

The gang waited in the shade of the willow, tails swishing at the mosquitoes and flies. Brownie stood over Virtue, doing his best to keep the pests off his blond-headed charge. They all looked at me, expectant and bemused.

What next?

I paced in the sunshine, gritting my teeth.

"It is so goddam hot!" I complained.

No one replied.

I gazed at the goat. She was once again full of milk – a mammalian wonder to behold! – and I knew it was time once again to place the child at her udders.

"Damn inconvenient," I muttered.

Virtue gazed up at me, waving off a biting insect wanting to light on her dainty cheek.

I rubbed my face in my hands. "Oh, all right."

I wonkily marched over and grabbed the goat and dragged her toward the blanket, positioning her sideways and so. I then snatched up Virtue and, working around my tender impediment, I knelt on one knee, holding the girl in feeding position beneath her shaggy wet nurse.

Virtue did not at first engage.

"Well?"

I knew I had offended the little girl's feelings with my rudeness, but I was too uncomfortable and put out to apologize.

"Oh, bother, child! I do not have time or patience for this indulgence. Either you take your meal now, or we will be on our way."

Reluctantly, the girl began to do her business, although it was with considerably diminished gusto from other repasts in the past.

I did my duty, but it was not with my customary tolerance and kindhearted maternity.

The goat nonchalantly chewed on a willow twig, seemingly undistracted by the work going on beneath her belly.

I ached.

Some minutes passed – a small eternity – until Virtue, at last, finished.

I plopped her back onto her blanket and stood, thinking what to do.

"Baah!" said the goat, in some pagan argot lost to the world, and she peered up at me with her sand-colored eyes.

"Oh, shut up!"

That was when I hit upon, what seemed at the moment, a good idea.

I rubbed my chin, considering.

I blinked my bleary eyes, sizing up the goat's assets.

I grabbed her by a horn. "Come on, goat."

And then I led her over the rise to the wallow and out of sight of the others.

DELIVERING VIRTUE

Admittedly, it was not one of my more chivalrous deeds. Far from it. And aside from the animal satisfaction I personally derived from the encounter, I mostly marveled at how similar it had been to many of my other experiences with professionals of my own species. The parallels were alarmingly many. And I will advise the novice that, outside of true love – the merits of which I have heard many a troubadour sing – no-name nanny goats are, more or less, as satisfying as your typical whore. Maybe even more so, as they do not require monetary payment in return for their ministrations.

At any rate, I achieved my relief.

The nanny and I sauntered back to the group, somewhat flushed from our tryst.

The others all seemed to know what had occurred.

Brownie looked away from me and pretended to be licking at the flies hovering over Virtue's head.

Virtue sat quiet on her blanket, hands folded in her lap.

Puck snorted his derision, and showed me his teeth.

"What are you grinning at, eunuch?"

It was a mean-spirited thing to say, and I immediately felt ashamed for it. He was a good horse, and no one likes to be called a eunuch. Least of all a eunuch.

NEXT MORNING, THE GOAT was dead. A victim, I deduced, of some noxious wildflower she had found along the riverbank and indiscriminately ingested.

She lay stiff and bloated, with her legs sticking out straight. Bluebottle flies had already settled in for a feast around her various openings. A whiff of mortality hovered above her.

"*Merde!*" I mumbled, when I first made the discovery.

I readied Virtue and the horses for the trail, and then they waited with their heads bowed behind me. I felt compelled to voice a reverential panegyric for their benefit. But try as I might to find a preordained oration befitting to the occasion of a goat's funeral, no poem immediately came to me, and so I was forced to ad lib with a tribute of my own. I held my hat in my hands before me.

"She was a good goat," I said prosaically. "Uncomplaining and willing to do what was asked of her for the greater good. She will be sorely missed."

I cleared my throat, for strangely, although my makeshift requiem was undoubtedly insipid, I found myself tearing up like some heart-broke sissy.

"She..." I said, and wiped my nose. "The nanny never had a name in this life, but forever will she be remembered for her servitude and gentle ways. Perhaps the angels will find a fitting tag by which to call her on the other side. That is," I shrugged, "assuming goats are allowed into heaven."

I considered this.

I tipped back and gazed into the cloudless sky, wondering.

Then I nodded and knelt before the goat's carcass. Reaching out, I laid a fingertip on her eyelid, attempting to slide it closed as a sign of harmonious finality. But the eye would not stay shut. I tried again. But it just snapped back open and stared up at me, dry and sandy and busy with bugs.

"Well, anyway." I stood, and put on my hat. "Amen, goat. And rest in peace."

THE GOAT'S DEMISE PUT us in a pickle that, at first glance, I did not fully appreciate. On the contrary. I suppose it was merely a sublimated shame that made me feel this way, but I found myself greatly gladdened not to have that bleating, horned creature tagging at our heels. She had always perturbed me in some inexplicable way – her annoyingly homogenized sandiness, her penchant for unceasing mastication – and now, especially after our love affair, her presence would only have served to remind me of my errant ways.

"So long, Old Sarah." I smiled secretly as we rode away. "Bless thee!"

Alas, we had not travelled many miles before it occurred to me that the nanny had been the little girl's primary source of food. I peered down at where the back of Virtue's blond head was resting close against my chest. Hmm, I thought. The girl was now able to nibble an occasional hardtack, or suck on a dried apple that I had mashed into a fruity wad of pulp – the only two good options out of the Spartan stuffs provided by Thurman's people – but I knew enough to realize that such fare was not sufficient for a growing child. Her innards were not yet established for such taxing acts of digestion. She needed the liquid nutrients of milk if she were to remain healthy, build her bone-works, and continue her vigorous rate of growth.

What to do?

I gazed down the trail ahead of us, cogitating speculatively on what lay ahead.

I glanced back over my shoulder, reviewing what we had left behind.

For one quick instant I contemplated the burgeoning milk-laden breasts of Shadrach. Surely their devout and indoctrinated proprietor would feel honored to provide sustenance for the Holy Betrothed. But once again I found myself appalled to be in league with such a dismal lot as that one led by Timotheus McDonald, and I could not make myself turn our course in reverse and travel all that long way back. Besides, hot as it was, I was still able to sniff the inevitable approach of winter lurking over the horizon. Time was our most valuable commodity, and not to be wasted.

At the end of my deliberations, both directions of forward and backward seemed equally lacking in immediate promise, so we just continued our onward-plodding course.

"Oh, well," I told myself. "Perhaps Jehovah and Zeus will collaborate to provide us with a cool river of milk."

I seriously doubted this, but it was an amusing distraction with which to pass the time. I even attempted to turn my clever notion into a poem, but lost interest when I could (with the exception of *galactic*) find no fitting rhyme for lactic.

BY AND BY, THAT searing day passed beneath our thudding hooves.

We had gone well beyond Virtue's regular stopping time for a meal, and I could tell by the way she fidgeted, and then decidedly, and somewhat downheartedly, ceased to fidget, that the thought of milk was on her mind. She must have understood that the goat was no more, and then surmised what that meant. She played distractedly with Brownie's mane. More than once I heard her little tummy rumble with hunger.

We encountered no one all afternoon – no settlers or nomads or derelicts of any kind. An occasional rabbit. A few birds. But no people.

Virtue grew listless and withdrawn.

I started to worry.

We stopped at day's end and built a fire on which to attempt the conjuration of a delicious supper.

"Try this," I said, and held a spoon to Virtue's pouting lips.

She timidly pecked at my offering of glop, but I knew straight away that I had no future as a cuisinère for children.

"It is just a biscuit," I enticed, "softened to perfection with water, and then puréed into a scrumptious, one-of-a-kind pâté."

When she showed no interest, I put a bit of the grayish matter into my own mouth, testing its palatability. "Mmm!" It was admittedly unappetizing, almost, one might say, repulsive. It tasted something like wet paper mixed with a soupçon of river mud, and I could not justifiably blame Virtue for her lack of enthusiasm.

"Maybe if I put a bit of sugar in it."

Virtue shook her head.

"You are right. Sugar-coated shit is still just shit." I tossed the spoon back into the pot and turned to spit into the fire. "Pardon my French," I said. "Well, we need to find something you can eat."

I regarded the river and considered trying to catch a fish. Maybe I could make a nice broth from a carp's head.

Virtue looked at me, and, reading my mind in that we way that she could, she shook her head once more.

I nodded. "Yes. You are probably right. A foolish idea." I rubbed my palms on my thighs. "Should I try to snare some game then? Maybe a partridge, or one of these marsh hares we see scampering about?"

She regarded me, giving me to know by the forward tilt of her head that such ideas were not appropriate. Not to mention that they were in direct contradiction to the seemingly evermore-ridiculous agreement I had signed way back in Independence.

I stood and walked over and brushed my hand along Puck's shoulder. "How are you holding up, Old Boy?" But he could tell that I was thinking of other things, and so did not indulge me with an answer.

I pondered, looking over the horse's back and on up the Platte moving slowly toward us in the failing light. I turned and peered into the sky. The first stars were just winking on in the east. It was a juvenile notion that came to me right then, and tellingly desperate, but I considered making a wish on one of those miniature candle points of light. Childish hope dies hard, it seems, even in a man's most secret heart.

I picked out one of the stars. Not the biggest of the bunch, but for some reason it caught my eye. It appeared to burn bluer than the rest, and seemed to have a sympathetic personality. I swallowed, and then whispered, "Oh, Star in the night, Oh, Star so bright, I wish I will..."

Before I could finish my exhortation, I heard another whisper joining with my own, overstepping and finishing my sentence before I had even mouthed the words and sent them out to heaven on a puff of my breath.

"I wish..." I said.

And then, "Milk."

I was greatly surprised, and stared more deeply at my star. Then I spun around, paranoid, half expecting to be ambushed or otherwise pillaged by some milk-maddened pervert hiding in the willows.

But there was no one there, just Puck and Brownie and Virtue.

Brownie's eyes shimmered with the firelight.

Virtue gazed up at me from where she sat near the pot of glop. She held her palms up to me. This time, with the full volume of her girlish voice, she said, clear as you please, "Milk."

Dazzled, I slowly bobbed my head. "Sure," I mumbled. "Of course. Milk."

Virtue let her hands drop slowly to her sides, seemingly satisfied that I had gotten her message. Then she busied herself with straightening the folds in her dress, before lying on her side in a restful position on the blanket.

I examined the stars for a long time, but could not find the one upon which I had originally begun to cast my wish. The sky seemed suddenly awash with innumerable shining eyes. Then I squinted up the dark river, hitting upon the only idea I could find in my taxed bonce.

"Well, we all need to get some good sleep." I spoke to the horses. "I am going to ask for much effort of you on the morrow. A forced march through even more perils."

Brownie whinnied, reassuring me that he was up to the task.

I went over and laid next to Virtue, once again peering up into the firmament. It occurred to me that I was, rather coincidentally, observing the Milky Way. It was like a great river surging through the sky. How deep it was! Going on for a billion miles. And I felt the overpowering sensation of being messed with for the amusement of the gods and their minions. I smiled at this great cosmic joke to which I was most assuredly the butt.

"Say," I whispered over to Virtue. "When did you learn to talk anyway?"

But the little wonder did not answer.

She was already somewhere in her dreams.

AMERICA!

The land for those seeking supreme satisfaction.

Be it God, gold nuggets, or syllabic idioms, there is something for everyone in this Garden of Earthly Delights.

And although I am reasonably certain historians will someday argue that this country was built up and made great by industrious entrepreneurs and enlightened spiritual mystics, a closer and more cynical peek beneath the ruins might reveal that it was just as soon raped and plundered by avaricious self-serving opportunists and delusional charismatic goofs who were merely erecting churches to house their own fantasies and most primitive, if cunningly masked, hungers.

Yet, on occasion, one came upon the manifestation of an idea so distilled, splendid, and removed from any immediate notions of recognizable human gratification, that it could only have been driven by something truly insane, childlike, or divine. Those three sources of inspiration being somewhat kissing cousins.

Puck and Brownie carried us at a lope all that next day. They seemed to understand Virtue's pressing need for milk, and so they did not let down on their efforts. They were lathered with sweat. Froth flowed feely from their panting mouths and dilated nostrils. But I did not need to encourage them even once to make this haste, and I was heartily impressed by their determination and selfless sense of duty. They caused me to wonder if I should perhaps reexamine my own sense of purpose. One could believe the animals truly cared for the child's wellbeing.

At long last, rooftops came into view.

Now the hamlet of Ablutia was, to state it mildly, singular. It was founded by a brazenly pious sect that was a northern offshoot of a western divergence of a southern belief system clinging to The New Testament model of John the Baptist. Ablutionites, as they dubbed themselves, believed that if a little baptism was good for the soul, a whole bunch must be even better. To this end, they had created a rather sophisticated canal system based – an outsider could only surmise – on the irrigation plan for the Gardens of Babylon. They had redirected the Platte into a web of waterways that wound like a tangle of wet worms throughout their village, and then flowed through openings in the foundations of all the houses. Inside each home was a wide spot in the middle of the floor, as broad and deep as three conjoined bathtubs, lined with stones, and full of muddy water.

The motivation for this communal water system came from Guilt – that ubiquitous force that has for so long been the prime motivator in Christianity. The logic followed that since a person can not help but think sinful thoughts, and since sinful thoughts are as good as the sin itself for direct passage into the deepest territories of hell, and, finally, since sins can be washed away with baptism, why not baptize oneself continually? Waiting for Sunday to come around, what with such vivid daydreams of thy neighbor's wife, was too risky, and so it made most sense to these devotees that when such wayward reflections infringed upon the mind, one should quick immerse him or herself in the atoning waters. An Ablutionite's greatest hope was that Jesus would find him soaking in his private pool of repentance when Gabriel's trumpet blast sounded the Last Judgment.

They were a wrinkled lot, perfumed with mildew, and not prone to getting much work done in any worldly sense of the word, but they seemed content in their sodden state. A passerby could find them always chanting and shivering and dripping, with sublime, blue-lipped smiles spread over their well-washed faces. They might have risen up to become one of the world's great religious powers – something akin to Rome, or Mecca – had it not been for providence deciding otherwise. Who is to say that theirs was any more farfetched than the well-established beliefs of, say, Judaism, Catholicism, Pantheism, or even Animism? Still, one has learned through close study of such institutions, that all isms are best approached with a healthy dose of skepticism.

As for myself, on that particular day, I was mostly interested in their milk cows. And yet, as we drew near, I experienced the growing realization that all was not right in Ablutia.

Ululations drifted on the air.

A single desolate voice punctuated the laments with an intermittent grunting and gnashing of teeth.

It caused the horses to stop in their tracks; it prompted the little hairs to prickle up under my collar.

"What in the most unholy perdition do you suppose that is?"

I tried to laugh with nonchalance, but my voice came out of me high-pitched, giving away my apprehension. I stood in the stirrups, attempting to see before us into the maze of lopsided buildings. A tangible shadow seemed to have inundated the village, even in the bright sunlight, and it was a most intimidating proposition to now penetrate that dark umbrella of gloom. At that particular moment, I would have just as soon skulked around the place, giving it a wide berth and continuing on our way. Decidedly, it was our want of milk that drove us forward, albeit with extremely inhibited enthusiasm.

"Come on." I bravely swallowed at the protuberance stuck sideways in my gullet, and wrapped a protective arm around Virtue. "Let us go and see."

Warily, we strode into Ablutia.

It was truly a wonderland of the sort contrived by Hieronymus Bosch, for nowhere else – outside of the lagoons of Venice – could one find such an otherworldly schema of ditches and sumps working so integrally with human habitation. Water was everywhere. A crisscross of footbridges. Here was a wide puddle with a handrail leading pointlessly into its muck. There was a small amphitheater erected before a recently excavated, but as yet unfilled, baptismal pond. A mute harpsichord teetered at its edge, and a hymnal lay fluttering on the ground like a wounded bird. Paddlewheels turned aimlessly in the slow brown streams flowing languidly into the maws of every house and building. Fountains gurgled and gagged with sludge.

As we penetrated the township, I spotted fat bullfrogs lounging in the ubiquitous mud. Occasionally one would lift off and snap at a hovering damselfly.

Water snakes fornicated in the lily pads, their golden eyes following us askance as we passed.

But the sight that was most surreal was the one we came to at the river's edge.

Puck spied it first, and reared up in repugnance and alarm.

"Mother of God!"

There, laid out in the figure of ghoulish crucifix, was the entire populace of Ablutia, by all appearances quite dead. A single living woman was bent over among the corpses, some of them puffed and stiff with rigor mortis, all of them dressed in their grimy white baptismal robes. The woman appeared to be sorting and arranging the bodies according to some design known only to her. She dragged a half-grown child to a gap in the cadaverous glyph, and then tucked it stiffly under the leg of a lifeless man lying face up to the sun. Once done, she dropped to her knees, lifted her hands to heaven, and wailed in a most unearthly primalism. At first the woman was unaware of our presence, but then when she heard our hooves, she whirled and saw us.

"Awhoooooooh!" she screeched, and stamped toward us with both her arms stretched before her, forming a cross with her index fingers.

Brownie shied.

"Get away, Dark Angel!" she shrieked. "Get away!"

My heart began beating wildly, as she was most worked up into a frenzied state and seemed capable of a drastic act.

"Woman!" I said. "Calm yourself! We mean you no harm."

She ceased her forward march, but continued to hold her crucifixal fingers toward us threateningly. Her glower gave us to know that she was most crazed. Her hair was asunder and all sticking out. Like the dead around her, she wore her baptismal robe, and I will say, at the risk of sounding inapposite, that she looked most stunning and perversely alluring, as if she had stepped straight out of some ancient Greek ode to Eros. Her diaphanous toga was wet and clung to all of her more voluptuous attributes. I dare say, too, that her lunacy added to her charm, and for a slender moment I considered that it might just be my magnanimous duty to let her tag along with us for a while, seeing as she was otherwise destitute and without living friends. Perhaps I could sooth her woes in manly fashion.

"Awoooooohooooohooooooooooo!" she howled, rather erotically.

When she was finished, I adjusted in the saddle and swept my arm toward the morbid scene before me. "What horrible plight, my lady, has befallen your people?"

"The Dark Angel!" she hissed. "He brought the sickness." She pointed at the river. "He put it in the water."

"The sickness?"

"The river fever. He spat it into our flow of life. He jacolated it into our well." She clenched her fists and looked at them. "And I alone survived."

I had heard that a vibrio poison sometimes infected these villages, as corrupted water is always a problem when too many people come together in one place without a proper sewer. The white man's disease had been known to wipe out entire populations of the natives. It had erased more than one upstart settlement of whites besides. But this was the first I had ever seen of it with my own eyes.

"Awoooh!" yowled the woman, and then she scurried to the river and, forming a cup with her hands, dipped them into the river. She then hurried back and flung it raining over the corpses. "Awoooooooooooooh! We must purify the souls," she explained. "We must keep them wet."

I was at a loss for how to help this wretched creature. In spite of my noble intentions, she seemed too far gone. I squinted up into the sky to where a dozen vultures had begun their slow and persistent gyrations. They never once flapped their wings, but rode on some invisible stream of air. One envied them their privileged vantage over the world. "Little birdy up so high," I whispered. "What keeps you up there...?"

"Awoooooooh!"

The woman had grabbed hold of the ankles of a dead old woman and was dragging her backwards to the water. "We must baptize their souls. We must not let them dry or their souls will belong to Him."

She backed right into the river, pulling the body in after her. It bobbed and floated, and then she pushed it out into the flow, in the manner of someone launching a skiff. A single stiffened arm lifted up above the surface, and one could almost believe the cadaver was waving farewell.

The crazy woman slogged back out of the water. "Awwooooooh!" She grabbed hold of a dead child and dragged it back to the river where she pushed it out into the sluggish dark stream.

"Woman!" I called.

"Awoooooh! And I alone ..." she moaned. "I alone survived."

She kept up her work of dragging corpses, disassembling the ghastly crucifix, and did not pay us any more attention.

"Well that is the way it is, I suppose."

Virtue sat slumped against my front side. I felt her tremble, and I knew we had to find the cows soon.

"Tck Tck," I clicked, and we turned and rode away.

It was with considerable dismay and heaviness of heart that we at last discovered the barnyard animals. Ten sheep, nine pigs, and three plump Jersey milk cows. All dead. The Dark Angel, it seemed, chose his victims without discrimination.

"Damn!"

I assessed the dead cows. Their bags were bloated and still full of milk, and for one desperate moment I considered tapping them where they lay. But then that would likely have only produced some vile phlegm, and I thought better of the idea.

"Hmm!" I conferred with the horses and Virtue. I knew that the child was in a desperate state. She shuddered like a withered leaf against me, and I must admit that this made me feel most miserable and sad. In short time, the little girl had become an important part of my life, and I cared for her, I suppose, in a way I have cared for few others. I did not want to let her die. Not to mention she was my grubstake.

"This puts us in a fix, to be sure. But let us not give up hope."

I gazed up the river. It appeared exceedingly ugly in the midday heat.

"I am becoming evermore disillusioned with this route, as it seems polluted with humanity and rife with hazard."

I looked to the south.

I considered the north.

We were traveling that portion of the country that gives way to uninterrupted grassland, and it occurred to me that we might be better off just navigating those rolling waves of wild pastureland instead of following the common trail of the westward settlers. It was doubtless a gamble. For few were the rivers of milk to be found on that barren plain. But I felt something peculiar stirring in my solar plexus right then, the likes of which I had never felt before in my life. If I had to give it a name, I might have called it Faith. What else could it be? It made no good sense, to be sure, but that was exactly how I had observed faith working its magic in others. It was as if I had been infected with it by association. And I suppose it was made all the more improbable considering I had just encountered a whole town of faithful who had recently met their demise largely, it appeared, as a result of their faith. But still, and again, I felt compelled to follow my hunch. The stars, although hidden behind that vault of vulture-cluttered blue, seemed to be whispering encouragement into my ear.

I placed my hand against Virtue's chest and gave her a reassuring squeeze. She placed her own little hand on mine.

"Let us follow another way," I said.

For what, at this juncture, did we have to lose?

SKY AND GRASS - THAT is all there was anywhere we looked – sky and grass – sky and grass.

The grass was shoulder high to the horses, and we felt to be fairly swimming through it. It became overwhelming and dreadfully monotonous and I found that if one contemplated the situation too heavily, one immediately found himself sinking towards a panic the likes known only to swimmers who have paddled too far out from sight of land.

Virtue languished further. I cuddled her against my middle and she held onto my thumb with both hands. Her head was bowed forward. She breathed in short gasps. She was yet alive, but I could feel her withering, like a cut flower left too long on the windowsill.

I began to doubt my inspired decision to leave the river. At first I believed every step forward could only be a step toward our ultimate salvation. Surely I had not misunderstood the stars' urging. One thought confidently that we were being looked out for by some force unseen. But then a single patient vulture took up dogging our slow headway, reeling above, round and round, like some feathered shark in the sky. His shadow passed over us again and again, and this began, rather methodically, to unravel my nerves. As the day progressed, my great faith gave way to a lesser hope, and then, with the incessant swishing of dry grass, my hope plummeted to the level of despair.

Puck and Brownie floundered forward.

The vulture soared tirelessly above.

My heart began to ache.

Like most sojourners on this earth, I have experienced the pain of having my heart muscle broke to pieces. Such, it seems, is the lot of every member of humanity. And I am not claiming that mine was any more or less poignant than the impending losses felt by, say, the citizens of Ablutia, as they watched their husbands and wives and children being felled all around them. Life is a trap into which we all are born, strewn with few enough joys, and many perils, and with no surefire escape but death. How that death arrives is, more or less, inconsequential. But a person's sadness – yes, his sadness – is his own, to be cherished and sheltered, and mine felt most significant to me that day because of the great sense of unfinished business it carried along with it as baggage.

I will not lie; I had been privately proud to be chosen for the job of delivering Virtue to the City of Rocks. At long last, a confirmation of my worth! I had fancied... Dare I say it? I had fancied that it had actually been a divine decision to use me and my special talents – the stuff of epic poems and heroic legend – and so maybe I was more than I had come, in these recent years, to think of myself. Perhaps I was *not* a shiftless ne'er-do-well. Maybe mine *was* a valiant soul after all, destined for greatness, just as I had always fancied myself to be since I was but a boy. But now, and regrettably, once again in my life I felt myself approaching the imminent edge of failure.

Mayhap it was only a bad habit resurfacing in time of need, the same way as some men might turn to whiskey or religion when circumstances become all too much for them to endure, but my own mind cowered from the harrowing situation in which we now found ourselves and began, as was its wont, to seek the solace and protection of poetry.

> "Oh lift me from the grass!" I spontaneously intoned.
> I die! I faint! I fail!
> Let thy love in kisses rain
> On my lips and eyelids pale.
> My cheek is cold and white, alas!
> My heart beats loud and fast; -
> Oh! Press it to thine own again,
> Where it will break at last."

Admittedly, it was not the most optimistic poem I could have quoted, but it was the one that had arisen from my secret internal stockpile, and I have found that verse, even laced with gloom, has the effect of a salve to the troubled soul. Those rhythms and sounds were good medicine for me. Still, I was the leader of this little band, and I comprehended straight away that even though I felt greatly calmed myself, I should perhaps recite something a bit more upbeat for the sake of my troops. I thumbed through the well worn pages in my brain and came up with this song –

> "When voices of children are heard on the green
> And laughing is heard on the hill,
> My heart is at rest within my breast
> And everything else is..."

Brownie halted; so did Puck.

"What?" I said.

They did not move.

"You want something about a happy pony? I have yet to write that one, but will just as soon as I..."

Puck neighed, as if to shut me up. "Listen, you self-consumed dullard!" he said to me in horse.

I sat quietly, if not a bit humiliated, until sure enough, there, over the hiss of the rustling grass, I heard what one supposed must be a song. Although unfamiliar in its cadence and language, it was eerily beautiful to hear, almost mesmerizing, like some beckoning siren tune. Brownie turned his head and bobbed it twice toward the direction of the music. He was, I decided, telling me to have a look.

I nodded obediently, and, holding Virtue close, raised myself up in the stirrups so that I might take a gander.

Grass and Sky.

Grass and Sky and vultures. Many of them now. All soaring down low in the distance. They swooped and dipped over the only mark of relief in all the prairie spread out around us – two scraggled trees of an unidentifiable species poking up out of the grassland. There was some commotion going on under the trees, and although ethereal, I deduced that the voice resonating from that spindly copse was not one of joy, but of a whelming sorrow.

"Bother!" I sighed. For I was growing sore weary of melancholia.

And yet, this disturbance in the otherwise uninterrupted expanse of our monotony did indicate, at the very least, a variation to our forlorn venture.

"Well," I said, wiping the sweat from my neck. "I suppose we had better go and see what is happening there."

My enthusiasm was thin, but perhaps God, plural or otherwise, had not abandoned us after all.

MISTER POE HIMSELF COULD not have contrived a spookier spectacle than the one that confronted us now. It even surpassed the ghastly ruins of Ablutia in its weirdness and gruesome spectacle. It solicited from the closet of my sublimated amnesia the memory of a nightmare I had suffered as a boy, and as all that childhood scariness came rushing back at me, I found myself somewhat paralyzed in the saddle, and loath to proceed forward. But Brownie seemed determined that this was where we needed to go. He disregarded my panicked tugging at his reins, blatantly overriding my command to halt and assess the situation from a safe and reasonable distance.

"Whoa, boy," I fairly whimpered. "Please whoa!"

But by the time he had finally stopped, we had reached the trees and were positioned right before the bizarre siren.

She stopped her song and squared to face us.

"Jesus Mary and Joseph!" I murmured.

Yes, I thought to myself, and marveled at my déjà vu. The witch was most assuredly an exact copy from my childhood dream. I could not guess how she had come to find herself manifested in physical form right here on the American Frontier, so far as it was in time and space from my darkened boyhood bedchamber across that wide fishpond of the Atlantic.

"Hello," I said, and perfunctorily tipped my hat.

She did not reply, only glared. Her face was painted with white clay, and her hair was chopped in haphazard fashion, at places right down to her scalp. Tufts of black hair hung like decorations on the tall stalks of grass, and appeared as if it had been sawed from her head with a bowie knife that was none too sharp. Her ripped skirt and blouse revealed secret glimpses of the cinnamon colored skin underneath, indicating that she was not Caucasian.

"Pardon me." I could not help but ask. "Have you ever been to Cherbourg, France?"

But she said nothing, only stood stock still, as if waiting for us to be on our way so that she might continue with her arcane rite.

Behind her, in the crotches of two stunted thorn trees, were what appeared to be giant cocoons made of buffalo hides. They were held in place with twisted ropes of grass. A white painted face stuck up out of each cocoon – one of a man, the other of an infant. One could have supposed that they were some sorts of human-bug-being crossbreeds wrestling to break free and take flight in the form of hideously mutated butterflies. The eyes were closed on each face, but someone – the siren – had drawn large wide-open eyes in black charcoal on their foreheads. This gave me a severe case of the willies, and an unsolicited tremor swept from the top of my hat to the toes of my boots. Both of the bug people were clearly deceased, and with their big unblinking eyes, it looked as if they were peering out from the other side of this earthly existence.

I quickly surmised that we had happened upon a private funeral to which we were not formally invited. Still, I was a deliverer with a mission, perhaps even chosen by God, and not to be daunted by the woman's stony manner.

"My name is Didier Rain," I said. "Versifier, word collector, and would-be entrepreneur. These are my associates, Puck and Brownie." I motioned toward each of my horses. "And this," I said, holding a hand against Virtue, "is my precious child." (The words just came out that way. I do not know why. I suppose it was my nerves that made it so.) "She is in a bad way, very thirsty for milk."

Virtue did not stir as I spoke, and I feared for an instant that she had already slipped away. But then I felt, very faintly, her heart was drumming softly once – twice – thrice against my palm.

The siren woman stood motionless, but for her eyes. Her gaze flitted over Virtue, and in spite of her preoccupation with her own personal sadness, the woman's white mask softened at the pathetic sight of the sick child bound with a strap to my front side.

"*Mon fils est mort,*" she rasped. "*Et mon mari.*"

I observed the corpses in the trees and deduced that they were the dead child and husband to which she referred.

"I am truly sorry for your loss," I said. "*Mes condoléances.*"

She slowly bobbed her shaggy head.

I gazed up into the sky, past the twirling vultures, looking to see if perchance I could catch a glimpse of my blue star. Then I looked back at the woman.

"Life," I said, "can be mysterious. *Tres mysteriuex.* The Big Spirit, it seems, has seen to it that our paths cross right when they should." I laced my fingers together in the air before me, for visual effect to my point. "We have a need. *Nous avons bessoin du lait.*" I laid my fingertips over the tattoo hidden under my shirtfront. "And you must now fill the hole that is in your broken heart."

She thought about this, and then nodded again, seeming to understand what I was getting at. A single tear glistened in her dark brown eye, and then trickled down, making a tiny rivulet in the white clay powdering her cheek.

I climbed down off of Brownie, hugging Virtue close, and stepped closer. "You have milk," I said, and gestured toward her breasts.

The woman looked down at the front of her torn blouse, lifting both of her hands like bowls beneath her bosom. It was every inch an exact duplicate to the gesture she had performed so long ago in my boyhood dream, and I knew right then that this life, for all of its grim reality and submerged joy, was more than it appeared on the surface.

The sad siren helped me transfer Virtue from my makeshift papoose into her own arms. She studied the girl's face. She fingered a tendril of Virtue's yellow hair.

"*Syatapis,*" she said, as if identifying something about Virtue that was familiar and significant. "*Syatapis!*"

It was an Indian word that I did not know, but it seemed to mean something important to the woman. She grew somewhat excited. She carried Virtue over to the foot of the tree with the dead child hanging in it, sat down on a root, and opened her blouse.

At first, Virtue did not take to the offering. She seemed to be in a coma and was unresponsive to the nipple being rubbed so enticingly across her withered lips.

I whispered something like a prayer to the sky.

I waited.

Then, a single droplet of milk leaked onto the girl's tongue. She squirmed. Her mouth puckered into a pout. Her tongue started going. And then, at long last, even from the depths of her sleep, Virtue began to drink.

I do not remember ever feeling more relieved. Maudlin tears gushed forth from out my eyeholes, and I had to turn away from the woman, pretending to adjust a saddle strap so that she would not get the wrong impression and think me a pansy.

"Maybe we will survive this ordeal after all," I mumbled to Brownie.

But then a vulture lit in the tree over the nursing siren. And then another. And another.

Foreboding. Evil. Ugly pink bald heads.

Dead people bound up in trees. Ghost faces. A half-starved white child taking suck from a crazy witch I had once met in a dream while scavengers wait above to dine on the dead folks' livers.

The whole situation was enormously disconcerting.

And at that moment I realized that – even though we had survived yet another in our continuing string of perils – there was just as much fighting against us as was fighting for us. Although there were no trees to see in any direction I turned, I felt for certain that we were not yet out of the proverbial woods.

Everything good has its bad side too.

I knew that for a fact.

It was a lesson I had learned long ago – the very platitude with which I had rebuilt my own broken heart.

THE SIREN'S NAME WAS Turtle Dove.

She came from the Blackfoot tribe of Indians, or "*Siksika*," as she called it.

At first, she was generally stoic in temperament, and not forthcoming with personal information, but in time I was successful enough in my interrogations to learn that her husband had been a Frenchman fur trapper who had made some trade for her as a wife. After Europe's demand for beaver pelts had fallen off, the trapper had found himself with too much idle time, grew introspective, and so, with nothing much better to occupy his days, became a seeker of God. Boredom being just one of the many byroads to sanctity. This inevitably led them to Ablutia where, after being filled up to the brim with fervor, the Frenchman had himself and his little son baptized. But as the Blackfoots are wary and respectful of the spirits who live under the waters, Turtle Dove had declined to partake in the soul-cleansing practices of the Ablutionites. This reluctance was to preserve her mortal life, as both her husband and child soon succumbed to the Dark Angel's dirty water plague. Although their spirits now most certainly were enjoying their new home in heaven.

After Turtle Dove revived Virtue, I was greatly gladdened. I felt as if a blacksmith's anvil had been lifted from my shoulders, and an arrow drawn from out my fretful heart.

"You had me worried, little darling."

DELIVERING VIRTUE

Virtue gazed up at me from Turtle Dove's lap, smiling like spring sunshine. "Rain," she said, just as clear and pretty as you please. "Rain."

That stirred in me an ineffable joy and wonderment. How magical was this reality! How miraculous this blond-headed creature in my care!

But it was not a very cheery spot in which to have a reunion, what with Turtle Dove's loved ones decomposing above our heads, and so after the woman gave a parting gesture to her family, she led us over a rise to where she had a pair of mares tethered in a lush patch of chicory and sweetgrass near a little spring.

They were truly gorgeous animals, both flaxen palominos sporting braided blond-white manes adorned tastefully with feathers and colored beads. If horses could blush, Brownie and Puck surely did upon meeting those fine equine demoiselles. I had not seen a more embarrassing display of fall-all-over-yourself since I was boy in the play yard. Most unbecoming of their noble stations as my aides du cachet, but quite hilarious to watch.

"Sabrina," said Turtle Dove, and laid her palm on the nose of one of the mares. She stepped toward the other animal. "Genevieve."

I tipped my hat to the beauties. "*Un plaisir.*"

Then Brownie, in a show of animal gentility lost to me, did the only thing he could think to do; he stridently emptied his bladder, creating a large puddle of shimmering amber in the flattened grass between his legs.

"That will surely make a favorable impression," I whispered, and grinned. But he was not paying attention to my good-hearted jibe. His full courtesy was on Sabrina, and I must say, had I been born a horse, I might likewise have been moved to give her my complete and flattering attention. For she was a most lovely creature to behold.

Puck, in turn, was doing his best to impress Genevieve. Again and again he lifted up his sockless foot, showing off his foppish flare for fashion. "Look at me," he stomped. "Look at me! Look at me!"

Sabrina and Genevieve regarded my horses as if they were silly schoolboys – tolerant of their antics, polite, but obviously uninterested in starting up a romance. This did not seem in the least to discourage my smitten lads. They kept up their attention-getting strategies. Still, I had to laugh. They did not own a single testicle between them, and I suppose it never occurred to them that a consummation of love would ultimately be improbable, if not downright impossible. I found myself feeling pity for them at first, but then, oddly, was moved to envy.

Removal of a man's procreative hardware would, after all, free him up for other enterprise, eliminating that pesky distraction that lured one into so much turmoil, discomfort, and woe. I scratched my chin. I looked down at myself, considering.

We all drank from the burbling spring. I filled our canteens, and then Turtle Dove commenced to wash up. I left her to her toilet, and busied myself with saddling the horses and tending to Virtue.

Already, after her much-needed imbibement at Turtle Dove's breast, Virtue appeared to have taken a small leap in vitality and size. It was as if she had rehydrated and had become more full and large. The cornflower dress she had been wearing these last few days was already looking to be exchanged for a size bigger. I found myself amazed.

Even her hair was longer.

And then she did something I wholly did not anticipate – she stood!

She walked!

A bit tipsy, to be sure, but very accomplished, considering.

I chuckled at my own surprise. "Child," I said. "You never fail to dumbfound."

She ambled over behind Genevieve and ran her fingers through the long blond hairs of her tail. I had encountered more than one stable boy who had been made dimwitted by the swift backward kick of a horse, but I was disinclined to worry just now. Virtue was blessed. I felt sure that the mare would do her no harm.

The little girl examined the horse's tail hairs, comparing them to the hair on her own head. I think it pleased her to meet another in this world who shared similarities, if only follicularly speaking.

"Pretty," she said, and smiled.

Genevieve stood still and patient throughout.

Turtle Dove came from the spring, all scrubbed clean of her clay mask. She had traded her tattered dress for a new one of white doeskin. She looked to be a different person altogether, and I found myself tipping my hat to her as she walked up, as if we were meeting for the first time. Yes, her blue-black hair was still hacked and teased, but I was deeply surprised at her loveliness otherwise displayed. Her face was fetching, with a white scar along her brown jawline, like a primitive mark of beauty. Her figure reminded an admirer of a Roman statuette.

"Well…" I said. "Uh… Wha…"

My lips somehow got twisted up with my tongue and teeth. My gift for eloquent gab took a momentary hiatus, and I was sore pressed to find words correct expressive of what to say I wanted.

My flusterment did not faze Turtle Dove. She walked past me and knelt before Virtue, speaking to her softly in a flowing mix of French and Blackfoot.

Virtue nodded at what she was saying.

Turtle Dove stood and lifted the child onto the back of Genevieve, and then she gracefully leapt up onto the horse's back herself, positioning Virtue so that she was right up close to her front. She reached around the girl, took hold of the reins, and peered down at me. She shrugged. "*Allons?*"

"Uh," I stammered. "Uh, sure. Let us now be on our way."

TURTLE DOVE USURPED THE role of nursemaid. Justifiably so, I suppose, as she was better equipped with the proper mammarian apparatus to fulfill such lactictory employment. My own duties were – if not exactly eliminated – significantly diminished. I admit with a blush that at first this caused me a small degree of jealous irritation. Yes, I *had* asked the Indian woman to step in, and again yes, I *did* appreciate her help (we were surely lost without her), but I did not expect to feel so worthless as a result.

I had grown accustomed to having Virtue near to me, making jokes with her along the way, and telling her parts of my favorite poems while holding her close. Now, and suddenly, I was thrust to the periphery – a minor moon orbiting the distant radiant sun – and I did not enjoy the lonesome sensation. One wondered if he was even needed at all. Turtle Dove was well versed in the ways of wilderness navigation – maybe even more so than myself – and seemed entirely capable of delivering Virtue to the Prophet without my assistance. I felt like a father who, after depositing his seed to the proper plot of feminine soil, was rendered obsolete, perhaps even no more than tolerated. (Albeit, it was an even more inequitable scenario since I had not even been allowed to enjoy that first husbandry stage of delivering my seed to said feminine plot.)

But by and by, I adjusted to my demotion, looking upon it as a paid holiday to be enjoyed. After all, that thirty thousand dollars would be mine, with or without help from collaborators along the way. Although we were still many treacherous miles from the City of Rocks, our success was looking surer with each passing day.

DELIVERING VIRTUE

In the evenings, in camp, my vacation continued.

Turtle Dove not only tended to Virtue, she did the cooking too. Our stuffs were running low, but no matter. The Indian woman knew no end to finding manna from Nature's cornucopia. She prepared flavorable stews made up of roots and savory grasses. She formed seed flour cakelets spiced with wild herbs. For dessert she always found some bounty hidden in the grass. One evening she came to me and held out a handful of crimson berries. I took pause, and did not immediately devour her succulent treat. In a fit of uncharacteristic discretion, I was unsure that it was wise to partake of such an offering of fruit from an unknown and exceedingly enigmatic woman. Perhaps she wanted me poisoned and out of her way. Perhaps she wanted Virtue for her own daughter, a replacement for the child she had lost.

It was a stupid insecurity, I admit, one born from that old dream I had suffered as an adolescent in which the same feminine archetype had molested and tortured and titillated me in nightmarish fashion.

Rain, I assured myself, this is not a dream, but waking life.

But still, my hand would not reach out to accept her gift.

"Amostsi míímistsi likááhsiiyaawa!" she said. She thrust the hand toward me. The berries glittered like rubies. "*Les fruits sont bons!*"

I smiled weakly, and held my hand over my belly. "I am quite sated," I said. "I do not have capacity for another bite."

But she only took hold of my hand, turned it upright, and spilled the berries into my palm. She took a single berry from the little mound and held it before me between her thumb and forefinger. "*Ouvrez votre bouche!*" she commanded.

I opened my mouth.

She placed the berry onto my tongue, and then, taking the top of my head in one hand, and my chin in the other, she closed my mouth for me. "*Mangez!*"

How could I refuse?

The berry rather exploded throughout my mouth cavity, filling it up with a tart and tasteful sensation that was not unpleasurable.

Turtle Dove smiled. "*C'est bon?*"

I nodded. "*Oui.* Very good."

I ate the rest of the berries, one by one, as she watched. I fully expected to die any minute, but ultimately did not.

Turtle Dove then went over and shared some berries with Virtue. They laughed quietly and talked, and then the woman let down her tunic and gave the girl her evening ration of milk.

"Berries with cream," I mumbled, and licked my lips.

I watched them nursing for a while over the dancing flames of our small buffalo chip campfire. But then Turtle Dove's eyes met mine, unblinking and staring impassively, and I found myself compelled to drop my gaze.

I rose, stretched insouciantly, and went to check on the horses.

Sabrina and Genevieve were kept on one side of the camp, while Puck and Brownie were kept on the other.

"*Bonsoir, mes demoiselles*," I said, and passed my hand over their withers. "Is there anything I can do for you ladies? Something to make your night more restful?"

But they only smiled kindly, humoring me.

I went over to my horses.

"Hello, boys."

Both Puck and Brownie stood side by side, trail weary, with their heads held down low. By now it had become apparent that the mares considered them no more than younger brothers – snot-nosed and still in their knickers. This solicited from my lads a hangdog demeanor that was uncharacteristic of their usual *bon vivance*.

"Cheer up, fellows," I said. "They are not as pretty as all that."

But of course that was untrue, and my attempts at commiseration only made things worse.

I brushed them out with a currycomb, and then left them to their sorrow.

I wandered the margin of the camp, just beyond the halo light of the fire. It was like watching into a lighted house from a darkened street. Voyeuristic to be honest, as I was somewhat spying on the Indian woman from the cover of darkness.

Most men would call such a lady a squaw, but most men are beasts. I knew too much about the underpinnings of words to use such derogatory nomenclature on such a fine specimen as Turtle Dove. "She deserves better," I whispered to myself.

A coyote yapped somewhere over the hills. And then another. And then dozens, or so it seemed. It was always hard to tell with them.

I thought about the word – Coyote. "Coy dog," I voiced. "Shy. Elusive. Full of secrets."

The stars sparkled up above. I tipped back and gazed into them, feeling like I was falling and falling into their depths. A joyful melancholy flooded my soul right then. One of those moments that is so hard to elucidate. How can unhappiness make a person so damn happy? How can tragedy become such a welcome comedy? How can etcetera and etcetera marry to become so etcetera? I looked for my own blue star. But to no avail. It was lost like some part of my self in the ever-widening expanses.

"Turtle Dove," I said quietly. Her name was lovely to contemplate. An amalgam of a primitive water creature with an elegant and ethereal creature of the sky. "The deep life mystery stuff of poems."

"Maybe I could write such a poem," I told myself. The solace of poetry. "Perhaps I will try."

The pen felt unfamiliar to my fingers.

The ink smelled like the exotic perfume of some long lost lover. My hands were fairly shaking as I held the little booklet of paper against my knees, and I had to grin at myself for my schoolboy anxiety. "One would think you were about to do battle with a dragon," I mumbled to myself.

Virtue and Turtle Dove both looked at me over the fire and I felt myself redden with discomfiture.

"Never mind," I said, and smiled a bit too broadly. "*Rien*. I was merely talking to myself."

They went back to their ladylike occupations.

I dipped the nib into the bottle of ink and then held it over the paper, poised and ready to compose a thing of utter beauty.

But then I froze stiff. I could not so much as make myself press the pen to the parchment. I could not find a symbol for the words and feelings that were dammed up in the deepest and most haunted pools of my turbid brain.

How on earth, I wondered, could anything once so simple and pleasurable have become so terrifying?

A tiny bubble of ink dripped from the pen to the paper, and I swear that it made a noise louder than that of a painful, bloodcurdling scream. I winced.

I swallowed hard, and then gazed over the flames at Virtue and Turtle Dove. How mind-bogglingly beautiful they were! Like a painting by George de la Tour. Their delicate features. In this starry night. With the coyotes playing a wild American symphony as background to it all! And I found myself overwhelmed by the magnitude of the colossal ruins of my life.

Oh, Rain, I internally moaned. Oh, Rain.

I was on the edge of despair, I will confess. I was on the verge of tossing my tools of poesy into that buffalo shit fire. For what was the use?

But then the girls came over and sat, one on each side, next to me. Turtle Dove was making busy cleaning the dirt from some roots she had gathered. She had a little heap of them before her, and a wooden bowl. She sat so close I could feel her warmth. I could smell her woman scent – a heady mix of milk and soft cinnamon skin.

Virtue held out a hairbrush made of porcupine quills. She smiled at me. She was so pretty there in the firelight. "Rain," she said. "Will you brush my hair?"

And so I did.

Gently, tenuously, working out the tangles of her fair yellow hair as if they were the knots binding my own heart.

It was quite a domestic scene.

One in which I never in my dreams imagined I could be a part.

We were like a happy little family.

THE SKY HAD FORGOTTEN how to rain.

Or so it seemed.

Nary a drop had fallen on our journey thus far.

The grass had grown dry and brittle. The dirt beneath our hooves had turned to powder. It all felt wrongful. Truly, it seemed as if some malign weather spirit was mad at us, or was at least enjoying the tawdry spectacle of our dry-throated suffering. Waterholes and streams were few and random, and we often found them all dried up – just cracked mud and fossilized bird tracks.

So it was with a giddy expectancy that one late afternoon I sighted a building of clouds on the western horizon. They scudded and clumped and rolled our direction, growing dark and heavy with promise.

"*Il pleut! Il pleut! Mais je suis heureux,*" I crooned. Although, in truth, it had not yet begun to so much as spit.

The evening swooped in fast, and with the clouds filling the heavens, a gothic velvet glow suffused the prairie. Was this our old familiar Earth? It appeared more whimsical and strange. The air was stagnant, the whole world seemingly held its breath.

As a child my mother had given me, as *un cadeau du Noël*, a miniature diorama. I would play with it for long hours, lost in my imagination. I manipulated a pair of marionettes – one of a knight, the other of a fair maiden – so that they acted out scenarios of heroism and chivalry in that fanciful make-believe world. Now, in this gloaming, I was overcome with a nostalgic sensation, bringing back to my mind my childhood toy. Only this time I felt my*self* to be the figurine. I peered up into that roiling purpled glow, but detected no puppet master working my strings. Still, the sensation remained.

Turtle Dove trotted abreast of me. Virtue had learned to ride in tandem behind her, and the girl sat on Genevieve's haunch with her arms wrapped around the Indian woman's waist. She smiled over at me, augmenting my growing happiness.

We rode side by side for a ways, myself in a state of naïve joy.

Then Turtle Dove spoke.

"*Le ciel est sec,*" she said. The sky is dry.

"No, no," I laughed. "It is fixing to rain. We had best to make camp, get under cover, and be ready for the downpour."

"*Non!*" She pointed at the darkling sky, a suggestion of anxiety in her gesture. "No rain."

We pulled up and assessed the situation. The clouds throbbed with electricality; the grumble of thunder swept toward us over the grassy swells – all indications of an impending tempest. Still, I had to concede, she was correct. There was no hint of water on the air, none of that usual wet smell of rain that precedes a shower. Just a sullenness mixed in with the stink of burnt ozone.

"Should we make camp?" I asked. "And hunker down?"

"*Non.*" She shook her head. "*Attendez!*"

"Wait for what?"

Turtle Dove turned her hand with her fingers pointed upward, wiggling them in the air between us.

I laughed. "What is that supposed to mean? Worms are going to fall from the clouds?"

She did not see the humor. A foreboding flash of lightning blinded me right then, followed directly by an earsplitting knell of thunder.

Once my blindness subsided, and I could find focus on the scene before me, Turtle Dove pointed toward the swiftly approaching storm. She turned her horse so she was squarely in front of me, and then, peering straight into my dilated eyes, she said, without hint of irony or accent – "Fire!"

At once, darkness consumed the world, punctuated heavily with flashes of bright blue light. A man's eyes could not adjust quickly enough to the back and forth interplay of gloom and brilliance.

The skeleton shapes of girls and horses burned like ghosts onto my eyeballs.

The dead air came to life with wind.

"Stay close!" I shouted. It would be easy for us all to be blown asunder. "Stay together!"

The horses had worked up into a frenzy, rearing and prancing. They nickered in trepidation, and I heard the dull thud of one animal's body colliding with another in the intermittent darkness. I feared someone might fall and get trampled.

"Stay still!" I shouted. "Do not move about!" But the thunder swallowed my words.

It was a most nerve-wracking circumstance. One instant you were alone in the darkness; and then in the next you were being pummeled with electrical light. The hairs stood out all over my body, the air crackled and sparkled, and I truly expected to be fried by lightning at any moment.

Soon, just as Turtle Dove had foretold, at a point where a lightning bolt had stabbed into the earth, a single flame began to dance in the distance. It appeared like the alluring radiance of a flower – albeit, in the garden of a demon. Another flame then came to bloom in another direction. And then another, and another – some close, some far away – all around us on that dry grass prairie. The wind whipped the flames up bigger and bigger. In no time, there was enough light to see the details of the panorama. Although indeed, there was nothing to see in any direction that did not cause the heart to pound with a doomful dread.

"*Allons!*" cried Turtle Dove.

She dug her heels into Genevieve's ribs and galloped off with Virtue into the fiery maelstrom. The rest of us followed without question. Puck. Sabrina. And finally, me and Brownie. The woman was leading us through the encroaching inferno toward a corridor of darkness – a passageway as of yet not engulfed by fire.

The flames joined on one side and became tall and orange-red, sweeping toward us in a hot wave driven by the wind. Smoke blew thickly over the plain, causing eyes to sting and throats to burn.

We sped toward safety, endeavoring to outrun the closing blaze.

The thunder boomed and boomed, and then, curiously, it grew into a constant rumble that built to a crescendo with the pounding of our hooves. A dark mass poured out of the surrounding flames and hinter reaches.

Wild eyes flashed on every side.

"Awhooo!" I cried. For I was overwhelmed with a sudden terror. It looked as if we were running with the very fiends of hell.

But they were not devils – only bison.

Thousands of them, just as scared as ourselves, and just as desperate to outrun the devouring flames. They swarmed in a stampede and swept us up into their pell-mell tumult. I was stunned, right there in the midst of it all, to be taken by the overriding bovine odor – the repugnant reek of animals in a panic. The stench mixed with the smoke, creating a pernicious aroma that gagged me, even as I drove blindly onward with the herd.

I could see my comrades ahead, drifting farther away. Virtue's blond hair. Sabrina's and Genevieve's pale rumps bouncing among the collective corpus of brown-black beasts. But there was nothing I could do to bring them back. It was as if we were in a violent stream, and were at the absolute mercy of the current.

The buffalo closed around me and Brownie. Their black horns sawed at the air along the horse's sides, threatening to disembowel him with any wrong move, or misplaced step. He gallantly managed the helter-skelter.

It became apparent to me that Brownie was struggling to inch himself toward the edge of the herd, easing sideways through the bounding bodies, pressing toward the outside so that we would not be in such danger of being crushed.

"Good boy!" I cried.

The corridor was narrowing, the flames closing in, causing the bison to funnel through an ever-constricting gap. One could feel the heat of fire on all sides. We were nearly at the outer edge of the mob when a bison's horn painfully grazed my shinbone.

"Ahhh!" I cried, and drew my legs up high out of the stirrups. But alas! This proved unwise, as it put me off balance in the saddle.

I fell.

Whump!

One somersault – bang! And then another.

My wind was knocked out, and I was sorely dazed. But I retained enough of my sense to get up quick. I leapt to my feet and spun around.

Wham!

A bison lowered his shoulder into my chest.

I rolled backward, tossed something like a rag doll. Legs and hooves flashed on all sides of me. Flames. The stench. Even in the midst of it, I saw my mother's face.

"Now my powers are all o'erthrown," I sighed, and held up my palms.

But no. Brownie had stood by, my noble steed. He positioned himself between my battered person and the beastly onslaught.

Rearing up. Making such a ruckus and racket that the animals shied away, parting around him. I struggled to stand. The tail end of the herd rolled by and then, of a sudden, Brownie and I were alone.

The thunder subsided, replaced now with the roar and crackle of hell.

Brownie stood heaving as I climbed onto his back.

We were completely surrounded by the conflagration.

Great licking tongues of flame; sparks spitting up into the clouds and stars.

Brownie paused for only one second, gathering, and then he raced off at a gallop. Faster and faster, directly toward the blaze. The heat closed around us like a clenching fist. Closer and closer. Brownie's hooves driving over the well-churned sod.

"Go! Go!" I shouted. "Take us through!"

At last Brownie leaped – high, high as a winged myth – through that looming wall of flame.

I DO NOT CLEARLY recall what happened next.

I must have pitched off my horse and tumbled onto the ground.

I have a nebulous recollection of imps laughing and dancing in the brimstone. They prodded me with tridents, and taunted me with the rudest of words. But I suppose that may well have been no more than a dazed hallucination brought on by a blow to my head. At any rate, I soon became cataleptic.

Everything went fuzzy, then black.

When I came to, the first thing I noticed was that my body had been replaced with pain. Every square iota of me hurt. Even my fingernails.

"Oooh!" I groaned.

My cheek felt to be on fire, but I could not yet lift my head. Opening my eyes was task enough to begin with.

The earth was cocked sideways, and scorched, and still smoldering before my face. I saw it stretching out from where I lay. I vaguely deduced that it was dawn. For a pale gray light suffused the seared landscape. It streamed in apocalyptic fashion through the drifting smoke, but it was not unlovely. There was something almost peaceful about it.

The wing-shadow of a bird flitted past.

I swallowed at the cinder in my throat.

I coughed.

And then Brownie stepped into view before me.

He dropped his nose close to mine, his nostrils blowing hot breath over my face. He nibbled at my ear with his rubbery lips, tickling me back to life.

I crawled into a seated position. The ground was covered with the feathery ash of burnt grass. It puffed up and disintegrated wherever it was disturbed. A mound of something indiscernible smoldered a few feet away to my right. I squinted at it, wondering if it was perhaps a human brain – maybe my own – but then decided it was only buffalo manure, and not something to be concerned with.

I looked at the back of my hands and arms. They were covered in ashes, and the hair seemed to be singed clean of the skin. I then reached up and ran my fingers through the hair on my head.

"Ah!" I chimed. What a disconcerting surprise!

My hair crumbled and came off in crispy clumps in my fingers, burnt and singed and stinking. I rubbed my head carefully, until, near as I could tell, I was bald. All the hairs had been toasted from off my topknot.

"How do I look?"

Brownie whinnied reassuringly, but I could hear in his voice that he was only being kind. He looked sound enough himself, a few small cuts, and a bit seared along the flanks. But otherwise no avulsed eyeballs, disgorged entrails, or other injuries glaringly displayed.

"You are my hero, friend," I said. "I owe you my life." I shrugged. "For what it is worth."

He nodded.

I stood.

I stretched.

I creaked.

I found my hat, dusted it off, and placed it with care onto my embarrassing head. And then I took my bearings. I put the pale light to my back and faced what I figured must be west.

"Any idea about the others?"

But no sooner had I asked then I saw spectral shadows taking shape in the smoke about a hundred feet away. I did not know if they be buffalo, Indians, Mormonic angels, or possibly Beelzebub himself, accompanied by an entourage of his dark genii. I braced myself, preparing for more hardship and peril. But hooray! The shapes soon became palpable silhouettes. And I knew them! They were three horses and a woman with a child.

"Halloo!" I called.

Puck snorted a salutation through the fog, and then they all trotted over the burnt earth to where Brownie and I were waiting.

"Are we all of a piece?" I asked when they came up close.

They none of them said anything at first. They only stared, wide-eyed, and perhaps a bit horrified. I suppose it was hard for them to recognize me – their dashing, fearless leader – in my newly donned mask of ashen ugliness.

Then Turtle Dove laughed.

"What?" I said, and held out my arms at my sides. "You do not like my latest style?"

She laughed again, and laughed some more. And then Puck started in, and then Sabrina and Genevieve. Virtue, bless her soul, only grinned.

I turned around for them, exhibiting my filthy garments and hideous maquillage. And then I began to laugh myself, although it much pained me to do so. We were greatly relieved to be reunited and, more or less, whole.

We laughed like that for a long time, right there in the midst of that smoldering wasteland, happy, happy to be alive.

OUR HORSES SMELLED WATER, and without trying to steer their course, we let them take us to it. They started in at a trot, raising their noses and sniffing at the smoky air, but soon they were cantering along, heads down, driven onward by their mighty thirst.

We reached the western edge of the burn – that place where the first lightning bolts had touched down – and magically the countryside appeared before us as if none of that stormy nightmare had ever occurred. It was like stepping through a doorway from one enormous room into another. The prairie was just as it had been before – all rolling hills covered in tall brown grass rustling on the too-warm breeze.

At last we came to a bluff, and beneath us, like a silver ribbon shimmering in the sunlight, a stream could be seen winding bucolically through a stand of willows and small trees, bringing to my mind something I had once seen in a painting by a Barbizon Master.

The water tasted strongly of minerals – rather sulfurous truly – but we did not send up grievances to the gods. Any liquid at all was welcome as we washed the ash from our well-parched gullets. We lined up side-by-side, horses and humans alike, gratefully lapping at that lowland beck.

Once our bellies were swollen with drink, we commenced to wash up.

"I will tend to the horses," I told Turtle Dove, "if you will see to Virtue's needs."

She bobbed her shaggy head, and after finding a change of dress for the child, led her by the hand through the willows towards a pool.

As was my gentlemanly wont, I saw to the girl horses first.

"Ladies," I said, and relieved them of their leather hardware and saddlebags. My bones were creaking, and it was all I could do to slide the saddles from their backs. I seemed to have cracked a rib or two in my collision with that bison, and I could feel a painful grinding sensation under my skin.

I led the mares to the stream bank and, using our cooking pot for a bucket, I poured water over their backs, washing away the sweat and ashes and singed hairs. After that, I combed them out with the currycomb, taking great care with their manes and tails, sorting and untangling the colored beads intertwined therein. The whole process was exceedingly tedious, but they looked much better afterwards – quite beautiful – and both seemed appreciative of my fumbling efforts at a professional coiffure.

They set to nibbling at the watercress growing in the stream, and then I went over to Puck and Brownie.

"Boys," I said. "Howdy-do?"

They both appeared a bit worse for wear. As I unburdened them of their saddles and sawbucks, they trembled and flinched with muscle tenderness. Puck was scorched across his chest, as if a flame had flared right up and roasted him good. And Brownie had more than one horn wound along his flanks and hip. Black bleeding cuts marked his filthy, ash-covered hide.

"You might look almost as bad as I do," I teased. But they were neither one in the mood for a joke.

I poured water over their backs, brushing them out with ginger strokes. They did not seem grateful, so much as tolerant. When I was finished, they only just stood there, asleep on their feet.

"My noble cohorts," I whispered. "Take a rest."

I then lined up the saddles on a log, arranging them like so, and trying to make a civilized camp with a semblance of order and discipline. Sabrina had been carrying the saddle and bags once used by Turtle Dove's deceased husband, and I had not taken stock of its contents, as the widow woman was always nearby, and it seemed intrusive to rummage through a dead man's belongings. But now circumstances seemed to justify my curiosity, although in retrospection, I do not know why I considered propriety to have changed any since before our fiery charge with the bison. Such, I suppose, are the workings of a fatigued, yet inquisitive mind. At any rate, I sat on the log with the heavy leather bags across my knees.

They were decorated with beads and feathers in the style most popular with mountain men and trappers of that time so recently past, especially those of the French persuasion. The men often had long braided hair, and wore elaborate fringed buckskins and furs, purely impractical, almost, one could say, like something from a fashionable

Parisian street scene, although with a strong Indian influence on their choice of garb and accessories. They were wild dandies, those boys, each outdoing the next in his attempts at style.

I opened the flap on the bag and pulled out the contents hidden inside.

First came a woolen shirt, red as a faded rose, and flouncy. Wrapped inside the shirt I found a battered and dog-eared Bible. I opened the book to Leviticus, for no good reason except that I had always liked the way that word sounded when spoken.

"Leviticus," I said, nodded at its sound, and then closed the book and laid it beside me on the log.

Next I found a twist of tobacco, a charm on a string, and a map scribbled on a piece of rabbit skin. I turned the map first this way, then that, but could make no sense of it. It looked to be something made by a child. The twirling blue line must be water, I ventured, and the brown lines were mountains, but the starry sky seemed to be underneath, and there was no way to tell if this side or that was north or south or forward or backward. For some reason I was unable to explain, the little diagram seemed to be lacking in any awareness of time. "Is it a map of foreverness?" One wondered. At any rate, it seemed like the kind of map that could, if followed too closely, lead a man to becoming profoundly and most hopelessly lost.

I reached more deeply into the pouch. And lo! "What, pray, is this?"

I pulled out a silver flask. It was decorated with a scene scratched onto its side that appeared to have been created by an apprentice metal smith, as it was crudely etched and unrefined in technique. There was a nude woman standing waist deep in a pool in a clearing. A smile was engraved on her face, and her hands were cupped toward the water. She had the tiniest nipples one could ever imagine. On the bank of the pool, playing his pipes, was a faun. The whole scene was too clumsy for my taste, and had it entered into a contemporary poem or piece of fiction I was reading, I would surely have smiled at its quaint attempt at allegory, but ultimately would not have taken it seriously, as such blatancies have always struck me as old fashioned and a mite heavy-handed and too sentimental to bear the weight of life's truest meanings. Nevertheless, I uncorked the flask and sniffed its contents.

I flinched. My eyes came to tears in a blink. "Hmmm," I said, and wrinkled my nose. It was a liquorous concoction of unknown derivation. Juniper frolicked with licorice in its depths. Intriguing, to say the least, and a tad bit frightful to contemplate.

I pressed the cork back in its place, and slipped the flask into the depths of my own saddlebag. "For later," I said. Although I did not know exactly to whom I was speaking. "When all this business is done with and we want to celebrate our success, we will surely have a nip of the dead man's tonic."

I looked at the sky. "Of course, not until that day."

The other bag proffered a kerchief, a pair of patched trousers, a tin fork, and a Francote Pinfire revolver, Belgian made. "Hmm," I said, and weighed the pistol in my palm. "Hmm."

I wrapped my fingers around its handle, letting my index finger find its proper place next to the smooth curve of the trigger. "Hmm."

Now it is a peculiar thing the way a gun can make a man feel more like a man. All of an instant. There I was one minute, unarmed and vulnerable, and now here I was again, armed and dangerous. A man likes to consider himself dangerous. He likes to feel formidable, a thing with which to contend. And while I could find no bullets for this particular piece of manliness, I still had some of that virile sensation surge through me just by holding that gun in my hand.

I lifted it up and aimed at a bird passing overhead. I lined up, following it along in the sights. "Poom!" I said, and made a mock recoil with my wrist. "Poom! Poom! Take that, you!"

I could almost smell the burnt gunpowder issuing forth from the barrel.

I could nearly imagine a puff of feathers, the bird plummeting toward the earth.

"Well," I said, admiring the gun. "Perhaps we will just put you away for a while." And I slipped the revolver into my own saddlebags alongside the flask.

I understand that an observer might wonder at my flagrant disregard for the agreement I had signed back in Independence – the very one handed to me by Brother Benjamin forbidding the bearing of firearms and the taking of strong drink. But I saw no violation of that pact in my actions thus far. I had, I might point out, not sipped from the flask. Carrying it along with me was not the same as imbibing its contents. So where was my sin?

As for the gun, if God did not want me to have it, why did he offer it to me as such an obvious gift from heaven? The Lord had merely provided. He must have suspected that I would have need of a gun some time upcoming, amended his commandment, and was now only providing safe passage for his Blessed Deliverer and Holy Betrothed. Besides, it had no bullets! One could hardly call a gun a gun if it came without bullets.

I closed up the dead man's bags and lay them across his saddle, and then I placed my own saddlebags at the other end of the log, so as to make them appear as if they had had no interaction with the dead man's bags.

I heard Turtle Dove and Virtue coming from the pool. I made to look as if I were gathering sticks for a campfire. They stepped from the willows, and I was deeply surprised at how fresh and clean Virtue could emerge so soon after our filthy ordeal in the ash and dust. She wore yet another new dress, this one blue as the sky. Her hair was washed clean and was brushed straight down, where it fell loosely over her thin shoulders.

"Well," I said. "Look at you, young lady. So pretty."

The girl bowed her head with genuine humility, and then said, "Thank you."

"Do you suppose a bath would do the same for me?"

She grinned. "I don't know," she said. "Maybe."

Turtle Dove held a handful of some ointment she had mixed up at the stream – wet clay and herbs and berry juice and whatnot. She went to Brownie, cooing to him in Blackfoot as she came near to his wounds. She gently administered the salve to his many cuts, smearing it with a finger along the blackened gashes. The horse's flesh twitched a bit, but he endured the discomfort without much show, and I was impressed with his manly forbearance.

When she was done with Brownie, Turtle Dove made for the other horses, treating their burns. She turned to me where I was watching with interest. "*Baignez vous*," she said, and made a face to indicate that I did not smell so good.

And so, like a good boy, I went to take a bath.

I REMOVED MY SOILED attire and rinsed it in the stream. The dirt and ash made a grayish cloud in the water that flowed down over the pebbles at the shallow edge of a deep pool. I saw a fish flash silver in the depths.

A little yellow bird hopped among the willows, curious at my task, warbling a sweet avian melody.

"*Bonjour, petit oiseau,*" I said, but I regretted it at once, as my voice only scared him away. It would have been nice to have his company.

I hung my dripping clothes to dry on the branches of a tree, although they were in such sad shape – so burnt and torn – I could not imagine ever wearing them again.

After that, I examined my lacerated shin.

The cut was about three inches long and went all the way to the bone. It made me queasy to look at. I did not know how best to care for it, but decided that it was surely wise to make it clean. I carefully let my feet down over the bank and into the water.

"Yow!" I cringed, sucking air through my gritted teeth.

The wound stung something awful when it met with that mineral rich water. A puff of blood hovered around my knee, then dissipated into the stream. After the chill had sufficiently numbed my lower leg, I let the rest of my body descend into the pool.

It was with a mix of hurt and relief that I floated weightless in that cool liquescence. The scorched places on my face and head came to life with painful awareness. My ribs ached, and I could imagine quite clearly just how they were detached from the rest of my ribcage. I felt like a broken doll. Still, the water was a balm. All in all, I began to feel better than I had before.

I gently rubbed the dirt from my skin.

I paddled back and forth like a happy duck.

I let myself sink away for a time, mindful of nothing, bobbing face-down like a drowned man, until I could no longer hold my breath.

Finally, I crawled out onto the grass and lay belly up in the resplendent sunshine.

An unreasonable and lighthearted tranquility settled over me in that moment. It defied the general anxiety of my circumstances. I felt exactly the opposite of ill at ease, or careworn with angst. I had known such moments only rarely in my adulthood, and the temptation was to reach out for it, trying to capture it, or befriend the feeling so as to never be alone and without it. But I have learned that such responses only scare peaceful times away, and so I endeavored to refrain from any knee-jerk moves, and just lay still.

"Om," I whispered to myself. "Om."

I was still basking in that good feeling when a shadow passed between my person and the sun. I felt an abrupt cooling on my skin. When I opened my eyes, I was confronted with a silhouette, and coming as I was from that drowsy and peaceful state of being, I was quite certain in that instant that I was at last experiencing a visitation sent by God. I blinked into the brightness, trying to discern the details of this beatific personage hovering before me.

"*Voici*," came a voice.

Surely she was an angel!

My pulse accelerated as I waited to receive some divine piece of doctrine, or at least some sort of a heavenly blessing, but I was surprised instead to have a bundle plop into the grass beside me. I sat up, shielding my eyes from the sun with my hand, and realizing that it was Turtle Dove who had spoken. Of a sudden, I was aware of my nakedness.

"Oh!" I stammered. "Uh."

She dropped to her knees beside me, mixing up some gooey potion with a stick on a piece of bark.

One never knows how to act in such situations. Time and again. A man does not want to seem overly coy when airing his wares in front of a lady, as such displays will surely lessen his appeal to that most essential part of a female. But one *does* feel somewhat embarrassed, especially if one is cursed with a member as gregarious and forthcoming as my own. I refrained from covering myself, but still I blushed pink all over when my penis began to grow like bean sprout right there between the Indian woman and myself.

She did not seem to notice, only tipped her chin toward the bundle and said, "*Les vĕtements sont pour vous.*"

I took the bundle, and rather too quickly stood up and twirled away. She had given me the red shirt and patched trousers from her dead husband's saddlebags. I held up the shirt by the shoulders.

"Leviticus," I mumbled sheepishly.

"*Portez la chemise*," said Turtle Dove. "*Et les pantalons.*"

"Sure," I said. "*Merci bien.*" They were not to my sense of style, and a bit too large for my frame, causing me to look like a boy who had been handed an older brother's castoffs, but I was eager to be clothed, so I slid into them quick as I could.

"*Ici.*" She said and patted the ground with her hand.

I sat.

"*Donnez-moi votre jambe.*"

I moved so that my leg was close to her, and rolled up the cuff, exposing my wounded shin. She studied it closely, then reached into a little pouch at her waist and pulled out a bone needle and black horsehair thread.

I blenched all the way to my loins when I saw it. "Heh, heh," I laughed meekly, but did not otherwise speak, since I feared that any words I said might come out ignoble and sissified under the strain of the circumstances.

After threading the needle, Turtle Dove took hold of my heel and fixed it snuggly in her lap.

I swallowed, and lay back, grabbing handfuls of grass in each of my fists as I prepared for the upcoming ordeal. My tranquil feeling had quite abandoned me by this time.

And then she set to work.

I felt the prick of the needle, the thrust of that steely shaft, and the long drawn out procedure of the thread dragging through the puckered edges of my parted flesh. "Sweet Jesus!" I howled within. "Holy Mother!" But I do not believe Turtle Dove suspected my sensational anguish, as I kept it well hidden. She went about her work like a seamstress stitching up a torn petticoat.

Strangely, for all the great discomfort I was experiencing otherwise, I marveled at how my penis did not seem to mind in the least. He was not even marginally intimidated by my excruciation otherwise endured, and if anything, found himself more stimulated and engorged. It seemed as if the little beast considered pain a sort of aphrodisiacal stimulator, and the more torturous the suffering, the more intense was his eagerness to perform. I lifted my head and glanced down my body at the elongated lump in the front of my baggy new trousers.

DELIVERING VIRTUE

A marvel of virile zeal!

Turtle Dove bent over my leg, one palm cupped behind my calf to hold it steady. Her shaggy hairdo was sticking out in the sun. I saw the white scar peeking out from under her brown jawline. Her feminine shapeliness moved about with a suggestion of sensuality inside the loose-fitting shell of her buckskin dress.

And that, in a flash, is when I again revisited my old nightmare – the same one in which Turtle Dove and I had first met, so many years ago, when I was adolescent. We are but the stuff of dreams, I thought. And then I marveled at how thin was the line between everything in this world. For surely dreams and waking life are not so far apart as we make them out to be. I recalled in that old dream how this same woman, with her painted white face, had come to me, teased and tortured me, and then, in the end, satisfied me in a way I have been trying to rediscover ever since. At the time, it had seemed to my young mind like the most confusing mix of sacred and profane a person could possibly endure. Quite horrifying. And quite wonderful. Assuredly it was the epitome of all that Father Bartholomew had ever warned me against. But it was a dream, out of my control, so where, I ask, was my sin?

"*Donc!*" said Turtle Dove. And then she put away her needle.

I lifted onto my elbows, greatly relieved to have it over with. But then the woman took up the piece of bark she had laid in the grass, and daubed at the goo with a stick. She then proceeded to slather the unguent over my freshly stitched foreleg.

"*Zut!*" I cried, and jerked up straight.

It felt as if the witch had applied a hot coal to my tattered flesh. I fairly sniveled. I regret that I might have allowed a tear or two to escape from the reservoir stored up inside my head.

"What have you done to me, woman?"

She only held up the bark and made a gesture toward my lower leg. "*Une fois, tous les jours.*"

"Not on your life," I said. "Never again!"

She shook her head. "*Oui! Tous les jours!*"

I was in no position to put up a fight. "We shall see," I said.

Then she moved toward my head. When I jerked away from her, I experienced a stab of pain in my ribs, and automatically grabbed at my side. Turtle Dove noted this, but it did not deter her from her intention of applying the fiery ointment to the seared skin on my face.

"*Non!*" she said, and whacked my thigh hard with her open palm, giving me to know that I was in deep trouble if I did not hold myself still. Perhaps it was the memory of my old dream that caused me to obey, but I behaved as she commanded and allowed her to administer her torture once again, this time to my cheek.

"Zounds galore!" I groaned, no longer hiding my physical anguish.

"*Ouvrez votre chemise*," she said, and I opened my shirt, just as she instructed.

Turtle Dove placed her hands inside my shirt and ran them gently over my back. I could feel her fingers investigating each bump of my ribs until – "Ouch!" – she found the ones that were broken. She drew out her hands and covered one palm with the herbal tincture. She then placed her sticky paw back into my shirt and laid it flat against my bruised and damaged ribcage, holding it there for a good long while.

I became aware of the air inflating and then evacuating my lungs, in and out, again and again, as the Indian woman's hand raised and fell with my breath. What had started out as quite a misery began to progress toward something more pleasing, even serene. It was good to have her hand there. I began to feel sorry for my earlier behavior. "Thank you," I said. "*Merci beaucoup.*"

She nodded.

The intimacy of the moment moved me to a boldness I might not otherwise have displayed, and I was inspired to ask her a question.

"Turtle Dove," I said. "Do you remember that we have met before?"

She narrowed her dark eyes, and looked at me.

"In a dream," I said. "When I was younger."

She smiled ambiguously, and shrugged. I got the impression that she had probably been asked this same absurd question before, perhaps even by her own husband. For she was a type as much an individual. She was the quintessential wild woman, to some extent, every man's idyll, and had most likely occupied more than one fellow's most primordial dreams.

Still, I persisted.

"Turtle Dove," I said. "Do you suppose – under the right conditions, of course – once my hair grows back, to be sure – that you could ever love a man like me?"

She drew her hand from out of my shirt and sat back on her heels, scrutinizing my expression. "Love?" she said.

One got the impression that it was the first time she had ever spoken the word. It came out sounding a bit foreign and innocent, and like nothing I had ever heard before. It came naked of meaning, as if it had been newly coined right there on the bank of that mineral spring.

"Yes," I said. "*Amour.*"

She shook her shaggy head and grinned. "*Qu'est que c'est – Amour?*"

"What is love?"

She nodded.

I must say I was stymied by the question. "Well," I said. "It is..." I looked past her to the pool. "It is..."

She knelt before me, waiting. I suddenly felt like a dictionary replete with blank pages. How does one define love for a child? How does one say it is the stuff that makes stars shine and poems weep and hearts to ache with hopeful yearning? How can such a sacred thing be defined?

The yellow bird had returned, and he warbled a long and drawn out refrain. I saw a flash of his sunshiny plumage in the willows across the pool.

"I suppose I do not know," I said. "There was time, but..." I hunched my shoulders helplessly. "What is love? *Je ne sais pas.*"

She wiped her hand in the grass and then leaned toward me, commencing to button up my shirt. That is when she spied my tattoo. She parted the lapels and squinted curiously at the drop of water inked onto my chest.

"Ooh!" she said.

Timidly, she reached out with her finger to the lobular glyph. White or brown, I have never met any woman who could resist doing this, and I will advise the young man considering a tattoo of his own – have it printed in a place on your person where you most want to be touched.

Turtle Dove's fingertip went hypnotically round and round the perimeter of my water drop. I could feel my heart picking up speed beneath her undulating touch.

"*Syatapis?*" she asked.

I recognized it as the same word she had uttered upon first meeting Virtue. I surmised that it was a favorable adjective to have directed at oneself, but could not guess its complete meaning.

"*Que veut dire?*" I asked. "*Syatapis?*"

She leaned back, taking her finger away from my chest. She pointed to the pool, and then made a gesture where one open hand undulated under the other. "*Les personnes qui habitant la monde sous l'eau.*"

The people who live under the water.

"*Vous-ĕtes Syatapis?*"

"Me?"

She nodded.

Now I had heard that the Blackfoot revered all the spirits of the underwater world, and I surmised that it might just be to my advantage to lay claim to such a lineage. After all, I had a water drop tattooed onto my chest, my name was Rain, and no one you will ever meet likes a cold draught of water better than myself, so perhaps I *was* one of these *Syatapis* without even knowing it. Surely it was a possibility. And so I nodded at the Indian woman kneeling before me.

"*Oui*," I said. "*Je suis Syatapis.*"

Turtle Dove's eyes grew large.

"And Virtue, too," I continued. "We are both *Syatapis*."

Turtle Dove smiled knowingly, as if she had always suspected this, but now had the proof she needed to truly believe. "Ooh," she said. "Ooh." Then she stood before me. I do not know what I expected exactly – something more familiar and stimulating, I suppose – but the Indian woman pointed back toward camp, indicating that that is where I needed now to be. "*Partez-vous*," she commanded.

"Sure," I said. "Yes, of course. I will go see to Virtue."

She waited for me to go.

I limped away through the willows and into the trees, peering once over my shoulder to where Turtle Dove was now standing on the edge of the pool. She pulled her dress off over her head, and moved toward the water. I feigned to continue on, but once I was behind a thick stand of brush, I dropped down out of sight. I crept with a stalker's skill back toward the pool, staying low, careful not to bump any of the willows or otherwise shake the foliage and give myself away.

Turtle Dove's brown backside was to me. The nut-brown lobes of her derriere. The shallow dimples on each side of the small of her back. I lay in the grass, watching. She let herself sink into the pool and it was as if she had let herself become submerged in my very own soul.

"Oh, Turtle Dove," I whispered, full of longing.

I could feel my member all warm and full between the ground and my belly. He, if anything, was more than ready to take advantage of the fair maid. But I held back. I exercised my gentlemanly respect for the female sex of my species. I am not saying it was an easy thing to do, but I knew that a lasting love could not be built on a man's spontaneous primality. I needed to bide my time. I needed to go through the proper courtship rituals, show her my plumage, if you will, and then make my move when the time was right. It was the most painful abstinence I have ever endured, but most noble. It was made all the more excruciating by the full frontal view now offered up of Turtle Dove's nudity.

"My mistress eyes are nothing like the sun," I whispered, and then swallowed at the large lump of anticipation stuck sideways in my throat. "If pale be fair, her breasts... her breasts are dun."

I licked my lips, took one last look, and then crawled slowly backwards out of my hiding place.

I did not want to leave, but the torture was too intense, and besides that, I was beginning to feel I had left Virtue too long unattended.

WE DECIDED TO STAY put for a while.

The horses were battered and bruised from their previous tribulations, and it made sense to let them have a good rest before putting them through the next perilous leg of our journey. I, too, was in need of some mending. The thought of bouncing all day in the saddle with my broken ribs was quite abominable to contemplate, so I was perfectly content with lollygagging by the pool. Yes, time *was* against us. And again, yes, winter *was* prowling out there somewhere over that western horizon. But how could we face the pending snows if we were all crippled up and in a weakened condition? It seemed best to wait a few days, allowing our bodies to heal.

The site was an earthly paradise – or near to it – right there on that wide lonesome prairie, and it might have been perfect if not for the profusion of sulfur and gypsum in the water. After a few days of drinking from the stream, I am embarrassed to say, it caused one to produce a vile wind. The horses blew continually, and I soon learned to give them a wide berth. I encouraged Puck and Brownie to graze far from the center of camp.

"The grass is so succulent and tasty in that direction," I urged. "Way over there, downwind, beyond the willows."

But then of course when they left there was no one else to blame for the lingering stench.

After my daily bath, Turtle Dove continued with her treatment to my wounds. Oddly, I found myself becoming somewhat addicted to the sting and pinch of her pungent potions as they were applied to my shinbone, and it was with an irrational regret that one day I noticed my lesion was beginning to heal. It seemed a slow progression toward intimacy was indeed occurring between the widow and myself, but at this lethargic snail's pace, I figured we would both be too old to consummate before we ever reached our amorous and matrimonial climax.

Yes, I will confess, I had grand designs on the Indian woman. In my most current daydreams I had constructed a scenario in which Turtle Dove and I lived in a little cabin just north of the City of Rocks. This would procure us privacy enough to enjoy our conjugal existence, while allowing us proximity to easily visit our dear Virtue, and her Prophet husband. I could not fully imagine this idyllic situation, as it was bursting with fancy and yet to be discovered details, but I knew at least that Turtle Dove and I would have a western window in our bedroom, and that we would lie under the blankets at night, cuddling and listening to the small rain tapping on our roof.

"Do you like the rain?" I asked one day, as my wife-to-be pressed her salve-covered palm against my healing ribcage. It was my best effort at leading small talk, but as Turtle Dove was a woman with a mix of disparate tongues, my meanings often were misunderstood as she substituted one wrong word of a language for another.

"*Aimez-vous?*"

"Oh," I chuckled. "Yes, my name is Rain. That is true. But I was referring to the heavenly substance that sometimes falls from the clouds." I held my open palm to the blue sky. "Sky tears," I said.

Turtle Dove gave me a confused grin, and then pointed at my tattoo. "*Vous-ětes pluie?*"

She thought that I was telling her that I was a drop of rain. I smiled at her childlike innocence. For she was appealingly naïve.

"No," I said. "I am not rain; I am Rain."

Her expression became more confused, and she shook her shaggy head.

"Just call me Didier," I said, boldly touching my fingers to her bare knee. "And I will call you Dove."

This intimacy was as close as I had come to forcing my hand with the lady, determined as I was to proceed with a gentleman's decorum. But I must say that feeling my fingertips come in contact with her skin caused my whole being to tingle and become rigid with a boyish excitement I had not experienced since long ago, when I had first spoken with a girl I met in Cherbourg. This was that same experience, I would estimate, only better, as I was more mature now, and more assuredly suave.

Turtle Dove glanced down at my bold fingers. Even under her dark skin, I believe I sensed a hint of blush. The moment seemed ripe as a piece of fruit, and it was left only for me to pick it deftly.

"Oh, Dove," I whispered with ardent innuendo, and leaned forward.

But this adjustment in my posture caused an abrupt and unexpected spasm in my bowels.

And that, I am dismayed to say, is when I unintentionally let flee a fart.

Rather loudly.

And with all the bouquet of a skunk who had just loaded up on a clutch of rotten eggs.

Turtle Dove recoiled with an expression of bemused horror. She held her hand over her nose and backed away, giggling and gagging, I thought, with uncalled for exaggeration.

"*Pardon!*" I said, and felt myself grow hot with shame. I waved at the polluted air between us, attempting to disperse the mustard cloud of gas, but there was no denying that the moment had passed in a switch from one of near bliss to one of pungent mortification.

Still laughing, Turtle Dove went to the pool and washed her hand.

"*Ce n'est pas moi!*" I exclaimed. "It is the water. *C'est l'eau.*"

But she just kept up laughing and making hyperbolic gagging gestures.

That stream, I decided, had betrayed me. And although I know it was a childish thought to think, I found myself mad at it, and even, in the manner of an animist, granted it a persona – one I did not like. "You sewer!" I whispered, and directed all of my wrath and frustration at that snakish twist of liquid. But I suppose, in reality, that water was just water, and probably did not mind my insult so much, as it surely lacked a brain and human feelings to do so. Still, I seethed with humiliation.

"Phooey!" I said, and left Turtle Dove at the pool, stomping off through the willows, I am loath to admit, like an angry nipper.

I MARCHED OFF, SPITTING mad.

"Of all the cursed luck!"

I did not know to where I was going, only that I needed to put some distance between myself and the scene of my most recent disgrace. I blindly trudged through the trees, past the camp, and on upstream. I kicked dirt. I punched air.

"Goddam!" I growled. "Is there anything more fundamentally maddening than unreciprocated affection?"

I looked to the sky, still stomping, awaiting an answer.

But, of course, the sky was mute as a splash of paint.

And worse yet, in glancing away from where I was placing my footfalls, I stepped into a rabbit hole, lost my balance, and toppled forward down a steep bank.

"Ahh!" I cried.

When I came to rest, I was head down, lying on my back on an incline, with my boots uphill. I was quite dazed, and my confusion was compounded by the upside down scene playing out before me. There, a few yards away, was a sinuous young girl with blonde-white hair. A host of tiny blue butterflies danced on the breeze. They all fluttered around her head and shoulders. The girl held her arm out to her side, and the butterflies resting in her palm lifted off into the ether, which, from my tweaked vantage, was where the ground was supposed to be. Those colorful winged creatures became the myriad fragments of the sky. It was quite beautiful to witness, if not a bit surreal.

The girl – still upside down – turned to me with an expression of concern. "Are you all right?" she asked.

I felt a shooting sensation in my shin, a throb in my ribs, and a nauseation in my general personage. "I do not know," I answered. The words came out of me with an amusing topsy-turvy voice. But for all my other bodily disorders, I found myself most self-conscious about my too-large hand-me-down clothes, and my blistered and peeling head. I must have appeared most ridiculous, something like a beat-up, par-roasted clown. "But I am certain," I continued, "that my pride has never been more aggrieved."

I then let my body slither and slump sideways down the embankment so that I was at a horizontal aspect to the earth. Then I sat up.

The girl, it turned out, was Virtue. She came to me, kneeling in the sand beside the stream. It struck me as truly peculiar how one sees things differently after being inadvertently inverted. It shakes things up. It reorganizes the parts, giving one a new perspective, as if examining a painting turned over and so being offered greater insight into the truer nuances of its composition. Now that I was upright, I was greatly impressed with the maturity and grace of my young charge. She had grown so much, and so fast. She was so ladylike. Her wrists were delicate and thin. Her eyes flashed with the same hue as of those butterflies.

A damp spot had seeped through the lower leg of my trousers, and when she saw it, Virtue gently rolled up the cuff, revealing that my wound had popped a couple of its stitches, and was oozing a thin pink liquid.

"Does it hurt much?" she asked.

"Nah," I said. "Only when I sit down, or stand up, or blink, or breathe."

She grinned at my joke, and all my troubles magically fluttered away. Virtue had that effect on me.

"And how are *you* holding up, young lady?"

"I'm fine. It's nice here."

I looked around. I spied the trickling stream, the very one with whom I had been so angry and put out just a few minutes prior. Virtue was correct – it *was* nice here. Unexpectedly, that stream was among the loveliest little rivulets I had ever beheld. It made a joyful and animated descant. I felt ashamed for my recent behavior, and nodded toward the water in apology. Surely it could not help that its contents were so conducive to malodorous intestinal wind. After all, we all have our faults. One would hope that that is exactly what makes us each one so endearing.

"I suppose our respite must soon come to an end," I said. "We have many miles left to travel before we get you to your ..."

I paused. I could not say that word – *husband*. It just would not come out of my mouth. It seemed too absurd. Inappropriate. But I could not think what else to call this enigmatic Nehi person toward whom we had been progressing. For the first time on this journey, I felt a niggling suspicion of wrongness in my assignment.

Virtue looked west, but she said nothing.

I sensed a trepidation in her demeanor.

"It will all work out," I assured her. "I make you that promise."

She looked back at me, rested her hand on my boot, and smiled.

And although I greatly wanted to mean what I said, I felt like a fool for ever saying it. I had lived too long in this world to ever give much credence to such guarantees of a fairytale ending.

PEOPLE WANT BEAUTY; THEY want that splendorous quality in their lives and in their streams and mountains, all the way up to the realm of the stars and moon and then back down to the deep blue seas. They want it in the melodious words they speak and read and hear directed at them from the lips of others. They want the beautiful country – the exquisite wild frontier tamed and made beautifully civilized according to their idealized standards. They want beauty in their homes and tea cozies and cotton nightshirts. They want it in their Holy Book covers, and in the doctrines and parables snugly packaged within those selfsame covers. They want it in the paintings they hang on their walls, the songbirds they have caged in their parlors, and in the bright flowers they keep in vases by the window. They want beauty in the various masks they choose to wear when going out into the day. They want it in their bobbles and accessories. People want the beautiful weather – the small rain coming down, and then the dripping hopeful sunny daybreak after that same small rain is finished. They want it in their drinking water. They want hallowed beauty in their stained glass churches and fortified towns and virtuous mates. They long so secretly, so silently, and so wholeheartedly for that exquisite fairytale moment when, like a perfectly discovered rhyme, everything in their lives comes together just so – that orgasmotic and magical blink of an eye when an anapestic happenchance works out beautifully to the rhythm of the poem of their dreams. They want beautiful love to sweep in beautifully and lift them beautifully up to their beautiful castles in the beautiful sky. They want beautiful Jesus, and beautiful salvation, and the elusive beautiful paradise. Oh, that sweet, sweet paradise! We seek it out in every moment of every day, and behind every pair of eyes. Surely it is as basic a need as food and water.

Beauty.

Here you are.

There you go.

Oh! To whither hast thou flown?

DELIVERING VIRTUE

Such were the random workings of my mind that day as I sat alone on the bluff overlooking our little late summer camp. My head was grinding with thought. Below me was a scene, to my eyes, of ineffable beauty.

The horses were at the edge of camp, beyond the trees, grazing in a picturesque configuration in the tall grass. There was a subliminal rightness in the variations of their postures and the assorted colors of their coats. It is difficult to explain such an abstract aspect of aesthetics, but had an artist painted the scene, he would have been sorely pressed to come up with a more telling combination of parts to express the underlying mix of wildness and docility contained within the combined personalities of those four beasts.

At the center of the composition was the camp itself, and like a strategically placed hue – a caesura of color – was Virtue. She was still wearing her blue dress, and she appeared like a singular forget-me-not on the edge of the stream. She was too far away to be seen with any exactitude, but one could tell, even with the distance, that she was engaged in a meditative interaction with Nature. Perhaps she was whispering with the butterflies; perhaps she was humming a tune in the language of angels or *Syatapis*; perhaps she was having a parley with God himself. Although ambiguous, her posture and elegance gave one to know that she represented a purity too seldom found in this terrestrial sphere.

The trees shimmered in the warm breeze, their leaves turning and quivering to show their silvery undersides in the afternoon sunlight.

And then, on the other side of the grove, came the third panel in the triptych – the pool. Turtle Dove's brown arms flashed in the water. The blurred outline of her naked body moved just under the rippling surface. Something there was just right in how she was both visible and obscured at once. It was as if she were known, and not known, all in the same instant. It was as if a dream were coming to life by way of her physical presence, not yet fully born from the depths, or complete with a soul, and so was filled with an implication that the dream world was reluctant or unable to divulge.

Anyway, I was mystified.

I was suffering all of that giddy and miserable sensation of revelatory arrest experienced when one is confronted with an object – manmade or otherwise – which offers up a fleeting and timeless beauty. And yet there I was, up on my lonesome hillock, observing that beauty as if through a window, or in a museum where it is forbidden to touch. I fairly pined to be a part of the picture below me, to stroke its parts.

But then I smirked at the thought. "Who are you fooling, Rain?"

With my patched, hand-me-down clothes, and uglified head – my masculine earnestness and clumsy manner – what would I have contributed to the scene but a note of ominous and muddled buffoonery?

"Just enjoy it from afar," I told myself. "Today, my friend, you are most surely on the outside."

It was a lonely thought to have, one that instantly filled me up with a deep and personal sadness.

"Anyway," I said. "The problem with beauty is that it is so damn evanescent."

I sat there with myself, watching, until the sun dropped so low on the western horizon that it blinded me with its celestial light.

Then I went down.

OVER SUPPER, I MADE the announcement.

"We have dawdled here long enough," I said, "like a bunch of holiday makers without a worry or care. It has been an enjoyable time." I glanced in the direction of the pool. "But if we mean to get to the City of Rocks before first snowfall, our dilly-dallying must come to its end."

I took a big gulp of water from my tin cup, broke wind with furtive skill, and nodded decisively.

"Tomorrow at dawn," I concluded, "we will be on our way."

No one seemed disapproving, nonplussed, disappointed or otherwise moved by my address. I do not know what I expected. No one seemed emotional at all – neither the geldings nor the ladies – and I wondered if I was the only member of the contingent whom the decision had effected. Had this entire vacation been for my benefit alone? Apparently mine was the only soul made glum by the prospect of leaving this camp behind. I peeked sideways at Turtle Dove, searching for some suggestion of remorse or nostalgia. After all, our courtship had begun here. Someday, with the gods willing, I hoped we would look back together upon this site as the place where our love's latent seed was first planted and watered and made to grow into the beautiful thing it was destined to become. Perhaps we would even return some years hence for an anniversary visit. I might even compose a villanelle in commemoration. But Turtle Dove appeared impassive in the firelight, not exhibiting any obvious display of emotion as she spooned a bit of steaming root broth between her parted lips.

"Well," I sighed, and quietly solaced myself. "At least I know that *I personally* will always hold a fondness in my heart for this little haven on the prairie."

The stream plinked and prattled in the darkness.

An owl hooted amidst the stars – first here – then over there.

My shinbone hurt.

And my ribs.

It seemed that my tumble down the embankment earlier in the day had served me poorly in my physicality. I wanted Turtle Dove to work her magic, maybe re-stitch my broken wound, or at least apply one of her hot-coal tincture treatments to my forelimb. I longed for that intimate torture, that feminine attention. It placated my manly afflictions, and kept my more base intentions at bay. But I was being cursed with an abnormally pungent and magniloquent case of intestinal turgidity, and I did not dare get too close to my affianced, as I could not bear another of her giggle-ridden spurnings.

I sat on the opposite side of the fire, safely back from the flames, gurgling with discomfort, secretly questioning the Almighty's design for the gut-works of a man.

Virtue caught my eye.

What an angel.

Her beatific smile alone was almost enough to ease any man's ailment.

Even in my distress, she made me think of blue butterflies.

I stood carefully, and then walked over to our makeshift livery, preparing for the next day's journey. I synched and braided a loose strap on Puck's sawbuck, making it more secure for the rigors of a rough ride. I turned my own saddle over in the near darkness, plucking the horsehairs that had worked between the seams in the leather, and then rolling them into a ball. Busy work, to be sure, but it served to keep me away from the girls. I looked over at the fire. Turtle Dove and Virtue were up to their usual business, laughing in a pidgin mix of Blackfoot and French (what I had come to call Frenchfoot), gabbing, I supposed, about girl stuff. I carelessly flopped my saddle over on the log, and when I did the stirrup swung down and whapped me directly on my injured shin.

I did not call out, but held my cry of pain inside of me. My eyes watered and I clenched my jaw, bending over with both hands gripping my knees. It hurt terribly, but damned if I would let on like some namby-pamby. For the benefit of the group, I had to make a show of strength that might be undermined by such a pusillanimous display of physical anguish. My worth as a leader had been compromised enough these last days, what with my humorous apparel and battered face and body, and now I needed every edge I could get if I were to reinstate my aptitude as the Blessed Deliverer.

I sat on the log, writhing.

I peered up into the sky, not as a romantic, but as a tortured sentient creature with a grimace needing a point upon which to focus. I did not even bother to seek out my own blue star. It was surely lost in the soup of stars swirling before my eyes. But then I was fairly astonished to spy a meteor blazing a quick bright path across a distant corner of the heavens. Its appearance served me like a tap on the shoulder, shaking my prudence, gently reminding me of possibilities I had otherwise discounted due to the constraints imposed on me by my distant Mormon employers.

And that is when I hit upon a suspicious impulse, albeit one cleverly disguised as a good idea.

Now the roundabout path of my subsequent logic might have struck an observer as a convoluted and unjustifiable attempt at justifying the unjustifiable. In hindsight, which is always embarrassingly sharp and uninterrupted by the myopic mists that so often plague a person at the end of a trying day, I can plainly see now that it was not necessarily the brilliant conclusion that I took it for in that particular moment. But physical torment can drive a man to lazy and erroneous philosophy, and so that very phenomenon is to what I attribute my ensuing actions.

My hand came to rest on my saddlebags, which were hanging over the log as if over the back of a horse. "Hmm!" I reached inside one compartment, groped its contents, and brought out the flask I had hidden there days before. I was well away from the campfire, but yet still close enough for its flickering luminance to show me the wraithlike scene etched into the canister's side. The woman. The pool. The faun. And perhaps it was only the fire's wavering glimmer that caused the apparition, but I swear that the faun let down his pipes, looked out from the scene, and, with what sounded like a Greek accent, whispered the imperative – "Take succor."

No man I know could argue with such a supernatural encouragement.

I glanced over my shoulder into the darkness, and then looked back to the flask, chewing at my bottom lip with deliberation. A spontaneous dialogue then commenced between the two halves of my self, each one representing an opposing argument to the subject at hand.

"Doctors sometimes use such tonic as medicine," said one sensible half of my conscience. "So if taken as such, where is the sin?"

"But you signed an agreement back in Independence. You made a promise to Benjamin as an honorable man that you would not let such substances cross your lips."

"Independence is a long ways away. And the constraints of that contract did not take into account the grueling and unforeseen circumstances of the trail, not to mention the physical discomfort you are suffering this evening."

"But you know how it is your habit to let one harmless nip lead never-endingly to another."

"But this journey is changing you. Surely you are no longer that hapless scalawag who once had a weakness for drink and its affiliate vices."

"Why take the chance?"

"Perhaps a chance should be taken, as a trial by firewater, if you will, so that you might prove once and for all that you have improved, and are no longer that reprehensible beast that once you were."

"But what if you *are* still what you were?"

"Well, nothing is learned through timidity. Take a taste and find out."

"Do not!"

"Do it."

"I warn you, it is a Pandora's Box!"

And so, on and so forth – blar, blar, blar – until the two voices joined in confusion and became one with the nonsensical babble of the stream.

Of course, I uncorked the bottle. Where was the harm in doing that?

DELIVERING VIRTUE

The flask seemed to gasp with relief, a little puff of acerbic vapor escaping like a genie from its spout. When it encountered my nostrils, a wellspring of slobber issued forth from the underside of my tongue, causing me to swallow.

"Medicine," I whispered. And as if to justify the substance as such, I then tugged up my pant cuff and spilled the tiniest bit of the liquor onto my wound. It sizzled along the edges of the cut, and caused me to grit my teeth. In the smallest way, it was a corresponding experience to the one enacted upon me by my lovely Turtle Dove, although minus the feminine interaction. Still, it was somewhat a consolation, and I felt a smidgeon of relief. The liquid slithered like a tiny snake down my foreleg and into my boot.

I held the flask to my nose, breathing deeply.

"Just one single sip," I promised myself. "And then we will most surely put it away for good."

BY THE THIRD SIP I was already feeling significantly improved in the areas of my shinbone, my ribs, and even in the tortured twist of entrails packaged within the lower reaches of those ribs. The source of my flatulence seemed dowsed by the magical liquid I had poured down my craw and into its flames. I let out a steamy little belch of licorice mixed with sulfur and juniper, and then ran my tongue over my lips.

"Well," I said, and winked at the maiden on the flask. "That was not so bad as all that, was it?"

She did not reply.

It was with an impressive self-control that I then took only one or two (at most, three) more sips before reinserting the cork and, without sentiment or ballyhoo, slid the flask back into my panniers.

I sat on the log for a moment, a comforting warmth spreading to the various corners of my body.

The owl screeched overhead, and this prompted me to lean back and peer into the stars once more.

How stunning they were!

So tranquil and bedazzling!

How beautiful it all and everything else besides suddenly was!

I spied the owl's dark shadow flashing between the heavenly points of light. This seemed dramatic and staged for my benefit in a paranormal, yet not-so-threatening way.

"Little *Oiseau*," I sang to myself. "*Petit* Birdy."

I found myself imagining what it might feel like to be up there so high, just flapping around in the stars over the dark and slumbering frontier. My mind plucked out and I fancied myself peering down on my dearest Turtle Dove as she sat with Virtue by the campfire. For some reason lost to me, the image made me in turns immeasurably happy, profoundly miserable, and then, again, immeasurably happy. Life, at times, can flop back and forth that way.

Then I discovered in myself a longing to join the very picture I was observing down below. This was simple enough, I realized, as I was not truly soaring overhead with the owl, but just squatting on a log. I had only to stand, walk over to the camp, and reconvene with the girls.

"First stand," I told myself.

I did, but I do not recall hearing my voice commanding me to take anymore of the steps required to get from one place to the next. And yet there now I was.

Turtle Dove and Virtue both looked up at me, expectantly.

I gazed down at them, hovering, an irrepressible grin spreading over my face.

"*Qu-est que c'est?*" asked my Dove.

Her voice was like silence mixed with music.

It stirred in me a passion – a tremor of joy and anticipation in the corresponding regions of my heart, my solar plexus, and also in that area farther down.

"Nothing," I finally answered. " *Rien.*" And then, in a fit of unanticipated inspiration, I blurted, "I think I will now write some verse!"

The girls stared at me blankly. Puck snorted from the edge of the darkness. They were all by now a tad wary of my attempts to bring ink and paper to any partnership for the sake of a beauteous and cadenced expression. And so I suppose they were less than impressed with my bold declaration. Still, Virtue smiled reassuringly.

"Good for you," she said. "Have fun."

Turtle Dove only shrugged, and gave me an indifferent nod.

This small measure of encouragement was enough to put a lift in my already elevated spirits, and so I turned decisively on my boot heel, strode back to my saddlebags, and found my paper pad and ink and pen. Yes, I confess, for good measure I took one more sip from the flask, although it was exceedingly small in quantity, barely a taste, truly. My thinking was that I did not dare let my shinbone start up hurting while I was in the throes of poetic composition, and the tonic seemed my greatest insurance that such an interruption would be kept at bay.

"Medicine," I whispered.

NIPPLE, I SOON DISCOVERED, is an exceedingly difficult word for which to find an appropriate rhyme.

Of course, Ripple came to mind almost at once, but by no way I turned it could I find any eloquent way to make a nipple ripple.

No doubt the motivation for such a beginning to my poem came from the scene playing out before me. Turtle Dove had pulled down her top, and was giving Virtue her evening allowance of milk. One envied them their intimate connection – that mother-child bond that is like no other. Virtue knelt on the ground beside her nursemaid, leaning over her front, her hand steadying her against Turtle Dove's upper thigh. They were so innocent and open about their task. So Sapphic. Never mind that Virtue had moved beyond infancy and was now a girl. Never mind that I, with thirsts of my own, was observing them in full view.

Turtle Dove's eyes fell on mine. They twinkled with firelight. She did not turn away, but held perfectly still. It was as if she were a detailed part of a bigger picture, fixed in a timeless application of paint, and would be looking out for generations to come at any viewer who passed, reminding them always, through subtle aide-memoire, of some inexpressible thing they had lost along the way.

I grew unexpectedly warm, and quickly, before I forgot what I was up to, tugged open the collar of my shirt, letting out some steam, and jotted both *Nipple* and *Ripple* at the bottom of the page, thinking I would work them in as my poem progressed.

I then endeavored to continue writing. I was out of practice, and it proved most difficult. My mind would not let go of the thought of Turtle Dove watching me, muse-like, as I wrote, and with her quintessence so fully ensconced in my mind, I penned the line – "Let us go then, you and I, when the evening is spread out against the sky, like…"

But I stopped right there.

DELIVERING VIRTUE

I lifted the pen from the parchment.

Now perhaps it was only a side effect brought on by the medicine I had earlier self-administered, but I realized a sensation that I had, on past occasions, felt before – once when I was a lad with a poem about a red wheelbarrow glazed with rain, and another time later on with a poem about two roads diverging in a yellowed wood. It is difficult to explain the sensation with any clarity, as it is mysterious and vague and somewhat disturbing. It was something like discovering that you are walking with one foot in a dream. But this was no ordinary dream; this was a dream belonging to someone who had not yet been born. And although we are all God's creatures, and no doubt connected in cosmic ways we cannot fathom as mortals, this particular sensation felt to be aberrant and distressing.

It is common, and perhaps inevitable, that a poet will lift lines and even whole stanzas from other versifiers in history. For the ever-rising temple of Poesy is surely built on the ink-soaked foundations laid down by those who came before us. And it could even be argued that certain holy books are, in fact, nothing more than restructurings of the dusty myth-laden epics of the foggy past. But to borrow from the unlived future seemed wrongful in ways that felt akin to playing God. One sensed Mephistopheles lurking in the shadows. There were some things that just should not be done, some lines that should never be crossed. And although I had most certainly stepped over more than one doubtful line in my life, this was the one Thou Shalt Not above all others that I refused to transgress. Such far-reaching necromantic plagiarism seemed similar to bringing forth a babe before it had fully ripened in the wellspring of the womb. How could such a fragile, par-souled being – be it a poem or a child – ever survive in the harshness of this waking life? Such creatures born ahead of their time are most assuredly doomed from the start.

But alas, this additional stricture on the free-flow of my syncopated musings only caused me more angst. How would I ever build a living, breathing poem of my own with all these rules circling round in my head?

"Maybe I just need to stretch my legs," I told myself, "And then perhaps the mind will follow."

I left Turtle Dove and Virtue to their business, and strolled about the camp, taking a circuitous route through the willows that led me inevitably to the log with my saddlebags.

As I walked, I happened upon a thought about the great poet Coleridge, and specifically about his poem Kubla Khan. It is widely understood among fellow poets that this masterwork was composed while its creator was in the throes of an opium-induced reverie. I had no opium.

"But," I whispered, as I pulled the flask from its hiding place, "I do have you."

I uncorked the canister once more, and said, "Merely a splash to oil the rusted cog-works of my mind." And then I tipped back and let a long draught of the liquid burn a stream of fire down my throat.

I replaced the flask, stood, wavered for a moment, steadied myself with a hand against the log, and then went back to my waiting paper and pen.

The word *Tipple* came to me as I walked, and I was most exhilarated at the thought of my opium substitute doing such good work on my poetic behalf. I quick wrote down the word *Tipple* next to *Ripple* and *Nipple*.

Virtue was finished with nursing, and as the evening was getting late, she decided to ready herself for bed. She brushed out her hair, while talking quietly with Turtle Dove.

I blinked and swallowed and struggled to rhyme something – anything – with something else.

Virtue came over when she was finished grooming. She had wound her hair into a long braid and tied it with a ribbon.

"Goodnight," she said, and reached out to me with her hand.

I lifted my own hand and took hold of hers. She gave my fingers a gentle squeeze. I cannot express how happy that made me. Then she turned and went to the far corner of the camp where there was a shallow compression in the grass where she and Turtle Dove had a Buffalo robe spread out with some blankets.

"Pleasant dreams," I called.

And then she sank down into the shadows.

The horses were snoozing on the perimeter.

Turtle Dove and I were left alone.

IT WAS THERE AND then, *sous les étoiles,* on that wild American frontier, with my own true love so picturesquely sorting herbs before me, that Bacchus saw fit to fling open the floodgates of poesy.

I fairly swooned at the rush of inspiration that so swiftly inundated my being.

My vision momentarily blurred.

I caught my breath.

But then, with my pen loaded up with ink, I set to work on my poem.

Oh, what a splendorous feeling to be once again composing!

The words flowed flowingly and flowingly flowed like a springtide freshet born from the lofty bosom of the mountains – twisting and undulating here – making a bend in a rhythm there – plashing headlong ever faster in a froth and forward tremulously onward. And I – I was but carried along – a gleeful bard of a boy abob on a musical gush of verbalistic flotsam.

Oh!

And oh!

When I was finished, I did not bother to reread what I had written. Instead, with confidence, I placed my pen and paper to the side, and leaned back, somewhat spent. My head was spinning. A ringing sounded in my ears. I silently burped up a sulfurous and licorice posset that burnt the inside of my nostrils. I swallowed and sniffed.

Turtle Dove was on the other side of the flames, gathering up the bowls and spoons and knives from our supper. She stacked the bowls together, one inside the next. She tossed a bit of uneaten biscuit into the fire, and then, without glancing my way, went off with the dishes through the trees toward the pool.

Now I have always been especially proud of my ability to interpret the nuances and mannerisms that so often elude non-speakers of a language – and I was feeling like a true master of words, even those unsaid. (Had I not just displayed a most impressive lingual dexterity with my poem?) And although understated, I took Turtle Dove's gestures for their secret meaning. "Come hither," she was most assuredly saying. "Follow me now into the shadows."

"Oh, Rain," I whispered. "Opportunity hath knocked sweetly upon thy garden gate."

And then, nervous as a youth, I hurried over and took one final drink from the flask, draining its contents in an effort to embolden myself for the interaction I sensed upcoming.

I then shuffled off toward the pool, falling only twice. My eyes had not yet adjusted to the darkness into which I entered, and the way was strewn with branches and holes and various other obstacles placed between my love and myself.

As I neared the clearing, I moved more slowly, and with more stealth. The stream babbled loudly enough to cover the sound of my footfalls. I crept closer, positioning myself behind a tree trunk, until Turtle Dove was only a single rod away. I could see her there now, kneeling on the bank, the starlight faintly illuminating her buxom feminine figure as she went about scrubbing out the bowls. The stars reflected in the pool, and it was difficult to tell where the sky stopped and the water began, as each one seemed to be a deliquesced extension of the other.

Turtle Dove hummed an Indian song as she worked. Primal and holy. It resonated in the deepest chambers of my heart, moving me to a great emotion. I was on the verge of joyful tears. I could have waited there behind that tree for all of eternity, so pristine was that teetering moment of anticipation. But then Turtle Dove did something that prompted the moment forward. She laid the bowls and utensils to the side. She slipped down the top of her buckskin dress, freeing her arms and shoulders of its encumbrance. And then, cupping a handful of water from the pool, she began to wash her breasts.

I took one step and fell.

"Umph!"

Turtle Dove spun and jumped to her feet.

She stood on the bank, covering herself with her arms.

I scrambled to my knees, and then, still on all fours, craned up at her. She was like something from a Botticelli, with the heavens as backdrop to her angelicism. I hesitated, but then, gathering myself, I mustered a composure worthy of my station.

"*Excusez-moi,*" I said. "*Uh... Bonsoir.*"

Turtle Dove did not at first reply. She feigned surprise, and I found myself all the more attracted to her for her courtly play at coyness.

I struggled to stand, and finally did. Although my fall had jarred me somewhat, causing me to feel a dizziness that resulted in a clumsy sidestep jig. I held my arms out to my sides for balance.

Turtle Dove stared at me. I could not clearly see her expression. I squinted at her face, but I could not clearly see her smile in the near darkness.

"*Qu-est que vous voulez?*" she asked.

Yes, I thought. Good question. What do I want? Simple things. A small rain coming down. Beauty. Peace. Paradise.

"*Un peu du lait,*" I said at last. The request surprised even me. It felt as if a part of myself unbeknownst to me had uttered its truest desire.

Turtle Dove did not move.

I stepped forward, and gestured with my open hand for her to sit on the ground. "Just a taste," I said. "*S'il vous plait.*"

It was impossible to know what was going on inside the woman's head. One could speculate that she was intrigued, excited, even eager. But, of course, one could not be certain. They are a mysterious sex. At any rate, after some moments of deliberation, she complied with my first wish that she sit in the grass by the pool. I knelt beside her.

I felt like a neophyte suitor hoping to get a first kiss. Uncertain. Sheepish. But subject to a great and overriding thirst.

To ease her discomfiture, I spoke soothingly, as a friend. "It is a lovely night," I said with casualness. "The stars are watching us. It reminds me very much of the nocturnal scene from my old dream – the very one in which you and I met before."

I searched the shadows of her face, looking for some indication of recollection. But she remained charmingly aloof, her arms still crossed over her chest. The stream plinked and clinked along the edges of the pool. The world seemed to have picked up speed in its spinning. Time felt to be running out, like an upturned bottle emptying of its contents.

I nodded toward her, and boldly laid my hand on her arm. "*Permettez-moi?*"

She drew back, half turning away, but when I pulled gently on her wrist, she did not resist too forcefully, and finally opened herself up to me.

I wet my lips with my tongue. Then, in the very manner I had observed Virtue doing the same, I leaned forward, rested my hand on Turtle Dove's thigh, and took suck.

HER MILK MADE ME drunk.

   With wistfulness.

   With adoration.

   With a wakened desire the power of which I did not know I had in me.

   Her sweetness stirred in me the queerest sensation. It was all joy and confusion, misery and hope. It was wild birds soaring on the wind; it was snow falling along invisible mountaintops. It was my childhood played out all over again in an instant – toys strewn on the floor, a lullaby sung softly at bedtime. It was sounds in the rainy street. Quiet laughter in the shadows. The clop of hooves. A moan, a whimper, and a scream. The dolorous clamor of bells in chorus with the eternal wash and hiss of the sea. It was truly a thousand things – the myriad jetsam of one's life – all coming together now in a single wave of longing.

   "Oh, Dove," I said at last, wiping my mouth on my sleeve.

   To live!

   To feel!

   To love!

   And Oh! – to be loved in return.

   "...behold, he cometh leaping upon the mountains... skipping upon the hills."

   I pressed her down into the grass, knocking over the freshly washed stack of bowls.

   "*Non!*" she called.

   "*Oui.*"

   (For a wise man once assured me that No, when translated from the language of a woman's heart, inevitably comes back around to meaning Yes.)

   She struggled, out of obligation, I suppose. Could I have respected her so much had she not?

   I held her wrists. "I am *Syatapis*," I said. "I am your man."

I pressed a gentle kiss onto her parted lips, and then took her hand and held it over my tattoo.

"And you," I told her. "You are my bride."

Her startled eyes sparkled with glints of stellar light, and then closed.

She let go of a deep deep sigh.

I heard the owl pass low over the pool, its beak clicking.

After that, she remained still and silent throughout.

WHEN I WAS A boy, and still in short pants, it was my daily habit to fling a dozen stones into the sea. I would wait for low tide, and toss one as far as I could, out beyond the waves. I would watch it splash in the sea foam, and then close my eyes, imagining it sinking away and away into the briny depths. Sometimes that stone dropped down through a school of little yellow fish, scattering them like flecks of sunlight. At other times, it bounced and rolled off the back of a silent leviathan cruising in that somnolent underworld. But always, before the first stone hit bottom, I would toss the next, repeating the procedure until my twelve stones were spent.

I had it in my mind that I was part of a sequence – a series of boys stretching from Adam all the way on up to some distant time in the future – and that we were all in league, over the generations, in a common effort to fill up the sea with stones. Someday, ages hence, some yet-to-be-born boy would be granted the privilege of tossing that last stone. The process would be complete. Then all we boys – ghosts of the past, standing shoulder to shoulder – would have completed our task. The continents would be joined. The Old World and the New would be a single contiguous mass.

One day, as I was tossing my stones, I heard some ladies talking and laughing behind me on the strand. It was common to see the wives of the wealthy merchants and ship owners taking their promenade in the afternoon. They dressed in all their finery, often sporting lace parasols, and wearing the most lavish of gowns. They were in an unspoken competition to see who could outdo the next in the elegance and fashionable statement of their attire.

One woman in particular always shined above the others. She was slightly taller than the rest, and thin, with a perfectly placed mole above her upper lip. I knew that her name was Chantal, and that she was my father's wife, although how I attained this information I do not recall. Through my father, she had connections in London and Paris, and so always outdid the other ladies with the latest cut of her dress. On top of that, she had the audacity to bring a small poodle as a sort of living accessory to her stylishness. The lap dog was nearly as done up as was she, all ribbons and coifed just so.

On that afternoon, while the ladies were busy jabbering about this thing and that, that mutt took an opportunity to quietly slip off his leash and go exploring. I watched him lift his nose to the breeze and sniff. If a dog could grin, he most assuredly did.

In no time, he had found the putrefied corpse of a cod that had washed up onto the sand. He ran his pink tongue along the corners of his mouth. And then, in a state of pure animal rapture, he rolled and rolled in that fly ridden offal. At last, completely satisfied with himself, the little scoundrel slunk back to his mistress.

I was down to my last stone, but I dared not turn away and miss the show I sensed forthcoming. Soon, I knew, that woman would catch a whiff of her dog's perfume. And sure enough...

"Oh!" she cried, and wheeled about.

The odor must have risen all at once, because, in unison, the other ladies politely, but urgently, placed their hands over their noses, smiling from behind their kerchiefs with pained expressions.

"Chou-Chou! Non!"

The poodle looked up, wagging the pompon on his tail. His curly black coat was decorated with fish scales and slime.

"Oh! Zut alors!"

The woman bent to pick up the dog, but then, thinking better of it, she instead furled her parasol onto its cane. She raised it up and brought it down with a whack on the little dog's back. Whack! Whack! While the other ladies watched.

I was a fair distance away, but my eyes met those of the dog. He just stood there, taking the blows, not even trying to run away. One could see that he was not a bit sorry for what he had done. He was merely suffering the wrath of fools.

"C'est la vie," he seemed to say to me. "It is how I am made. What is one to do?"

I looked down at the last stone resting in my palm. It was nicely shaped and curiously blue. It looked very much like a stone teardrop. I took and tossed it as far as I could into the surge and swell of the ocean – Plunk!

Whack! Whack! went the woman's parasol, even over the hiss of the waves.

The blue stone sunk into the depths, just one of the many stones yet to come.

"*Donc!*" I said, and then I turned and ran down the beach just as fast as I could go.

I DID NOT RECALL falling to sleep, but now, abruptly, I found myself surfacing in the waking world.

The vestige of some beautiful specter wavered in the shadows before me, and then slipped into the pool. I heard it part the waters and sink away. I felt myself reaching after, but sensed, from that confusing middle ground of dreams, that I had in truth remained motionless the whole time, and had not so much as lifted my little finger.

I laid there, gathering the disparate fragments of my cognizance. It was a problematic act to accomplish. I felt rather like a puzzle scattered on the ground – nonsensical, and in pieces. But eventually, those pieces began to join together, more or less in order.

I became aware of an inordinate pressure building in my brain. I was certain that a horse had his hoof resting on my forehead and was pressing down, testing to see at what point my skull would bust open like a ripe carbuncle. But when my eyes fluttered open, there was no horse standing over me – only air and sky. And blurred stars – far away – winking out, one by one, in the grayish glow.

"Dawn," I croaked, swallowing at the terrific dryness that had embraced the region of my larynx. "But where art thy rosy fingers?"

I licked my lips with a withered tongue, and was delighted to find them dampened with dew.

Everything felt to be saturated with a heavy condensation. It soaked coolly through my shirt. It was wet on the back of my hands, and on my face. That dew was the closest thing to rain I had experienced in such a long time, and although somewhat chilling and uncomfortable in its penetrating sogginess, it was just as soon refreshing besides. The dew felt somewhat cleansing, like, of sorts, a naturally occurring spit bath.

My mind mists began to lift, and I was able to sort the remnants of my dreams and separate them from the more tangible parts of the preceding night. I remembered the owl.

A taste of milk.

The touch of skin coming together with warm skin.

A resounding whack.

And then, in a rush, everything came back to me properly categorized.

I quick struggled to lift myself from the grass. The weight of my head was excessive and unmanageable. The ground shifted and tipped beneath me as I raised up – like the deck of a ship riding a rough sea – eliciting from my stomach pit an intense queasiness that instigated a surge of nervy sweat from all the pores of my body. I nearly upheaved, but only belched – a foul licorice-scented bile that stung my nostrils and seared my throat tube all the way back down to my innards. I gagged a bit, coughed, and then, resting on an elbow, turned to the side.

Turtle Dove!

She lay in the grass, still sleeping.

My Indian Princess. *Ma Belle Sauvage.*

Lost to her own secretive dreams.

She lay picturesquely among the scattered bowls. A nearly nonexistent smile graced her mouth. The dew, like tiny jewels, beaded her upturned breasts. I fancied myself taking up a lover's symbolic residence in the gentle heart sheltered beneath those breasts.

> "When the midnight of absence the day-scene pervading
> Distills its dew o'er the bosom of love…"

Oh, what splendor!

I smiled to myself. I surely could have admired her forever. But I was eager that she should wake, and that we should take our first steps forward in this life as a man and woman joined in the singularity of marriage. I placed my hand on her belly. I felt the dew drops disperse between my fingers and her skin. It was a sensation I knew, even then, that I would remember for the rest of my days.

"Dove," I whispered, and gave her a tender shake.

Her flesh rocked gently beneath my touch, causing the dewdrops to stream down the slopes of her breasts and pool in the shallow valley lying between.

"My love," I said more loudly, and then, with a smile, "Mrs. Rain."

But then my own heart dropped away inside of me. My calls fell on deaf ears.

She could not hear me now from where she was. That world was too far away.

"Oh!" I said. "Oh, love!"

I fell forward upon her lifeless form.

Like a babe, I clung to her.

And then I commenced to weep and weep.

HOW MANY TIMES CAN a man's heart be broke before it will cease to mend?

This I wondered as, dulled by grief, I swaddled Turtle Dove's body within the folds of her buffalo robe.

The others stood behind me near the pool, watching. I did not endeavor to hide my tears, and they, likewise, did not conceal their own sorrow. The horses held their heads bowed low. Virtue waited silently beside them.

"I can only guess..." I told the group, and sniffled. "I can only guess that the Dark Angel's latent poison must have finally dislodged inside of our dear Turtle Dove, and then promptly worked its evil." For there had been no indication that she was sick.

I tucked the robe in tight under her arms and legs, and bound it around the Indian woman with a length of rope, doing my best to mimic the way she had prepared her dead husband and son. I tried to make a fashion of that same style of odd, if not macabre, cocoon. Her head remained sticking out the top. My intentions were to respect her Blackfoot ways, enact her Indian rites, although in truth, I felt to be a bit of a white man muddler in my efforts at this undertaking.

I then went to a stagnant little backwater down the stream and brought up heaping handfuls of clay churned with white gypsum mud. I carried the dripping glob back and gently rubbed it on Turtle Dove's face all over. The clay began to dry at once with the warmth of the sunshine, and her countenance hardened under its alabaster death mask. She looked very much the same as she had when we had first met in my boyish dream, only now her eyes were closed, and I felt a whelming upsurge of sorrow at this thought of what we both had lost, and what we never now would have.

I applied the white clay to my own face as well. Had I had any hair to chop off, I most assuredly would have. I am certain I looked pathetic and grotesque in the eyes of those around me, but I did not care. I had adored her, and this was the only way now that I could find to express that fact.

With a piece of charcoal, I then drew a pair of eyes on her white forehead, again, in the manner I had seen used on her dead family. My efforts were a bit clumsy – the eyes were of mismatched sizes – but all in all, it was a respectable attempt considering. I blew the bits of cinder away, and then, kneeling, struggled to lift her into my arms.

I staggered to a nearby cottonwood tree with a trunk that forked about five feet off the ground. I adjusted the cocoon over my shoulder so that I might more easily heft it into the tree's crotch. It was not easy to do. At first I failed to get her high enough, and then, once I had, the body tumbled down onto the ground with a thump. This was disconcerting, and not at all according to the idealized choreography of the ritual I had mapped out in my head.

I sighed, and steadied myself with a hand against the tree, waiting for my wooziness to subside. Admittedly, the liquor opiate I had ingested the evening before was now affecting my equilibrium and causing an intermittent seasickness that made any physical act most challenging. But soon my vertigo passed, and I attempted once again to lift the corpse into the tree. I was about to fail once more, when I sensed Virtue beside me, placing her hands on the bundle and pushing upwards. Her help was enough to complete the task, and at last, Turtle Dove's shrouded body rested in the crotch of the tree.

"Thank you," I said.

Virtue smiled and stepped away.

I used another piece of rope to secure Turtle Dove to the tree, insuring that she would not be pulled down by a coyote, or toppled by the weight of the inevitable vultures. I then stepped backwards and, with sorrow, assessed my work.

I was surprised to see that my old clothes – the very shirt and trousers so burnt and torn during our ordeal with the prairie fire – were still hanging in the branches of the tree where, on that very first day at the pool, I had left them out to dry. They waved languidly in the breeze. I was about to step forward and yank them down, when it occurred to me to leave them be. I did not know clearly what they represented – perhaps some vestige of my former self – but they seemed appropriately placed there near to my dearly departed Turtle Dove. In a way, I suppose, I imagined it to be symbolic of our togetherness, although such logic was surely thin and personal. At any rate, they remained in the tree, flapping and empty.

DELIVERING VIRTUE

Turtle Dove's vantage afforded her a peaceful view of the pool. So much had happened here in these last few days. So much good and bad. Time had seemed to stand still. Her painted eyes peered out onto the scene. That grassy plot was where she had stitched my shin, and touched my tattoo. There was where she had swum in the pool's coolness. And of course, there was where we had effectuated our love, and from where, soon after, her soul had left this earthly world behind.

"Oh, Dove!" I whispered, and set forth on producing a new round of teardrops.

The others waited.

I did not want to leave her there now. The moment felt incomplete. But then I suppose that is always how it is when someone dies prematurely and of a sudden. So many things are left unsaid; so many loose ends are left undone.

The pool kept up its plinking and tinkling dirge.

The sun beat down.

And then I remembered something. How could I have forgotten?

"I'll be right back," I told Virtue and the horses.

In a minute, I returned with the poem I had composed the evening before. "Let us gather round," I said to my friends.

The horses and Virtue moved closer, forming a half circle before the cocoon.

"I will now read this bit of verse, inspired by Turtle Dove, as an encomium to her everlasting loveliness."

Now I had not reread the poem as of yet, or revised its lines to make it a more smooth flowing and polished work of art, but as I was still inspired by the thought of Coleridge's Kubla Khan, I boldly began to read.

> "Oh, Turtle Dove! Oh, Turtle Dove!
> I crave your love, Oh, Turtle Dove!
> Blue butterflies are in the sky,
> Darkened now by night.
> I see the stars flash in their wings -
> A beatific sight.

I hear your voice upon the stream,
Recalling now our white-faced dream.
You sing a song of water,
While Sweet Virtue sleeps like a daughter.
I smell your milk across the way, Oh,
Its honey doth my heart asway!
I long to suck your nipple..."

At this point I paused and cleared my throat, forcing down a surge of nausea.

"And from your breast now take a tipple..."

I was feeling bad.

"As I hear the plash and ripple...
Of..."

And then, in ill-timed fashion, I retched.

A great upsurge of licorice muck issued forth from selected orifices on my mud-caked face.

I doubled over, heaving and heaving, painfully purgating the poisons that had been percolating on my insides. This went on for some time.

At last, my convulsions ceased. But alas! My vomitus had splashed all over my hands, and over the poem held therein. I stood in a puddle of corruption, assessing the damage.

"Whoa!" I moaned, "Oooh-Ahhh!"

I tried to wipe the filth from my paper pad, hoping to finish my eulogy, but saw that it was hopeless. The ink had run, and the text was too marred to be deciphered. The poem was lost almost before it had been found.

I stood hunched over, considering this. "Oh, well," I said, and shrugged. "It needed considerable work anyway."

And then I tossed the poem to the side.

Turtle Dove looked down on us from on high. Even from under her deathly vestments and mask, she exuded a loveliness that seemed almost holy. "Go now," she seemed to say. "And take my memory with you."

I tipped my hat to her. "Farewell, my love."

Virtue went and laid a flower at her feet.

And then we prepared to move on, wondering what perils could possibly surpass this latest blow to our spirits and sense of purpose.

TURTLE DOVE'S PASSING ALL but sapped our collective enthusiasm. It was hard now to remember our objective, or why it even mattered. The horses clumped along with their eyes half closed, as if after a long and tedious day of pulling a plow. Virtue – riding Genevieve – rarely spoke. She traveled in a sort of hypnotic meditation. She seemed placid enough, but one could only guess at what she might have been thinking. I especially felt to be wandering aimlessly, aimlessly, leading everyone more or less in a westerly direction, toward the setting sun, but with no great sense of urgency. My heart ached. What did it matter if we made the City of Rocks by first snow? In the big picture, who cared if Nehi ever got his bride, or me my thirty thousand dollars?

"Hell," I muttered. "What if I never scribble another line of verse as long as I live?"

Would the human race be any the worse for it?

In the throes of those dark days, I greatly doubted that it would.

By and by, the terrain began to transform around us. The prairie at last surrendered to a rougher ground, with withered scrub brush and sage and the occasional stunted hackberry tree replacing the ubiquitous tall grass. This new landscape was unlovely to gaze upon. It was crisscrossed with dry ravines, bony ridges, and studded with sandstone plateaus placed like colossal headstones across the bleak topography. One sensed that we were gaining elevation, creeping ever upward on a ramp of slightly tipped earth that would lift us ultimately to the Continental Divide – that north-south crest that runs down the American map like a wrinkle in the backside of a whore's bloomers. The air was cooler too, causing one to feel that summer was most assuredly at its end. I suppose this change in scenery and subtle sense of progress might have marginally shaken our apathy, but not to any extent we noticed.

Our sorrow was too great.

After a few days, my clay mourning mask began to itch something dreadful, what with my whiskers sprouting underneath and trying to work their way through its impermeable plaster consistency. It did no good to scratch, as I only came away with bits of chalk under my nails, affording me no relief. I was beginning to think I might go mad with the irritation, when at last we came to an ugly little stream winding in the bottom of a gully. The hollow was choked with stinkweed and brush and brambles. We were in need of water – our continuous necessity – and although this creek had little to recommend it, we could not be sure how long before we would find one better. We rode along its high bank for a ways until we came to a place where we could get down to the water.

"We will fill our bellies and our canteens," I told the others. "And we will rest for a short time." I regarded the unlikely picnic ground, and shrugged. "Anyway, make yourselves as comfortable as you can. I need to do some work on my face."

I walked a ways downstream, so as not to foul the water for the others. And then I dropped to my knees, placed my hat to the side, and, taking a big breath, sank my head into the stream, endeavoring to loosen the mortar that clung so perniciously to my cheeks and earlobes. This procedure had no result at first – the mud was too petrified to dislodge – but at last, with repetitive dunkings, the veneer softened and began to peel away from my jowls.

"Christ almighty!"

It was a painful procedure. A goodly amount of my facial hair came off with the mask, plucking from out my jaw skin, and this was quite torturous to endure. Droplets of blood splashed in the water beneath me.

I had been working at this for a good long while when I heard a hubbub upstream. I knelt there on the stream's edge, looking back, my face dripping water and blood all down my front.

The air felt suspicious.

Tense.

Virtue, Brownie, Puck and Genevieve were holding themselves quite still, but Sabrina was nickering and carrying on as if she had seen a snake. She reared up on her hind legs, her eyes wild with fear.

I wiped the water from my face and stood.

"Say there," I called. "What is hap...?"

But in that instant a brown blur burst forth from the bushes with a roar.

I stepped backwards and fell into the stream.

The horses reared and bucked as the lurching bear swiped his great paw across Sabrina's shoulder.

She screamed and staggered sideways, but in the next blink she bolted up the bank and was out of sight.

The bear started to chase after, but then he whirled about, facing the others who were now trapped between him and a thicket.

I was sitting in the stream, watching the drama, expecting to see that bear murder each of my friends one at a time.

Would that I had had a gun!

To their heroic credit, Puck and Brownie both stepped forward, their hooves swatting in the air toward the grizzly. This caused the bear to pause, as they appeared most formidable and full of business. But then the bear growled again – an unearthly roar that gave one to know that the situation was hopeless, and we all might just as well lie down and have it over with.

The bear stalked forward.

I grabbed a rock from the bottom of the stream, staggered to my feet, and tossed it with all my might at this beastly Goliath.

"Hey yah!" I yelled.

The rock bounced off the bear's rump. He did not so much as turn to see who threw it.

That was when Virtue stepped forward. She laid her hands on both Puck's and Brownie's chests and pushed them back. Then she turned to face the bear.

"Oh, God!" I moaned.

She would barely provide a mouthful for this enormous monster. I could hardly watch.

But Virtue did not seem afraid in the least. And perhaps it was this fearless quality that caused the bear to tarry in his dining. What does this small creature know, he must have wondered, that makes her so brave?

I wondered the same thing myself.

Virtue was so exquisite there. Her blond hair was brushed back in a ponytail, and she wore a black dress. The grizzly raised up onto his back legs and towered above her. Long strings of drool hung down from his yellowed teeth. I fully anticipated this to be the last image I would have of Virtue before she was no more.

But the bear did not move forward; Virtue did not back down. She kept her gaze on the bear's eyes. They stood facing one another like that for what seemed a full minute. At last, she raised her arm and pointed to the side, as if directing the creature to where she wanted him to go.

The bear let out another roar, long and loud and full of threat. His claws flashed like daggers.

Virtue thrust her arm in the air more deliberately, gesturing to the side.

The bear dropped to all fours. He glared at the girl before him.

And then, with a huff, he turned and ambled away into the brush.

I nearly pissed myself with fear and relief.

I scrambled out of the stream and scuttled forward.

"Oh, Darling!"

I laughed nervously, embracing Virtue and maladroitly soaking the front of her dress.

"Oh, Virtue! I thought sure you were lost for good." I held her at arms' length. "Are you all of a piece?"

She smiled. "I'm fine."

It was true; there was not a blond hair out of place on her beautiful head.

I glanced to the large hole in the thicket into which the bruin had disappeared, but felt confident that he would not return. Virtue had sent him on his merry way, with nary a taste of pilgrim on his lips. A miracle!

I turned to the others. "Puck!" I said. "Brownie! That was the purest case of intrepid manliness I have ever seen displayed by horseflesh or human either one. You boys deserve gold medals."

They both were still breathing hard, and Puck was skittery, but Brownie, in his usual manner, remained easygoing. He bobbed his head and whinnied softly. I laid my hand on each of their necks. "Fine warriors," I said. "I am proud to know you."

Then at last I stepped toward Genevieve. She was visibly shaking, and the wild fear look had not yet left her eyes. So much had changed for her in these last few days, what with Turtle Dove's departure. I suspect she felt to be fairly at a loss without her other feminine companion near her side.

"Whoa, girl."

She was reluctant to let me touch her, and kept backing away, but then Virtue stepped past me and soothed her with a few soft words in Blackfoot. The girl laid her hand on the mare's nose and rubbed her cheek against her own, cooing. Genevieve became calm directly. The gesture reminded me very much of Turtle Dove's tender way.

Virtue turned to me. "We should find Sabrina."

"Oh, yes." I looked to the place where the panicked mare had leapt up the crumbling bank. The sand and dirt was scarred with her thrusting hoof marks to the point at which they went out of sight over the rim.

"I would not think she would wander too far afield," I said. "If you will wait here, and put things right with the others, I will go and fetch Sabrina."

In hindsight, which, as I have mentioned, is usually so crystal clear in its detail, I do not know now if this decision for me to go solo was ill advised, or if it was the option that would ultimately offer our contingent the best of the possible results. It certainly led me into a world of trouble. But I do shudder at contemplation of what might have happened had we all gone off together.

MY CLOTHES WERE UNCOMFORTABLY wet and baggy. As they were too big for me in the first place, I walked with my hands gripping the waistband, holding up my soaked trousers as I trudged along. My cuffs dragged in the dirt and became caked with mud. My boots squished and squirked in rhythm with my encumbered steps. I nearly turned back to get Brownie, thinking it would surely be more effectual to ride after Sabrina than to walk, but the mare's trail was easy to follow – what with the sandy soil so distinctly churned up by her hooves – that it offered no interruption or pause, and I found myself continuing on in spite of my soggy discomfort, assuming all along that I must be getting close to where the mare was waiting.

I galumphed onward.

And onward.

"Damn!"

I was about to give up when I saw Sabrina's tracks disappearing over a swell that dropped back down into another reach of the stream. At this point, Virtue and the others were about a mile away, wondering, I supposed, where the hell we were.

"I will check here," I told myself, "but if Sabrina is not visible from yonder rise, I will turn back."

When I reached the high bank and peered down – there she was – drinking at the creek. Even from up high, I could see the four red stripes where the bear had swiped her shoulder. I knew she would be jumpy, so I let her know, by way of a soft call, that I was coming.

"Sabrina," I cooed loudly.

She jerked up and leapt into the stream.

"Whoa, honey. Whoa. It is I, Didier."

She turned and glared up the hill.

I waved and smiled reassuringly. "All is well, my lady. Ursus Horribilis is handily vanquished."

She stomped at the stream, splashing and whinnying. She did not come up to me, so I climbed down to her.

"Whoa, girl," I purred, and waded into the stream. "Everything is fine. Your friend Mister Rain is here to help."

Although she was still considerably worked up, she let me come near, and even allowed me to stroke her neck. "Yes. Yes. Everything is fine."

Sabrina had a light duty with the company. She carried only the saddle and kit of Turtle Dove's deceased husband. To make her load more comfortable, it was my habit not to pull the saddle cinch too tightly, as there seemed no need without a rider. But now that saddle was all hanging off to one side, a single stirrup dragging the ground, the straps all twisted and tangled as a result of her rollicking escape from the bear.

"First, let us unburden you of this twisted mess."

I tossed the saddlebags and bedroll onto the ground. I removed the saddle and blanket and laid it beside them. And then I peered more closely at her wounds. They were clean, straight-edged scars about a foot long, as if made with four sharp barber's razors, and they only went as deep as her flaxen hide, not penetrating the flesh underneath. They had not bled much, even with her heart pumping so in a panic. I was relieved, and felt confident that the cuts would heal nicely, without much doctoring required on my part.

"They will merely leave a mark of character, Sabrina, enhancing your already astonishing beauty. A memento by which to start up conversation with some dandy boy stallion in your future."

Neither Sabrina nor Genevieve had ever appreciated my attempts at a joke, and she continued this indifference to my witticisms now, snorting and, if possible for a horse, rolling her eyes. No matter. I was too relieved at her overall good health to be hurt by her manner. It was looking as if we had survived this recent peril, and that made me glad.

"Let us get back to the others," I said. "They will surely be wondering about your wellbeing."

I bent to pick up the saddle, but when I did, Sabrina nickered fretfully.

"What? I am merely going to put you back together."

Her head started going up and down in that way horses do when they are agitated, and I felt perhaps my relief was premature, and that I still had some soothing to do with Sabrina before she would readily take her load.

That is when I heard a rooster crow.

"Err er Err er Errrrrrr!"

"What on earth?"

I was greatly surprised, as such fowl generally indicate domesticity and farms, and we seemed to be far from anywhere conducive to such a civilized habitation or agrarian enterprise. I peered up the far bank to where the sound was coming – nothing.

Then I heard the bark of a dog, only this time a bit off to the side.

I scratched my chin, squinting at the opposite swell, but saw neither chickens nor dogs in plain view.

I heard the sudden braying of a jackass.

I stood on the edge of the stream, holding up my pants, perplexed by this cacophony of farmyard noises sounding from a hillside populated, as far as I could see, by nothing more than a few scraggly bushes and rocks.

And that is when I heard laughter.

Raucous, belly-splitting laughter.

My bewilderment compounded, and I called out. "Who is there?"

To my astonishment, three figures materialized from out of the hillside. They appeared to rise right up out of the ground at the different points where the animals had earlier been heard. I deduced straight away that there had been no animals at all, only these three fellows here. Even with the distance, it was not difficult to tell that they were unusual variations of the human species – men, one supposed, as they were standing on two legs, but peculiar in the extreme.

"Greetings," I called, and put on a smile. "You had me going, what with your animal sounds. That is quite a talent."

One of them called over to the others, saying something I did not catch. It must have been quite hilarious, because they all three started in on another round of knee-slapping laughter. They seemed unable to stop.

I waited while they laughed and laughed.

They were all well muscled and tall; one could see that much even over the distance. None of them wore shirts. One had suspenders holding up his buckskin pants, but the other two just went bare-chested. Their hair was long and unkempt, never apparently having encountered a comb, and it reminded me of the matted backsides of sheep who had gone too long before shearing. They each had beards, too, long and snarled and full of burrs. Each one had a rifle hanging by a strap over his shoulder. These rifles appeared to be Hawkens, the variety so favored by trappers and buffalo hunters.

DELIVERING VIRTUE

At that moment, I felt fairly confident that these boys were a good lot, just a bit weird. They certainly had a jovial nature, and their laughter did not sound malicious or suggestive of hazard. Still, I intentionally resisted shooting a gaze in the direction of Virtue and the others, just in case such a move might bring them into an unforeseen net of danger.

Still laughing, the bearded boys all three came down to meet me. Sabrina was uneasy, and kept threatening to run away. "Be calm, girl. Let us see what these bewhiskered, chortling yahoos are about."

They waded the stream and stood close around me and the mare, somewhat looming over us because of their extraordinary height. They were all grins.

"Hello," I said. "My name is Didier Rain – versifier, word collector, and would-be..."

The one with the suspenders cut me off and said something, once again, that I did not understand. The others laughed and wagged their heads.

I tried to smile in friendly fashion, but their rudeness had somewhat jarred my sense of etiquette.

When they stopped laughing, I tried again. "A bruin attacked my horse." I pointed to Sabrina's wounds. "And she led me here to this beck where, now, I am pleased to make your acquaintance." I tipped my hat.

One of them – the one with the longest beard – stepped forward and laid his long and soiled fingers on side of my face, plucking a bit of clay that still remained attached to my jaw.

"Ouch!" I said, and tried to laugh.

The bearded fellow held up the chunk of clay for his companions to examine. They looked at it and, of course, laughed.

"Thank you," I continued. "I must have missed that particular crumb when I was at my toilet. I have no mirror, and so grooming can be problematic, as you probably know."

They started talking amongst themselves, waving their hands and gesturing with shoulders shrugs and fluttering fingers. It was most extraordinary to watch, and even more so to hear. They seemed to be speaking a language that, as near as I could decipher, was something from before language. It was all burps and yawps and grunts and hoots. I sensed no immediate connection to any Proto-Indo-European origins, or any other origins for that matter.

"Shhh#oo*!! G^lem~," said the suspendered one.

The other two stomped their feet and answered with what sounded like a sneeze crossed with a fart. For I can find no better way to describe it. They seemed to be discussing the situation at hand, but for all I knew, they might have been talking politics or religion.

"Say," I asked. "From where do you fine gentlemen hail?"

They ignored me and continued up with their primordial communications. It was entertaining, if not a tad distressing, to witness. Even the most learned polyglot would have himself a time deciphering their patois.

At any rate, it unsettled Sabrina to the extent that she felt the need to leave. And quickly! While the three characters were jabbering on, she suddenly bolted and reared away, turning on her hind legs and galloping up the same slope from where she had come earlier.

The three stopped their talking and calmly watched her go.

I looked at them, and then turned to watch the horse as well.

Sabrina seemed to be in the same state she had been when fleeing the bear, and I wondered at her panic. Did she know something that I did not? Was she savvy to some undercurrent in these men's talk that led her to be sore afraid? Apparently so.

I watched her run, her beautiful blond mane and tail waving in the sunlight. Her muscles rippled under her skin and she was most stunning to observe. She was almost at the rim, just about to disappear over the top, when I was startled by the report of a Hawken. I flinched, but did not take my eyes from the fleeing mare. She collapsed directly.

She flipped backwards and tumbled down the slope, her legs writhing as if she were still running. She lurched and plunged down and down. When she reached bottom, she lay perfectly still.

I was stunned.

The three fellows started in cackling and hooraying beside me. When I turned their way, a cloud of blue smoke hung in the air above them. One of the trio was holding up his rifle, as if in triumph.

"Say," I asked, attempting to smile. "Was that an absolutely necessary thing to do?"

Without taking time out from his laughing, the shooter stepped toward me. Then, by way of an answer, he raised his rifle butt into the air, bashing me hard alongside the head.

NOW I WAS USED to the state of stupor; I had visited there many times before. And as a curious fellow, I have always been intrigued that something so basic could come with so much variety. I had known drunken stupor – feverish stupor – weary stupor – falling-off-your-horse-into-the-mud stupor – the stupor of sensual arousal – as well as a pocketful of other stupors, all more or less similar in their sensation and general wooziness. But never had I been stupefied by way of the butt of a Hawken. It was largely unpleasant, causing a sensational agony in my cranial nut, and yet it did open a certain window that I might not otherwise have noticed. I peered through said window, and stepped into a scene that was bucolic and most inviting.

A quiet pool appeared before me, wide and calm. On yonder bank, I spied the gathering of a picnic. My old friend Delight was there, naked, kneeling on the grass before a child. This child had blue wings and a white face and I recognized him as Turtle Dove's little boy who had died. He was giggling and playing pata-cake with Delight while Turtle Dove's husband sat watching from the side, eating red berries from a bowl, one at a time. He, too, sported a pair of beautiful blue wings, his face white like paper.

Turtle Dove then glided down out of the trees and came over to the edge of the water. She stepped right out onto the surface of the pool and walked three paces in my direction.

I was amazed. "Say," I called over to her. "That is quite a trick. Do you think you can teach me how to do it?"

She did not smile, but lifted her hand toward me, in a gesture indicating that I should come hither. She spoke some words, but they only came out sounding like water rippling over rocks, and although I failed to understand them exactly, I sensed that she was urging me forward in that way a mother does when trying to prompt her child to take his first steps.

Now I wanted to walk on water. Who would not? And I most certainly wanted to join again with my beloved Turtle Dove. The memory of her sweet milk still lingered on my lips. But when I looked down into the pool, I saw dark shadows cruising in the depths. I could not decide if they be benign or malignant. Dare I take the chance?

No.

I called over once more. "I am sorry, but I am the Blessed Deliverer. I have unfinished business to which I must attend." I peered back over my shoulder, but there was nothing awaiting but darkness, and it occurred to me that it was somewhat unreasonable to choose such gloom over the pastoral scene before me. And yet...

"I will be back," I called. "Please save me some berries."

And then I turned on my boot heel, squirming back through the window just as it was about to close.

When I came to, I found myself slumped against a wall, gazing out at a long windowless room. The walls were earthen, apparently made of sod and dried mud, and timbered with bent and twisted hackberry limbs. The warren was dimly lit, with only a few small candles dispersed like votives in a church, but this offered enough illumination to see that the place was untidy. Pelts and traps and rags were strewn across the floor. A cooking fire flickered at the far end of the hall, its smoke swirling up through a hole in the high ceiling. The hole itself was black and glittering with intermittent stars, leading me to understand that it was nighttime. A large rack of ribs hung over the flames on a spit, dripping fat and filling the air with an aroma I found most repulsive. The three hoodlums sat hunkered around the fire, casting misshapen shadows up the dirt walls, while drinking from buffalo horns and gnawing at fistfuls of meat. They did not appear to notice that I had rejoined them here in the waking world.

They continued to laugh at every little thing.

My head ached horribly, and I was disheartened to realize myself viewing everything solely through my left eye, as my other eyehole was swollen shut tight. I touched the side of my head. It was tender and puffed. The metallic taste of my own blood was on my tongue. I feared my noggin had been fractured and now essential portions of my brain were leaking out through a fissure in my skull. It hurt to think.

One of the trio stood and went to a barrel, dipping his horn tankard into its depths. I was surprised to see he wore my faded red shirt wrapped like a turban around his head. A single sleeve dangled down his bare back. He was otherwise naked as a proverbial jaybird.

Hmmm, I thought. If he is wearing my shirt, what is this I am wearing myself?

I looked down at my body.

"Ho!" I said. I was staggered to find myself in a dress. "Oh!"

It was admittedly a lovely cut of velvety fabric – quite soft, with crenulated ribbing all around its midriff. I felt, oddly, that I had interacted with this dress before, and had I not known it was improbable, I would have sworn it had been plucked directly from Delight Tuttles's wardrobe. I laid my fingers on its front, tenderly stroking its fineness.

"Ha Hoooo!"

I looked up to find one of the fellows pointing my way. The other two turned to see. They all laughed and stood and laughed some more.

"!GLOR^_~`!" they shouted, and raised their drinking horns my direction.

Except that they were unclothed, and rather disconcertingly disported erect members the size of wapiti femurs, it was almost a comfort to receive their greeting. For these boys seemed genuinely pleased to see me.

The one fellow wearing my shirt tore a rib from the meat hanging over the fire. He then marched over the cluttered floor and brought me a bit of supper. He waved the rib beneath my nose.

"Oh," I said, and tried to smile graciously. "Thank you all the same. But I am a sworn vegetablearian, and do not partake of the sensate foods."

Like any good host, he would not take my No for an answer, and tried to force the meat betwixt my teeth. I reluctantly took the bone in my hands, and nibbled off a bit of the charred flesh. I suppose having gone so long without eating such fare made me inordinately sensitive to its taste. It was all I could do not to gag.

They all cheered when I swallowed, and then one of them gave me his flagon of drink. I sensed straight away that the concoction held therein was of a disreputable derivation – something like fermented sagebrush and dung – and although I wanted nothing to do with it, I was sorely in need of something to cleanse the taste of meat from my palate. I raised the horn in a gesture of thanks, put it to my lips, and poured a bit down my gullet.

The liquor blazed a path down my insides.

They cheered again.

Thus began the party.

The drink was strong and effective. It blurred the details of the subsequent events, and I suppose, all in all, I should consider myself thankful for that small blessing.

The festivities commenced with a game that was most daring and unusual. The boy wearing my shirt for a hat took one of the candles resting in a dirt alcove. Then, while the other two looked eagerly on, he delicately balanced the little torch on the end of his rigid, upturned penis. He slowly let his hands rise out to his sides, until they were as high as his shoulders, and then he strolled across the room, skillfully stepping over the debris, balancing as if he were walking atop a pole fence. The little flame wavered, but did not topple. When he reached the far wall, he took the candle and held it high over his head, melted wax dripping into his matted hair, crowing like a rooster.

Everyone laughed. Then they turned and looked at me, as if to ask, "Are you not impressed with our circus trick?"

I nodded with faux enthusiasm. "Remarkable," I said weakly. "Bravo!"

This balancing game was played for some time, the candle trading penises again and again, punctuated only by bouts of stuffing me with meat, and then chasing it down with the rude liquor. The meat had a familiarity to it that I could not quite place – a sweet spiciness that I somehow knew – but it was not until I spied the party-wear of one of my hosts that I understood whose flesh I was consuming.

"Oh!" I gulped. "Oh, No!"

The fellow had a horsetail dangling over his backside, tied around his waist by a thong, wearing it as if it were his own. Of course, it was lovely and long and blond, decorated with colorful beads and feathers.

I glanced at the partially consumed rack of ribs cooking over the fire. I had never much cared for the flavor of horsemeat, and liked it even less upon realizing that it was the selfsame flesh that had so recently housed the soul of my dear friend Sabrina.

"I am truly sorry, my lady." I felt that I had failed her dreadfully, and now, eating her, only made that failure more poignant and insulting.

Of course, I retched up. But by then, admittedly, the damage had long been done.

I imbibed the sagebrush solution, seeking a door by which to escape into some more favorable oblivion.

After the candle game, there was a wrestling match. And then the boys took their rifles and shot bones from off each other's heads. The bones exploded and the slugs thunked into the walls, raising puffs of dust, and sending down little fountains of dirt streaming onto the floor.

The room filled up with gun smoke.

Through it all, the laughter never ceased.

The whole time, I felt as if they were competing for my attention. "Look at me," they seemed to say. "Look at me!"

"No! Look at me!"

I felt, rather correctly it turned out, like the sole whore at a brothel.

Ultimately, after they had exhausted their games, they turned my way.

I prefer not to dwell on the happenings that ensued. Suffice it to say that Brother Bartholomew had been correct about the essential animal natures of certain men. And yet I found myself unwilling to immediately condemn their actions, even as they were inflicted upon me. After all, it could get awfully lonely out here on the frontier, without much by way of diversion. Things get so distorted in one's morality. I knew that for a fact myself. And in truth, I did not think they were as despicable as they might have seemed to anyone coming from a more civilized environment, just misdirected, and perhaps left out a little too long in the wilds. But in the end, so to speak, I simply felt that if I were to judge them, it would be unfair. I would only prove myself to be some sort of hypocrite, casting – as that old Bible story warns us not to do – a self-righteous stone at someone no more a sinner than oneself.

They twirled me around and around, always laughing.

And then, after a bout of bickering, they took their turns with me.

"Careful," I requested, with some fearfulness and dread, "that you do not mar my velvet dress."

DID THAT BACCHANALIA LAST a single night, or was it spread out over a collection of many nights? I could not rightly say. My non-lucid condition made it impossible for me to know. But I do remember being greatly relieved when my hosts at last wearied of prodding and promulgating my amenities, and then, one by one, collapsed in a heap on the floor. This should have been my opportunity to slip away. After all, enough merrymaking is most certainly enough. But the last fellow standing thought it prudent to tie my wrists to a weighty stone in the corner, thus preventing my timely departure.

So there I sat, alone, tethered, contemplating the stars I saw turning slowly above the smoke hole.

The candles sputtered in their alcoves.

The cooking fire dwindled, only a small portion of carbonized horse ribs dangling on the spit over the glowing coals.

The three hooligans snored and snored.

"Oh, Rain," I whispered, as if calling to myself from afar. "Oh, Mister Didier Rain, at what juncture didst thou turn so terribly astray?"

I was worried about Virtue and the others. Surely they had heard the shot that felled Sabrina, and then were moved to fretfulness and confusion. I trusted it to the gods that they were all right. I even went so far as to mutter what one might call a prayer, although I merely cast it out the smoke hole, with no particular deity in mind. I was only being hopeful that it would find a compassionate and capable agent to my troop's wellbeing.

Thinking about Virtue brought her vividly to my mind. Her face. Her freshet blue eyes. Her gentle ways and wizened mien. I remembered her mother way back in Independence, how she had touched me so tenderly, like a lover, and I was amazed to see, as if I had conjured her from within my reverie, a younger copy of that same beautiful woman now parting the buffalo blanket that covered the door-hole at the other end of the room. She wore a black dress, and her blond hair was drawn back into a ponytail. The girl glided my direction, silently avoiding the clutter and sleeping brutes strewn asunder. Was she the Angel of Death come to free me from the shackles of my despair? I was still convinced that the young lady was no more than a drunkard's hallucination when she stopped before me, kneeling close. She peered into my good eye.

I felt her breath on my face; I smelled wildflowers by a brook.

"Virtue?"

She placed a finger to my lips, giving me to know I should be quiet.

"But..."

She shook her head.

I was both delighted to see her, and fearful that the ruffians might find her out.

She took the knife and, all business, began to saw through the ropes binding my wrists.

Once freed, I stretched my fingers, urging the feeling back into my hands. Virtue then laid down her blade and took hold of one of those hands, helping me to my feet. I started to fall, but she held me steady until I was over my feet. She then gestured that we should stealthily make our way back to the door. She led, and I followed. As a precaution, I picked up the knife and held it at the ready.

My feet were not directly connected to my brain right then, and it was most challenging to keep them from stubbing on the disorderly floor. I had to walk slowly, with my arms held out to my sides. The ground seemed to pitch and swell. But eventually, and without too much clopping, I made it as far as the sleeping pile of sodomites.

There they lay, flaccid, each one donning a blissful smile within the greasy tangle of his beard. Virtue was at the door, holding the flap open and waiting, but I stopped. I regarded the knife I held in my hand. I thought to myself, surely they are so lost to their inebriated slumber that they would not even notice if, one by one, I slit their throats, or plunged my dagger into their hearts.

I felt strongly compelled to avenge Sabrina.

What kind of Deliverer would I be if I let these three get away with their murder?

I brandished the blade over their bodies, considering where to begin. One of the bastards still wore my shirt on his head. Another used my trousers for a pillow. But then I suffered a wave of vertigo – the three beasts blurred into one – and it was all I could do not to topple over on top of them. The spell soon passed, but within that intermezzo I decided that a righteous massacre was ill advised at this particular time.

You may not possess the faculties to pull it off, I warned myself. And besides... I looked down at my dress. Bloodstains are all but impossible to remove from such a finely brushed velvet.

I abandoned my scheme and made toward Virtue and the doorway.

Unfortunately, distracted by my woolgathering, I kicked a bone, and it went clattering loudly across the floor.

I froze, gazing down at the trinity of miscreants below me.

One of them squirmed, and wiggled his nose. His snoring stopped. He held his breath, as if in indecision. And then, much to my vexation, his eyes flickered open, and he gazed up into my face.

I DID NOT, WITH the conscientious protocol of a good-hearted whore, wait around to enquire if the whiskered gent had enjoyed a pleasant and restful repose after his last night's raucous indulgence in my orificial endowments. Rather, fast as a one-eyed, intoxicated man in a dress is able, I scampered for the door.

Virtue took hold of my hand and led me running into the chilly dawn. A rosy glow illuminated the ragged landscape into which we fled. Behind us, one could hear the clamor of my former captors rousing to wakefulness.

A rooster crowing!

The bark of a dog!

A jackass braying as if stung by a bee!

I clutched the front of my dress with my free hand, lifting it clear of my feet so that I might take more galloping strides. But in truth, my gait was less than impressive, and I found myself – even in the midst of my distress – developing a newfound respect for the female variant of my species. How cumbersome, if comely, these dresses were!

I fell – "Oomph!" – losing hold of Virtue's hand.

Once I had sorted my flailing limbs from the mountain of velvet in which I was encased, I found myself on my hands and knees, wheezing.

Virtue waited.

"Go!" I gasped. "You must not let them catch you!"

But she only leaned down and tugged at my arm, raising me to my feet. I did not see much hope for escape at that moment, and it fretted me terribly to think of those three candle-balancers catching up to Virtue.

"You should go!" I pleaded. "I will follow as best I can."

She said nothing, only pulled me forward, and I found myself running once again.

The hoots and hollers of our pursuers seemed to be growing imminently near.

Virtue led me onward, urging my haste. Who now, I had to ask myself, is delivering whom?

We sprinted through the sagebrush, over a swell in the earth, to where Puck, Brownie, and Genevieve awaited our arrival. Seeing them all there saddled and stamping at the ground put a lift in my step. I grew slightly encouraged, and ran harder those last few rods.

Virtue mounted Genevieve in a wink, and then I, with much effort and rustling of fabric, managed to heave myself into the saddle on Brownie's back. The horses did not wait for a command, but took off at once, running as fast as they could go.

I glanced back to see the naked man-creatures bounding over the rise. They carried their rifles strapped over their shoulders. They howled and leapt the bushes, taking great strides in our direction. They seemed to be gaining ground on us, even as our horses ran at top speed.

The race continued for most of a mile. We fled down a dry riverbed, kicking up the sand and gravel, using it as a road for our escape.

Our pursuers loped along on the high banks, two on one side, one on the other, maintaining their awesome pace. How could they run so fast?

"Go, Brownie! Go!"

Our horses sped onward, and at last, we appeared to be outdistancing the wild men. They called after us, howling and bawling like mournful coyotes, as if truly saddened to see us go. I grinned with relief when I sensed they had given up the chase.

But alas! My celebration was premature. Of a sudden, I felt a bite in my lower ear. I flinched and nearly pitched from Brownie's back, barely catching hold of the saddle horn. And then I heard the belated rifle shots behind me. I reached up and was sore distressed to find my ear all throbbing and mangled. I brought my hand down and saw that it was sticky with blood.

A farewell volley had nearly hit me in the back of the head.

I suppose I should have been grateful I was alive, but I could only lament that my head – already so badly burned and bashed and peeled – was now further despoiled by the shredded and dangling adornment of what remained of my left ear.

"Zounds!"

WE RODE HARD ALL morning, somewhat in fear that our tormentors might have mustered more endurance and were still on our trail. They were, after all, not your typical flat-footed trappers. But by middle of the day, with the horses exhausted and slathered in sweat, we trusted we had outrun them for good, and so we slowed to a trot, albeit, with much glancing back over our shoulders.

Virtue rode beside me, leaning over and scrutinizing the damage to my earflap.

"I have known dandies," I said, "who have pierced their lobes with awls so that they might wear gold hoops. But the results were largely cleaner and more exact than this makeshift method of using a musket ball fired at a hundred paces."

Virtue squinted at the side of my head, trying to discern my ear from the gore. I felt embarrassed, ludicrous, and more unbeautiful than ever in my life. My arse-hole burned. My head felt like a child's kickball. My right eye was blackened and swollen shut. My left ear – what remained of it – dangled from the side of my head like a piece of chewed-up, spit-out gristle.

And I was wearing a dress!

In that moment, seeing myself from the young lady's vantage, I began to giggle. It made my ribs hurt, but I could not help myself. For I was greatly relieved, and strangely giddy.

Virtue regarded me with a puzzled smile.

"Darling," I said. "I am just *so* pleased that you avoided that particular peril. It was most unsavory, and not something I would have wished you to endure." I shifted in my saddle. "And I am, likewise, so thankful that you were able to procure my rescue." I lifted my hands in a gesture to include the horses. "Thank you all." And then I giggled some more.

Of course, my merriment was in bad taste considering that we had just lost our dear Sabrina, and so with some considerable effort, I forced myself to stop. The recollection of my cannibalism made this easier to do. The sober thought that some of Sabrina's flesh might still be rotting in my belly shut me up quick.

"We should stop soon," I suggested, "and respect a moment for our lost friend."

It seemed to me that Genevieve grew sad at the mention of her golden partner.

Puck and Brownie, too, became noticeably introspective.

We plodded in silence for a ways, our thoughts full of mortality's omnipresence, and of our narrow escape from its ever-grasping clutches.

And so it came to pass that we paused on a high hill, gazing out in the easterly direction from where we had come. I had lost my hat somewhere along the way, or I would have taken it off in reverence. As it were, we just bowed our heads and turned our minds to Sabrina, and, at least for myself, to Turtle Dove as well.

I sighed at last, folded my hands against my dress front, and raised my eye to the scene.

A hawk wheeled loftily in the blue sky.

The land seemed profoundly indifferent to our plight and paltry human struggles. It just *was*. Whatever that might mean.

Maybe this whole life, I considered, is nothing but an accident – just something that happens because something must.

I could not have begun to explain this sentiment, as it made that kind of oblique sense to me that is impossible to elucidate, even to oneself. But I felt no need to utter a line from a poem, or even mumble some condoling eulogy ad libitum. Words can be so tiresome at times. So meaningless.

So hollow.

So full of wind and feathers.

THAT NIGHT IN CAMP, Virtue stitched my ear back together with needle and thread. She then swabbed it with Turtle Dove's potent herbal ointment. Yes, it hurt something awful. But pain had become my constant state of being, I had grown accustomed to its irritations, and so I did not so much as cringe throughout the entire operation. I was most manly, even considering my velvety choice of eveningwear.

"*Merci bien,*" I said.

Virtue put away her kit. She placed a stick onto our little campfire and sat opposite me, wrapped in a blanket.

The air was nippy, and I tucked my velvet folds around me, holding myself within the embrace of my own two arms.

A single coyote sang us a serenade from afar.

A whisper of moon traveled like a distant sail over Virtue's shoulder – a delightful and befitting backdrop to her feminine presence. Except that we were fully surrounded by the American wilderness – with all of its perfidy and peril – the feeling as a whole was one of domestic calm, somewhat like sitting of an evening in one's cozy parlor.

"I used to read poems to my mother," I said, "while she worked at her dress designs."

Virtue looked at me and nodded.

"She was a seamstress – the best in Cherbourg, it was said by those who appreciated such things." I laughed to myself. "I do not believe I have worn a dress since she had me pose as a mannequin so that she might work a hem into one of her gowns."

I ran my fingers against the nap of velvet on my sleeve, remembering.

"I read her all of the English Romantics, of whom I was most enamored, even though she did not know English well enough to understand the words. She always told me that it was pleasant and adequate just to hear the rhythms and sounds – those galloping thuds and bumps and sighs. She believed that that was all one need hear in order to comprehend the deeper resonance of the poetry's meaning."

I pondered this. As a youth – arrogant and book-learned – I had considered that idea somewhat ignorant, but now, listening to that coyote singing his aria of loneliness and open spaces, I came to believe that maybe my mother had been correct. After all, she *was* a sensitive woman.

"O, Wild West Wind, thou breath of Autumn's being,
Thou, from whose unseen presence the leaves dead
Are driven, like ghosts from an enchantress fleeing."

I regarded Virtue over the wavering flames. "Shelly," I explained. "He was our favorite."

"It's nice."

"Yes," I said. "He had a lovely way with words."

I found it immensely pleasing to talk about my mother and my boyhood. I had not done so for many years, and had all but forgotten anything that had ever happened to me before growing into an adult. Virtue had stirred those memories, all throughout this long journey, like some revelatory agent to a dream I had believed to be irrevocably submerged.

"Life is mysterious." I said. "We go around in a state of sleepwalk, oblivious to those miracles that surround us at every turn, too entrenched in our own misery to take notice of the magic." I nodded philosophically to the flames. "Sometimes it seems we are all just pieces of a big game, pushed around willy-nilly by some invisible hand. One surely sees where a man's ideas of God come from. What better explanation for the way one's life keeps looping back around on itself in ever-widening circles?"

Now sometimes talk can be a salve. It eases the heart pains and the soul weariness of one's tawdry existence. Surely that is why a person has friends. Undoubtedly, at the bottom of it, that is why one so willingly airs his sins to a priest. It feels good to confess, to admit that you are fallible and astray in those dark proverbial woods. One wants to explain himself. I do not know why this is so, only that it most assuredly is. And I had gone too many years without anyone to whom I might speak so freely. Virtue did not seem to mind my cathartic blabber. If anything, she was waiting for me to continue. She peered at me over the fire and smiled. There was nothing in the world like that smile for putting me at ease. I took it as my cue to continue and, rather sybaritically, began a rambling, free-flowing monologue. Once begun, I could not seem to stop.

The floodgates had been flung wide open.

I LIVED WITH MY mother above her dress shop. Her name was Marie DeRosier. My father, you see, lived across town with his wife, inhabiting one of those big houses looking out over the shipyards. His name was Horatio Rain – an American entrepreneur who made his fortune in shipping goods between the continents. My mother had been his callow mistress, and I, regrettably, had been the mishap who complicated their whole clandestine arrangement. From what I inferred, after my birth my father withheld his affections. This caused my mother great loneliness and stress. She had, in that unreasonable bent of an idealistic demoiselle, loved him, and had hoped he would divorce his wife and marry her instead, maybe even taking her to America where they could start anew. But that was not to be. And now as a girl in her situation – a young woman with a child, but no man – she was in danger of being poorly regarded by society. Such a deflowered lass is destined to live a life of loneliness and seclusion, eking out a livelihood as a washerwoman, a rag picker, or even a prostitute. She was fraught with despair. Fortunately for my mother, Monsieur Rain felt the inclination to set her up with her own trade. He provided the secret funding for her dress shop, and even encouraged a clientele by way of his wife and her friends. Although I am sure this was a humiliation to my mother, she accepted it without complaint. Understand, I was Horatio Rain's only child – his Ishmael, so to speak. His wife Chantal must have been unable to bring forth offspring. And so somehow, by what must have seemed a cruel twist, I was the sole heir to his fortune. This no doubt vexed him. And yet, a man's prideful sense of legacy can overwhelm his reason. He wants to hand something forward through the generations. He wants his name and enterprise to survive as a monument to his existence. As a result of this vanity, I was provided for.

My mother and I were close. Too close, I suppose. We had only each other to turn to. If I bumped my chin, my mother was there to give it a kiss. If she was feeling gloomy, I was the living doll she held while she wept. Which is not to say she was one much given to weeping. If anything, she taught me the trick of putting on a smile even in the most dire of situations.

I helped her in her shop. I especially liked to sort needles, or wind the colored threads onto spools. As I have said, she often employed me as a mannequin, and I would stand there on a stool for hours while she measured and cut and stitched. I enjoyed this enormously. It was like a game to see how long I could hold myself still.

In the evenings, after long days of toil, she told me stories of courtly love and valor – tall tales in which knights or heroic shepherd boys would overcome villains or slay dragons to win the heart of some fair skinned beauty. I would often fall to sleep with these romantic images in my head, the sound of the sea beyond the window, sometimes with raindrops tapping against the glass. I fancied myself as that hero. I vanquished demons and saved damsels. My mother and I shared a bed, and I would snuggle up to her as she sang a lullaby in the darkness, happy as a lamb. At that point I was quite oblivious to the complications that shadowed my life. Everything seemed blissful and good in my boyish mind.

Horatio Rain never came around. I would not have known him if I had seen him on the street. But one day a stranger stepped into my mother's shop to speak to her of business matters. He was a popinjay who sported drooping mustaches and the eyes of a fox. He carried a little pearl-handled pistol on his hip. He smelled of cigars and sweet cologne. I developed an intuitive hatred for the man at once. I would have gladly left the room, but I was in a vulnerable position. I was at my station balancing atop my stool, adorned in a gown undergoing the process of alteration. It was – even now, I remember clearly – of a chiffon silk, peach in color, with billowing sleeves. I held these sleeves out straight from my sides, my shoulders burning with fatigue. I urgently needed for my mother to remove the pins that threatened to pierce me if I should lower my trembling arms, but this self-important fop had interrupted her task, profoundly agitating her with his presence.

"*Maman*," I muttered. "*S'il vous plaît.*"

But she paid me no heed.

Who was this man who made me so suddenly invisible? Who was he who could so easily befuddle my mother and move her to a state of happy tears?

She leaned into him, pressing her bosom against his chest, and kissing his hand. Confused and uncomfortable, I could only watch. I grew even more bewildered when the man led my mother into her fitting room and began making love to her, right there in the light of day. Apparently her forthcoming charms had overwhelmed his good sense and commitment to abstinence in regard to her sensual bounties. The two of them made quite a lot of noise. Much moaning and rhythmic thumping, the very essence of a primordial poesy.

I stood there awkwardly throughout, doing my best not to harm the expensive, pin-laden piece of fabric in which I was so cumbersomely swathed. My quivering arms remained spread wide. I felt very much like pictures I had seen of Prometheus chained to a stone, or Christ nailed to a cross.

When they were quite finished, and had put themselves back together, they came into the room where I still awaited help. By now sweat was poring down my backbone. My shoulder muscles were on fire. Still, my mother, flushed and happy, paid me no attention. She tucked the disheveled tendrils of her hair back into place behind her ears, doing her best, it seemed, to pretty up for this rooster bird.

The man then stepped toward me, his face close to mine. His breath reeked of wormwood. He combed his mustache with his fingers and scrutinized me closely.

"*Il est une fille,*" he said, and smirked. He is a girl.

"*Mais non!*" replied my mother. "*Il est un bon garçon.*"

The man guffawed and shook his head, regarding me there in my eveningwear. "Sissy!" he said. "Pansy!"

And then with a laugh, he left the shop.

I did not remember letting my arms fall to my sides. I did not notice the pins sticking me all over, piercing me and leaving me in the attitude of some Saint Sebastian. For my father's disdainful words had cut me far more deeply.

"*Ah!*" yelled my mother.

She stepped forward and raised my arms.

"*Zut alors!*"

There, all down my sides, and on the insides of my arms, were a dozen little droplets of my bright red blood seeping through that silk chiffon.

ᵞ

DELIVERING VIRTUE

Soon after, Horatio Rain decided that I should be sent off to the country to attend a parochial school for boys. It was not the religious education that my father so wanted me to have, but rather a more rugged life among other lads, one full of scrapping and spitting and developing my more masculine characteristics. I needed to be a man if I were to someday represent his name. My mother was against the idea. "Who will help me in the shop?" she asked. But Monsieur Rain was adamant, and so off to school I went.

I missed my mother terribly, and wept into my pillow most nights of those first few months. The other boys were cruel and cunning and took advantage of my ignorance and delicate nature. I did not know how to be a boy myself. I had had no male upon whom to model myself, and I was way behind in all those little traits and talents that a would-be man must acquire in order to prosper in this world. Still, I enjoyed the formal learning. I loved the smell of the books in the library, and I was deeply moved by the sounds of Latin and Greek Bible stories uttered forth from the professors' lips within those stone halls. I proved to have quite a talent for those languages myself, and soon impressed my mentors.

On holidays I was allowed to travel back to Cherbourg and visit my mother. That is when I read her the poems. I had just discovered the poets, and was eager to share with her what I had learned. Our bond never weakened, although I would be remiss to say it had not changed. In my absence my mother had taken on an orphan girl as her apprentice – one Marguerite. She had appropriated my role as thread-winder and mannequin. She also was learning how to do some sewing herself, and my mother's business was expanding with her skillful help. At first I was as jealous as a cuckold. How could my mother dare to replace me with this waif? But soon, rather strangely, my jealousy of the girl evolved to admiration, moved on to fondness, and then finally grew into a most staggering infatuation.

Ah, Marguerite!

She became my star, my blue light, the very point around which all my life revolved. I felt that destiny had brought her to me. Although looking back, I would be hard pressed to explain why this was so. I put it down to my boyish stupidity and longing for a maiden toward whom I could direct my burgeoning romantic sensibilities.

She was not at all like the fair maidens my mother had so often mentioned in her fairytales. A drop of gypsy blood ran in her veins. Her eyes were dark, her hair. She had a smile that came easily, but did not reveal its meaning. Was she hiding a secret? It seemed she was.

And I made it my objective in life to find it out, be a part of that secret, to wrap myself around it and become it. Although, in truth, Marguerite generally paid me no mind. My passion was my own to hide away in my heart. But, I vowed that someday I would find a way to offer it up to her. And then... Ah, and then she would be mine!

My school years passed, and upon the day of my graduation I was introduced to a man named Winston Dirge. That truly was his name.

"I am a friend of your father's," he told me. "He and I have enjoyed many an adventure together. He has asked that I take you into my tutelage, and guide you in some of life's more valuable lessons."

He was charming and well mannered, with broad shoulders and a whimsical, but wise, demeanor. I liked him at once. It also turned out that Mister Dirge was a talented linguist. This was his primary diversion. He was, rather optimistically, amassing a dictionary of all the languages of the world, complete with cross-references, and he was now on his way to Greece and the Holy Land to trace down some long lost derivations.

"Would you care to join me in this enterprise?" he asked.

I was eager to return to my mother and, admittedly, to Marguerite. But I sensed that before me was an open door that I dare not let close. There is nothing like a well-traveled man to impress a lady, and I was in the midst of hatching a plan to win my true love's heart.

"Yes," I answered. "I will go."

Rather than voyage by ship, we traveled a circuitous route across the continent. We stopped at art collections and cathedrals along the way, studying the paintings and sculpture, and assessing the architecture. We went to operas and concerts. We spoke Italian and Latin and Greek. We read poetry, and even rendezvoused with certain of the poets themselves, as they were all acquaintances of Mister Dirge. I toured with wide-eyed enthusiasm. Never had I experienced so many wonderful encounters with culture and civilization. Never had I been more inspired.

But there was one aspect of my apprenticeship that I found most troubling. Winston Dirge, so debonair and civilized by day, became something else entirely by night. No matter where we were, he was able, by way of some well-honed skill, to find himself a bawdy encounter.

"A man has two natures, Didier. And he is only half a man if he exercises but one of them."

He encouraged me to join him in these perversely sexual revels. "Your father most certainly would have," he assured me. And that, in part, may well have been what dissuaded me. I had no desire whatsoever to be like my father, whom, I had learned, was little more than a wealthy whoremonger. I strived for something more elevated, something worthy of my dear, pure Marguerite. To this end, I would forego Dirge's invitations, and instead spend my evenings curled over my pen, working out my poems.

I had it in my mind to create a collection of sonnets, something like those of the great Bard himself, all dedicated to Marguerite, and all brimming with my heart's most strident song. Upon return from my travels, I would present her with my verse, confess my love, and she would then have no choice but to take me as her lover. We would be married, and I would begin my illustrious career as a poet.

For now, all I needed was to work hard, and keep my virtue intact. I had not yet lain with a woman, as I was saving myself for Marguerite. But I was a young man, full of simmering virility, and it pained me often to endure those earliest phases of what would become my life-long affliction. The pressure was great, and what with Winston Dirge's gallivanting, the opportunities were many to alleviate its niggling bother. But I refrained.

We crisscrossed Greece, sailed between its islands, explored its ruins, and scribbled down its words in long lists, always investigating their undercurrents, matching them with the sounds we found hidden in other languages. We then traveled on to the Holy Land, doing the same with Arabic and Hebrew and other tribal tongues, wandering the shores of the salty Dead Sea, searching, searching for those secret words lost under the many miles of sand.

"In the beginning was the Word," Dirge told me. "And the Word was God."

He sincerely believed this. It was his religion. Winston Dirge most devoutly believed that in order to reach what one might call God, one must dive into the deepest pools of language, and rediscover that first pure Word. This was a man's only hope of salvation. Only then could he enter into paradise.

I grew to share Dirge's enthusiasm for the search. I even grew to believe there was truth in what he said. But through it all, my mind never abandoned Marguerite. My dreams were full of her. Any word she uttered was, for me, *the* Word. For surely she was an angel.

Two years passed. I returned to Cherbourg with my poems in my hand, and my hope in my heart.

In that short time, Marguerite had developed from a girl into a woman. Upon first encountering her in my mother's shop, I could not help but stare at her breasts. I admonished myself for this, but still – they were so round and full and inviting, almost to burst from inside her apron. The vision that leapt to my mind was of myself ripping apart those lapels and burying my face between those fleshy mounds, breathing deeply of her skin, gasping like a boy in blissful danger of being drowned.

I had rehearsed the moment of our reunion a thousand times in my mind, knowing full well what I would say, and how. It was to be moving and gentle and persuasive. But Marguerite's burgeoning femininity had unarmed me. It stopped my tongue and clouded my brain.

"*Voila!*" was all I could manage to get out. And, blushing red, I handed her my sheaf of sonnets. "I wrote these for you."

"Oh, Didier," she said, and regarded the packet that I so hoped would touch her deepest soul. She turned it over. "*Merci*," she said, and smiled kindly. "But you must know I do not read."

And then, indifferently, she handed me back my poems and walked away to fetch a bolt of cloth.

I stood there.

With my worthless words.

For the longest time.

Unbelieving.

DELIVERING VIRTUE

How was it that I never knew Marguerite was illiterate? It had never occurred to me. Not once. I had always imagined her lying in her bed that night, a candle illuminating my verse, her heart swooning at my cleverness and rhythmic confessions of love.

But now...

I was at a loss.

I spent the remainder of that painful day traipsing stuporously along the piers and beaches. They were the same as they had always been, but different to me now. My experiences in life, my travels, had drained my boyhood haunts of their color. It was April – *le mois le plus creullement* – and it was raining a cold and penetrating rain. Cherbourg was most ugly. I felt to be wandering in a wasteland. I had all but abandoned my hope, had all but given up on my dreams of Marguerite, when I was struck with an inspiration.

"*Bien Sur!*"

I would simply read my poems aloud to her. The thought both thrilled and horrified me. It would take great courage and composure. It would be most challenging not to let the passion of my words cloud their delivery, but I would do it as if my life depended upon it. Surely, in so many ways, it did. I plucked up a stone and threw it resolutely into the waves. And then, before my courage abandoned me – before that stone touched the bottom of the sea – I ran up the strand through the darkness to Marguerite.

She did not share my mother's apartment, but lived in a room of her own on the next street over. I had never been inside, but knew which room was hers. I had many times crept up the stairs to her door and lay my hand on its coolness, willing myself into her dreams. But this night would be different. Tonight I would step through that door to the other side. My heart galloped at the notion.

Now I can only guess that when I was traveling through old Hellas, I had inadvertently disrespected the gods on their mountaintop, making them sore angry with me. I have felt ever since that they have hounded my steps with their cruel and ironical manipulations of my fate. But never have those malign immortals moved the game pieces around so much that they have ever surpassed the wry humor inflicted upon me that night. It must have been a most amusing drama to watch from on high.

I stood with my poems before Marguerite's door. I did not know if I was shaking from fear, or from the dampness of my clothes. I took a deep breath, and rapped my knuckles timidly against the wood, softly calling her name. "Marguerite." Part of me almost hoped she would not answer. But then I heard her voice through the panel. I did not understand clearly what she had called – it was as if she were speaking from under water – but I assumed she had summoned me to enter. And so I did.

Boldly.

Throwing the door wide and stepping in.

The room was small, barely spacious enough for a table, a wardrobe, and a bed. A short window hung on one wall. A lamp burned with low light from atop the table. But the overriding sensation that met me was the repellent and odoriferous wave of sweat and sweet cologne. The room had a vulgar aroma that I did not expect. And then I heard the moans, and saw the confusing tangle of arms and legs of the two-backed beast bucking on the bed.

I stood there for the longest time, trying to understand just what I was seeing.

At last, it occurred to me that my dear Marguerite was pinned beneath that mass of heaving masculine flesh. Fortuitously, I had arrived just in time to save her. I quickly scanned the room, looking for what I could use to bludgeon the brute. That is when I saw the man's clothes on the floor. That is when I spied the pistol on his belt.

I fired a single shot into the man's bare back.

Someone screamed in pain.

The man arched and tensed, and then, without spectacle, withered to lifelessness.

I tossed the gun into the corner and, dropping my poems, leapt forward, pulling the dead man from off of Marguerite. His carcass thumped onto the floor, rolling face up. Of course, it had been my father all along. An expression of shock and wonder was frozen onto his face, as if he had been granted a startling vision just at the instant of his demise. I do not wish to be gratuitous, or even to disrespect the dead (no matter how much I might have disrespected them in life), but it struck me as most odd that his member remained erect. But I did not waste time on him, and instead turned to help my poor Marguerite.

She lay on her back, trembling. I could not, even in that terrible moment, avert my eyes from her stunning naked body. It glowed warmly in the lamplight, a wilderness of feminine mystery.

"Oh, Love," I said. "It will be all right. I have saved you. I have delivered you from that beast."

But the look on her face gave me to know that she had not been asking for salvation. Her expression was one of contempt. Her smile gave me to know that she held onto her secret, and that I would always be separate of it. I could not meet her eyes, and averted my gaze downward.

"Rain," she whispered, and stopped shivering. "*Pluie*."

That is when I saw the hole in her chest.

That is when I understood that she was dead.

The bullet had missed my father's ribs, and had passed through him into her dark heart.

"Oh!" I wept.

Even still, the gods were not yet done with their fun.

I knew that I would be found out soon. Surely someone had heard the pop of my father's pistol, or Marguerite's scream. At the least, Marguerite or Horatio would be found missing on the morrow, and an investigation would ensue, leading to my capture. So much had changed so quickly. My life seemed over just as it was set to begin. Stunned, I stumbled my way to my mother's apartment.

"*Maman!*"

"*Didier?*" she called. "*Je suis ici.*"

I burst into her bedroom only to find her stepping from out of her bath.

"*Alors!*" she said, but did not cover herself. In that confusing instant, with me in a state of such childish distress, it was as if we had returned to our past.

I was her little boy again.

She was my doting mother.

And we resumed that easy way with each other that we had enjoyed so many years before.

"*Qu'est que c'est?*" she asked, and stepped from the steaming tub. She began toweling herself dry.

"*Oh, maman!*" I cried, and went to her.

She could tell I was distressed, and that something most dreadful had happened. But she did not ask me questions just yet. Instead, she held me to her bare damp skin. She squeezed me tight. She kissed me.

Again and again.

OUR LITTLE CAMPFIRE SNAPPED and spit some sparks up into the darkness, shaking me from my painful reverie. I was shocked to find myself trembling so terribly with the effects of the frigid night air. Summer was most definitely past. I squeezed myself tighter within the paltry protection of my velvet dress. I looked up to see Virtue still sitting in her blanket before me. She was a blurry image, but then, after I had wiped the moisture from my only good eye, she appeared more well defined and striking. Truly an angel. I bit my lip, insecure at my erstwhile candor, and shrugged.

"Well," I said.

Virtue seemed to be waiting for me to continue, but I knew it was my choice. She was leaving it to me if I wanted to tell more. She was allowing me to decide just how much of this embarrassingly histrionic and verbose catharsis I was in need. I felt I had said too much already. My speech was surely inappropriate for a young girl's ears. And at the same time, I sensed I was being carried down a swiftly moving river, one that had yet to dump me out into a calming pool. I had a ways left to go.

I picked up a nearby branch of sage, tossing it skillfully onto the fire.

"Anyhow," I continued. "I have since determined... after putting the pieces back together in a thousand different ways... that my mother's loneliness... mixed up, as it was, with my own pendant and sabotaged romantic expectations for that evening... along with the fateful timing of my entrance into her private boudoir... resulted in the interaction we therein wrought. That is to say..." I cleared the smoke from my throat. "My mother and I became lovers." I nodded to the rising flames, barely believing the audacity of my words. "She was my first."

A rush of whelming disconcertment passed through my body right then. Followed by an enormous outbreath of relief. I all but fell over dead with the sudden liberation of that secret factoid. It flapped away into the night like a startled bird. I realized just how many years I had been holding that confession caged inside of me, without ever really being conscious that I was. No one knew that part of my story but myself and Marie DeRosier – my mother.

A long moment passed before I could lift my gaze to Virtue. I feared she would be so appalled at my aforementioned deviance that she would now regard me as the loathsome animal I truly was. Such a response from the young lady might well have shattered my heart for a final time. I so valued her friendship and opinion. But her reaction was one of calm composure. I saw it in her face. She held that same equipoise and wizened demeanor I had perceived in her from the first moment we had met, way back when I had held her in my arms as a babe.

"How," she asked, "did you come to America?"

"Oh. My mother snuck me onto a ship that very night – one of Horatio Rain's own – a cargo vessel that happened to be casting away at dawn. In a matter of hours, I was bound westward over the dark and slopping waves of the Atlantic."

The very recollection of that voyage moved me to seasickness. I felt I might heave up right there. But I did not.

"I decided during that crossing that I would rebuild my life. I would learn the American Vernacular as best I could, submerging my foreign accent beneath its idioms and syntax. I would travel farther west, out into the wild territories, and seek out a new truth around which to exist. What had happened had happened – undeniably, regrettably – but now I would take that experience and give back to humanity in order to absolve my sins. I would create an epic – something to rival Milton, one Joseph Smith, or even Mister Alighieri himself. My previous sonnets had been naïve. But now I was poised for something far greater. The gods had granted me a second chance. I had, in a sense, been reborn."

I felt a surge of that old thrill of when I had first devised my plan. I felt a youthful vigor and hopefulness stirring deep inside of me. But then, almost at once, I recalled all the intervening years since that day. All that wasted time! All that dissolution! All those squandered nights of never jotting so much as a single line! And then I felt myself once again plunged into regret. It was quite a push and pull journey between euphoria and despair. Most exhausting.

"Well..." I forced a smile. I rubbed my palms conclusively on my velvet-clad thighs and peered with my one eye up into the stars. The coyote had stopped his singing some time ago, without me even noticing that he had. The moon had slipped behind the western horizon with a silent hiss. "Maybe," I said with feigned bravado, "I will write that epic yet."

Virtue did not reply except for a small, almost imperceptible, forward bob of her head. I abruptly became aware of my self-indulgence. I was disgusted with myself for taking this whole evening to, so to speak, wash out my laundry. What of Virtue herself? She was surely burdened with a certain degree of apprehension about her upcoming meeting with the Prophet. Forget your own already traveled path, I told myself. Consider the girl.

"You remind me of your mother," I said.

She blushed a bit, and smiled coyly. "Truly?"

"Yes. Very much." I felt I was recalling a dream, so long ago had been that encounter beneath the catalpa tree in Independence, but there was truth in what I said. "She is lovely, too," I continued. "And with a quiet way of strength. You are much alike."

This pleased the girl immensely. She could not hide her joy, and that made me feel very good. "I am sure," I continued, "that she would be most proud if she could see how you have developed."

I was surprised to see the young lady's eyes shining with tears. In all this time we had passed together – seemingly years and years by now – I had never known her to cry. It was most endearing to witness. Her face contorted into a lovely expression as she struggled to hold back her emotions. I did not know what else to say.

Virtue looked at me over the flames and smiled weakly, wiping her fingers across her cheeks. At last she lifted herself up and stood. The fire lit her beautiful nubile form. A backdrop of heaven spread out behind her. It was a most stunning scene to behold. Then, with her blanket folded in her arms, she stepped around the fire and came close to me, standing between the flames so that her face was darkened in shadow. She held her hand down to me. I lifted my hand to her. I confess, I was a bit flummoxed. I was not sure how to respond, or to what degree she was pulling me forward into the next moment. She held my hand in that cold air, her own warm fingers gently squeezing mine. I realized rather incongruently that I was suffering from a merciless thirst, as if I had had nothing to drink for years but salt tears. Another moment passed, eternal, full of my hesitance. Then she let me go.

"*Bonne nuit, Didier*," she said at last. "Thank you for delivering me."

I could but nod.

Virtue moved away to where she had made a bed beyond the penumbral light of the fire. I watched her drop to her knees, smooth her bedroll, and then sink away into the shadows. I admit to feeling very much like a drowning boy right then – one who had just let escape his last chance at salvation. My heart fairly beat itself to death inside of me. I was sore confused.

I sat for a while, considering the circumstances – the various Thou-shalt-nots of the moment. For god's sake, I was a beat-up, middle-aged, one-eyed nincompoop in a dress. What was allowed to such a character in that particular situation? If this had been a novel, or a play, what would I be preordained to do? But then life is not like that in actuality. There are no fanciful miracles here. I realized this by and by. And so after a time, I quietly stood and stretched my aching back, peering once more into the stars. Of all things, I saw mine own star amidst the stellar chaos. I was sure that this was the selfsame one upon which I had once cast my wish. I recognized its bluish hue. Surely there was meaning in this. And yet, one learns to doubt such impromptu justification for hope. Such confidence is the stuff of fools and zealots. Nevertheless, I made my way hopefully over to where Virtue lay in her bed.

I stood above her, hovering somewhat, it occurred to me, like a dark angel. The light was minimal, affording only that quiet luminance of the stars, but I could clearly see her face. Her slightly parted lips. Her closed eyes. She was sleeping. Was she somewhere in a far away dream, even as she lay here before me? Could I, I dared to wonder, be a part of that dream? Her breath came and went from inside of her – her animating force – intermittently lifting the blanket draped over her breasts.

I watched, enchanted.

All good things, I reminded myself, have a dark side, too.

But how do we discern one from the other?

Experience. And through our mistakes.

Well you certainly have made a few of those.

I rubbed my face in my hands.

Oh! And, Oh! It all seemed a quagmire.

You, Mister Rain, have some decisions to make.

I blew a long plume of frosty breath into the air before my face. And then, trembling, I looked once more, almost pleadingly, into the sky. But the stars were silent. Maybe... Perhaps... I heard some laughter drifting from beyond the distant horizon. But otherwise, those stars were unforthcoming of any guidance. And so I did what I always do when faced with loneliness and desperate sadness. I reached down into myself and pulled out a comforting poem. I turned it over in my mind, admiring it, remembering it from when I had first discovered its deepest meanings so long ago on the waves of the sea. I whispered it to dear Virtue as a gift, hoping, I suppose, that my presence would work its way into her soul, and find residence therein.

> "The moon has gone
> The Pleiades gone
> In dead of night
> Time passes on
> I lie alone"

Simple as that.
I peered down at her one more time.
So lovely.
I thought of my mother.
And then I forced myself to turn away.

THE CONTINENTAL DIVIDE CAME and went. It can be a most dramatic example of geologic wonder, complete with soaring peaks and ramparts of up-thrusted stone. But the portion we passed over was unimpressive – no more than a broad plateau inhabited by twisted sage and sparsely scattered pinion pines. A brotherhood of magpies flapped and swooped over the monotony. A cold and sunny wind buffeted us from the north, tossing up a grit that stung our eyes and ground between our teeth. It was some time before I felt any sense of having dropped over to the other side, as the terrain was generally undulating in character. I saw mountains in the distance, to both our left and our right – pale blue silhouettes looming like the backs of breaching whales on those horizons – and for a time these were the only milestones by which to mark our progress. But then I noticed the subtle shift indicating our drop in elevation. The air felt changed. And then one realized oneself adjusting accordingly in the saddle, leaning back a single degree of angle to accommodate the downwardness of the trail. Of course, this was partly an aberration. There was surely plenty more uphill travel in our future. But one felt a huge leap in our progress. We were drawing closer to the City of Rocks. All the rain and snow that fell on us from this point on was destined for the big pond of the Pacific.

We were not far now from the regular route of the westward bound travelers. At times I almost believed I could smell people – their soaps and sweat, their smoke and filth. We were more or less traveling parallel to their dusty wagon roadway. And yes, it did occur to me to go there and see if I might possibly make a trade of my velvet dress for a pair of trousers and perhaps a fine woolen shirt. But I chose not to. The premonition of such a humiliating encounter overpowered my desire to be attired in a more masculine style. Maybe I would wait for my hair to grow a bit more, and for my eye and ear to heal up completely. People can be so mean to anomalous creatures, especially the ugly ones. And I was not yet up to the challenge of dealing with humanity and all of its twofaced judgments. Besides, I greatly preferred the harmonious privacy of our band of misfits. We were, in many ways, like a little family. Although I would have been sore pressed to explain just who of us played what role in the traditions of your typical familial potpourri.

Who had Virtue become in such a scenario?

Who were the horses?

And who, pray tell, was I?

No doubt some of this confusion came from my wearing that velvet gown. Not to mention the varying differences in our species.

I developed a fever. It came and went intermittently throughout the subsequent days. Sometimes it was quite severe, causing me to generate a cold perspiration that damped my clothes. At other times it was less of a presence, just a headache and general chilliness. But it refused to go away.

"Woe unto you, Didier," I whispered. "It seems your wanton ways are catching you up."

I determined that the plentitude of poisons I had so recently ingested – the liquors and horsemeat and dubious water sources, as well as the various other venoms that had so menacingly been thrust upon me by my recent captors – were totaling up to an abominable mélange lodged within my physical being. Add to that the other maladies I was healing – my ribs and shinbone, my eyeball and earflap – and it seemed obvious that more than one door had been left open to let in some infection, or demon otherwise disguised. At any rate, I was not much enjoying myself.

Virtue noticed my juddering and asked, "Should we stop for a while?"

I shook my head and tried to smile reassuringly. "I do not believe that it would matter one way or the other. I will be fine. We might as well keep moving."

So we tramped onward, with me swaying woozily on my horse's back.

I wished I had not lost my hat.

My sickness was worse in the mornings, accompanied by nausea, somewhat subsiding as the day progressed. Sometimes I felt to be traveling in a hallucinatory condition. Such a thin veil hung between my reveries and the actualities of the world through which we moved.

We traveled along a riverbed, dry and without much indication that it had ever channeled water any time in the last hundred years. It was like a slow healing scar on the land. I was thinking much about my childhood. My recent recounting of that time had kept it in the fore of my mind, and I now found myself rehashing those old memories. On that particular day, I was recalling my boyhood games of slaying dragons, of how I used to swing a wooden sword at such denizens of the imagination, when lo! There before me, in the high sandstone bank of that river, I was faced with the full sized skeleton of just such a beast.

I stopped Brownie, and squinted at the bones held suspended in the wall.

"Am I truly seeing this?" I asked.

Brownie whinnied that yes I was.

The bones had turned brown over the ages, but they appeared to be all there. The creature seemed frozen in an instant of long ago time. It was taller than three horses. Such teeth it had!

"I greatly doubt," I laughed to myself, "that my puny rapier would have done much good against this big fellow."

At this, with a grinding dirt sound, the bony brute turned his enormous head from out of the sandstone, looking me up and down. I peered into his vacant eyeholes. I nearly fell over dead with amazement.

The moment passed quickly, but so vivid was the experience that I could not be sure it had not truly occurred. The dragon creature resumed his position in his sandy crypt.

Brownie moved forward apathetically.

I was deeply shaken, with cold beads of water gushing down my face.

Another time, we came over a rise below which was spread a wide valley. In one instant it was vacant, just a wilderness of silence and desolation. But then in the next moment, I saw a sprawling city of unusual buildings. They were not beautiful in their architecture and materials, just rectangles and squares with garish ornaments of bright lettering. The signs were too far to read, but I noticed one that stood out from the others. It had large golden arcs looming on a pole above its rooftop. These arches formed a letter M, and I was certain almost at once that the building was a church, and that the monogram stood for Mormons. For what else could it be but some declaration of religious pride and wherewithal – a sort of beacon drawing at the disparate members of a sect?

Soon the vision disappeared, returning to the wilderness valley inhabited only by rabbits and squirrels. But I noted in my delirium a likeness to that same sensation I have had of stealing from poems not yet written. This experience was much the same, only more sickly in its general impression, and I found myself wondering for the first time how true prophets could stomach their visions. Granted, mine were only fever-induced daydreams, but they held a doomful god-like ability, and were not something to be endured by a mere mortal like myself.

This Nehi character must be something quite extraordinary, I told myself. Truly a vicar of God.

Maybe prophecy was only a form of disease. My own brushes with the prophetic arts had only made me want to retch.

I GREW EVERMORE SICK.

I could neither eat nor drink.

Every bit of food or water that passed my lips just as soon passed back out with a violent upheaval. I felt myself growing thinner, wasting away.

> "That time of year thou mayest in me behold,
> When yellow leaves, or none, or few, do hang,
> Upon those boughs which shake against the cold..."

My dress turned baggy on my withering frame. My ribs rubbed disconcertingly on the inside of my gown's crenulated bodice. There seemed nothing I could do to halt the downward progression of my wellbeing.

One dawn, after a restless night of dreaming about my father and dragons, I could not lift myself from my bed. I knew it was time to get up and hit the trail, but I could not so much as move a muscle. I was drenched in sweat. I was quivering like a distempered cur. I glanced around the camp for Virtue and the horses, but they were not to be seen.

"Virtue!" I called, my voice no more than a croak. "Brownie?"

The fire had not been lit, and was nothing but a shallow pit of ashes.

It became apparent that I was alone.

"Oh," I said. "I see."

Had they gone without me? I could not blame them if they had.

Still, I found myself edging toward a panic, until I heard footfalls coming through the brush behind me. When I rolled that direction, I was pleased and somewhat astonished at whom I saw coming my way.

"Oh, Dove!" I said. "You are truly a sight for my sore eye."

She did not smile at my paltry joke, but came near to me and knelt on the ground. Her hair had grown out since last I saw her.

"You look very pretty," I told her.

Her face was scrubbed clean.

"I am not feeling well," I confided. And then, through a sudden spate of sobbing, I said, "I think maybe I am dying."

She reached under my blanket and laid her hand on my chest, feeling for where my heart was thumping weakly beneath its velveteen shell. I could not tell from her blank expression if she agreed with my prognosis.

"What is it like?" I asked in a whisper. "Should I be afraid?"

But she did not indulge me with an answer. Instead, she opened the pouch on her belt, and pulled out a single red berry.

"*Ouvrez votre bouche,*" she commanded.

Either the berry was poison, or it was not. What did it matter now? I felt disinclined to put up a fight. So I opened my mouth as she had bid.

She placed the fruit on my tongue.

"*Mangez!*"

I chewed. I was greatly astonished to find that the berry tasted just like Turtle Dove's milk.

"Oh!" I exclaimed. "May I have some more?"

She shook her head, and laid her fingers over my mouth. "*Ça suffit.*"

I closed my eye, savoring that lingering flavor. "I am sorry," I said, "for what I did to you. Please, I hope you can forgive me." But when I opened my eye back up, I was disappointed to find that Turtle Dove had gone.

I waited.

A ragged crow flapped above me through the blue sky.

At last, with much effort, I forced myself to rise. I slipped into my boots and stumbled out of camp. I did not know where I was going. The ground and brush was all laden with a hoary mantle of frost. I passed amidst the branches and boulders with no small effort, pausing regularly to catch my breath. And then I kept on. It seemed I had walked a thousand miles when I at last came to a clearing. I blinked at the scene before me, trying to discern the figures I saw through the mists rising over the meadow.

Brownie and Puck and Genevieve were all there. They grazed without looking my way. I could hear them tearing up big mouthfuls of the frosty grass and chewing. A ways off to the side, on the edge of the little vale, I saw a mule deer doe and her fawn. The fawn glanced over at me and flicked her tail. I noted that the little creature's spots were gone from her coat, indicating that she was moving out of her animal childhood and into maturity. The doe herself stood quite still. I could not fairly believe to what I was now a witness.

Life is a mysterious experience, I assured myself.

Virtue knelt beneath the doe and was partaking of her milk. I stood quietly watching. I had the same sensation I had always felt when I had watched the girl taking suck from Turtle Dove's breast. Albeit, now my own desires were somewhat mitigated, no doubt as a result of my sickness.

When she had finished, Virtue held one hand cupped beneath the doe's soft udders, while using her other hand to wring the teats. She then stood, resting her empty hand on the doe's flank. She leaned and spoke some words into the deer's large gray ear. Virtue walked across the meadow to where I was waiting. Oh, her smile.

When she came close, I nodded. "I did not know where you were," I explained with some embarrassment. "So I came looking."

She held her cupped hand up to me. "Here," she said. "Drink this while it's still warm."

I leaned forward and, awkwardly, lapped up the milk from her palm, working my tongue along the wrinkles at the base of her fingers. It was intimate and very nice to do. I straightened up and wiped my chin. "It tastes like berries."

"Yes," said Virtue.

"Thank you."

She nodded and then took hold of my hand. "Let's get you back to your bed."

Virtue led me back the way I had come. We felt to be fairly floating over the ground. At last we reached the camp and I lay down in my blankets. I did not know if I would now die as I sank back into my sleep. At that point I did not figure it much mattered. I would be disappointed not to deliver Virtue in person to her destination, but I felt that she could probably make it from here without much help from such a pitiful deliverer as myself.

ONCE MORE, I OPENED my eyes.

Was it a day later, a single minute, or as much as a week?

I could not rightly say.

A ragged crow flapped above me through the blue sky.

I felt very sleepy and wrung out, but not necessarily dead.

I clenched my fists and stretched my legs beneath the blanket.

I heard the fire cracking and turned to see Virtue bent over the flames. She dipped a tin cup into our cooking pot and then came to me, kneeling by my bed.

"Here."

I raised myself onto an elbow and took the cup, gulping its steaming contents. I was very thirsty, and this herbal beverage was quite delicious. I felt it going down into me, spreading a comforting warmth all throughout my vacant innards. I licked my lips, and handed the cup back to Virtue. "Thank you."

I half expected the tea to come back up in an instant, but it did not, and I realized that I was feeling somewhat improved.

"Do you want food?" asked Virtue.

I shook my head. "But more tea would be nice."

I was able to sit up without my morning sickness, and after being ill for such a long while, I found it quite pleasant to do the simplest things.

I sipped my tea.

I watched Virtue.

She had changed from her dark mourning dress to one that was slate gray. Her lithe figure filled the dress nicely. Her blond hair was drawn back and she was as stunning a young woman as one could ever imagine. I gazed down at my own dusty, sweat-stained dress and immediately felt self-conscious. But I did notice that I was at least seeing the world through both of my eyes, and the tenderness was all but gone from alongside my right cheekbone. I combed my fingers through my sprouting hair.

"How would you assess my ear?"

Virtue examined the side of my head. "Good," she said. "Shall I pull the stitches?"

And so I was on the mend. I still felt like a beat up, stomped on puppet doll – weak, and none too pleasant to look at – but things were generally improving all around. Before we broke camp, I had Virtue trim my hair in a more civilized style. And then I shaved the whisker stubble from my chin. Except that I was still wearing a dress, I was beginning to feel more like a man.

At such times, one feels a need to thank someone – some compassionate spirit, or guardian angel – although why this is so, I could not say. A person could just as soon curse the gods for ever allowing him to reach such a nadir in the first place. Nevertheless, I offered up a bit of gratitude to any deities who might have been listening.

"Thank you very much for the reprieve," I muttered. "I promise now to do my best in delivering Virtue to her rightful destination." I nodded to the sky. "You have my word."

I did not honestly know what *my* word might have been worth right then. And I admit to feeling somewhat silly in saying anything at all. But one senses that it is always wise to appease the powers that be. There are plenty of stories, Biblical and otherwise, offering dire examples of those who had failed to do so.

A WIDE WALL OF peaks stood between us and our westward progress.

They emerged from the horizon, stretching out in both directions of north and south, growing higher and steeper with the closing distance, until we drew near to the foot of the range.

"The Ute Indians call these the *Wasatch*," I explained to my companions, "Which I understand to mean something like *passage over the mountains*."

The massif towered before us – imposing, and none too diminutive in stature. But I was pleased to see that no new snow had fallen on the interior hillsides. There were only a few dwindling snowfields gleaming in the angular sunlight striking the uppermost slopes. This bit of luck was reassuring. We would not have to travel around the range, but could find a speedier route by way of the zigzagging canyons that bisected the mountains.

We picked our way north along the hills for a few miles, until we found a sizeable stream tumbling out of a wide gulch. After deciding it was highway enough to afford us passage, we entered into the mountains.

The autumnal sun was low; the days short.

We traveled mostly in deep canyon shadow, following game trails and an old Indian pathway that had been in use for a thousand years. The stream was generally swift and tumbling, but in the back eddies and pools one could find fringes of ice that did not melt away throughout the day. Trout fanned beneath these ice windows, their blood red gills pumping in the clear water. There were many aspen trees in the ravines, bright gold and dropping their coin-shaped leaves on our heads as we passed beneath their branches. Otherwise the forest was made up of fir and pines. The air was chill and delicious to breathe. I wore my blanket wrapped around my shoulders. Virtue had found a wool coat in one of the trunks, and she wore this as we picked our way.

Nighttime was too cold to sleep. I was still getting over my previous bout of illness and was all but skin and bone, with little fat to insulate my emaciated body. I built a sizeable fire and sat close to it while Virtue slumbered near the horses.

The night dragged on.

Milk-blue moonlight splashed across the ridgelines high above me. A handful of stars turned slowly in the narrow band of sky that opened between the steep walls of the canyon.

I passed the time with thoughts of poetry.

I was feeling something inside of me – a stirring. It is hard to explain, but I felt like a new vivacity was taking shape within the wilderness of my soul, a burgeoning life where there had been no life at all. I recognized it was a poem, and I knew it wanted out into the world. But damned if I knew how to deliver it! It seemed all my previous genius had slipped away with the years. I was a washed up rhymester, cut-rate and hackneyed and without much of a way with words.

"Perhaps I could write it in French, and that would rejuvenate my muse."

But my mother tongue was so deeply submerged that I feared I could never bring it back with any fluidity and wit.

"Well," I shrugged, "what about writing it down in Ute?"

For a moment I entertained the idea of settling in with the local Indians and learning their philological mode of expression. I would get myself closer to The Word that Winston Dirge had so earnestly sought. Surely the Indians were nearer to it than any of us. But my talent for acquiring new languages had become less than impressive, and so it seemed unlikely that I would ever speak Ute with fluency enough to create a great work. Besides, everyone knew that the big languages were swallowing up the little ones. What kind of future could a poem hope to enjoy if it is written in such a soon-to-be dead dialect?

There will surely come a day, I reminded myself, when no one will remember Homer either.

This thought sobered me. I felt all poured out and sad. I felt like the very essence of humanity itself was slipping away into the stars.

I peered up into those stars, squinting, wondering if I could feel any sense of myself tumbling away into that stellar dust. I almost thought I could, when I was startled by a sound in the brush, and what I took to be a splashing noise.

I turned to face the shadows. Of course there was nothing but forest darkness beyond the light of the fire. Still, I was sure I had heard something, and felt myself being watched.

The stream clinked along its icy bank. Perhaps I had only heard a trout leaping at the reflectory light of the stars.

"Rain," I grinned to myself. "I do believe you are growing goosey with your advancing years."

But my private joke did not make me feel any more at ease. I stood, and then took two steps toward the darkness. My heart picked up its beat. I shivered and wrapped my blanket tight around me.

"Who is there?"

My voice gave way my dread.

"If you know what is for your good, you will show yourself to me now."

I felt unthreatening in my velvet dress and state of gunlessness, and knew that if scoundrels were afoot, I was most assuredly dead. I leaned forward, trying to see.

"Marguerite?"

But no one answered my challenge. The woods grew silent. The stars. I gazed over to where Virtue was sleeping. She had not stirred. Brownie was watching me curiously, but the other horses kept their eyes closed.

I shrugged to my friend and explained, "I thought I heard a noise."

Brownie let his head dip forward, and then he went back to sleep.

NEXT MORNING, WE TREKKED as far as the headwaters of our little stream, climbed to a col, and then dropped down into the headwaters of another stream on the other side. This new waterway flowed west, into what the Mormons called Deseret. I had always figured this was nothing more than an inspired and poetic misspelling of desert. The word had a Francophonic twist to it that gave it a certain exoticism, something akin to the paradisiacal insinuations of Xanadu, Eden, or El Dorado. But in general, the place was rather bleak in character. The basin beyond the Wasatch was arid and not the stuff of your typical oasis. The soil seemed largely composed of salt and sand. It offered little to recommend it as a place to settle down. But the Mormons had proven themselves a determined bunch of enthusiastic procreators, tireless and devout and not easily exterminated, and so one suspected that unless some Dark Angel felt inclined to erase them from the map, an empire was surely in the offing on this barren plain. A blue-white emptiness filled the horizon to the southwest. I knew this to be the Great Salt Lake – America's answer to the Dead Sea.

But then Brigham Young's Mormon promised land was *not* our destination. We were bound for an offshoot of that particular truth, "a tributary of a purer verity," as Thurman had so articulately explained it to me back in Independence.

We left the Wasatch behind, directing our westerly course in a somewhat northbound angulation toward the City of Rocks.

"Thirty thousand dollars."

We were close enough now to our objective that I was beginning to smell the sweet and encouraging scent of possibility. Perhaps financial solvency would help me to feel more secure and capable of settling down to my life's task. "Maybe that is all that I have lacked." One presumes that poverty is an impediment to creative thought, and I had most assuredly been under its tyrannical influence for the last many years. Not having to worry about where one is going to get his supper might just free up some mind room to enjoy a bit of literary toil. I was eager to find out.

As for my good friend Cedric Dallon, I had been doing some thinking about his role in this enterprise. He was a good sort, and I surely owed him much. After all, I would not have this job without his footwork and diligence. But what, besides connecting me with Thurman's people, had he done to deserve such a hefty recompense? I was the one who had endured the perils. I was the one who had been stampeded upon by buffalo. I was the one who had been burnt and heartbroken and masculinarily compromised. I was the hero of this story, not he. And so I had come around to thinking that maybe he did not deserve a full cut of the treasure. Surely an industrious sort like Dallon would, through thrift and discretion, make a good investment of only a third of the entire sum, or even, for that matter, a fourth. At any rate, he did not seem deserving of a full half, and I was determined that I might adjust his payment accordingly. That is, just as soon as I got it in my hands.

I laughed out loud, and turned to Virtue. "I do believe we are going to make it."

She was noticeably less enthusiastic than me, and I scolded myself for my overt indifference to her pending nuptial bondage. At once I felt bad. Virtue was more to me than a commodity, I realized. Much more.

I will not deny that I had – since concluding my period of mourning for Turtle Dove – entertained a fanciful scheme that placed Virtue in the role of my own wife. I blush to admit. But sometimes all the money in the world does not seem worth the loneliness one must trade it for. Maybe, I considered, True Love is the muse by which to create a genuine epic, not currency. One suspected as much. But having had neither in my life, I was unsure which was a surer route to contentment. Could money *buy* me that love? I greatly doubted it. Although I was sure that cleaner and prettier whores could be mine for a larger fee than I was used to paying. Still, one mistrusted that such was the purer variety of amour that had so inspired the great works of poesy throughout the ages. Surely Dante's adoration of Beatrice overrode his fiscal stability when putting his pen to paper.

But then all this guesswork assumed that my love for Virtue was reciprocal.

What, friend, makes you think the girl could feel any love for such a bombastic failure and scalawag as yourself?

No. Perhaps I had mistranslated the few small gestures she had made. Perhaps mine was a notion too absurd to be considered. And yet, consider it I did.

We trotted along toward some inevitable climax. I knew that if I never found out how Virtue felt about me I would be haunted by the possibilities throughout my days and, most especially, my nights. I needed that one piece of information – positive or not – to move forward into the rest of my earthly existence. Hell! I needed it in order to move into the next day. Her answer would surely sway my inclinations toward the Prophet or otherwise. For the promise of Love, I might even be willing to defy Providence.

The thought of laying my heart before her made me very nervous. I laughed at myself for this. What is it that makes the possibility of rejection so intimidating in such situations? And yet, I could not have been more mortified. I went over and over in my head how to most gracefully broach the subject. I was fairly driving myself mad with possible scenarios. I felt to be tying a knot, ever larger and ever tighter, all around my Adam's apple.

Oh, Rain! I told myself. Simply force the moment to its crisis!

We were passing through a valley hemmed on both sides by rolling hills. A few crooked trees leaned against an invisible wind. The site was not picturesque or otherwise memorable. But I could not stand the thought of waiting to find a lovelier place to pose my pressing question. It was now, I decided, or never.

"Whoa, Brownie."

I took a deep breath of air, hoping to calm my nerves. And then I climbed down off my horse.

Virtue and Puck and Genevieve came alongside and stopped. I felt them watching me and waiting for an answer as to why I had pulled up here, but I could not make myself turn and face them. I pretended to be checking the straps on my saddle. I swallowed, closed my eyes, and bowed my head, whispering a little prayer for courage. And then I turned to Virtue.

Oh, she was lovely!

The many miles of the trail had done nothing to diminish her charm and beauty. She most certainly *was* virtue – unsullied and good.

It struck me as absurd that someone like myself could ever hope to be loved by someone so pure. Hope dies a hard and miserable death.

Again and again.

I stepped close to her, and rested my hand on her horse's shoulder, letting my knuckles boldly come into contact with her slate gray dress. I was fairly shaking with fear. I wanted to look handsome for her, someone for whom a lady could feel affection, but I felt less than charismatic right then. Perhaps it was my own dress that undermined my poise. Maybe it was my age and trampled demeanor. I do not know. I tried to overcome all of these failings, but the words were hard to find.

"Virtue," I said, and coughed. "Darling."

She gazed down on me from her mount. I could not read her look. Did she suspect what I intended?

"Virtue," I repeated myself. "Darling. I just wanted you to know... before we reach... I just want you to know that it has been a privilege to be with you all these hard miles."

She bobbed her head toward me, bolstering my mettle.

"And also, I want you to know that I have come to care a great deal for you. A *great* deal." I took a small fold of her dress and rubbed it betwixt my fingers, noting the fine texture of the fabric. "And so I was wondering," I said. "Well... I was wondering if... You know, if here – in front of God and everyone – if you... Well, if you, could ever in a thousand years..."

I was still struggling to put together the correct sequence of words when, from nowhere, there came a thwiiiiiit! sound, abruptly punctuated by a thwang-g-g-g!

Puck jerked, and my glance went to where he was standing close by. I was amazed to see what appeared to be a long-stemmed sunflower blooming from out the side of one of the trunks slung over his sawbuck. How peculiar! So distracted was I by my effort to speak to Virtue that it took a long second for me to notice that the flower was not a flower, but an arrow. One fletched with meadowlark feathers.

I squinted at it.

I placed my finger to my chin.

"Oh, Cupid," I murmured, "Thy dart hath shot wide."

I TURNED AND SPIED seven mounted Indians galloping toward us from over the hill.

"Bother!"

It seemed pointless to run away. I was flat footed on the ground, and they held the advantage of momentum. They were sure to overtake us if we fled. We might as well save our strength. They poured silently down the slope, like wolves closing in on a band of sheep.

"Virtue," I said, all afluster. "In this remaining moment of tenderness... As I was saying before were so inconsiderately disturbed... Well, if this imminent encounter does not go well, please know that I, your Didier..."

I was determined that I would complete my confession of love to the girl if it was the last act I ever completed. It appeared as if it might be just that. But by the time I had sorted my words for eloquent delivery, the natives were upon us and had taken Virtue's attention away from me.

"Bother and vexation!"

They rode around us in a circle, each with an arrow nocked in his bow and aiming our way. They seemed to be sizing us up. I, in turn, assessed their degree of apparent threat. They were certainly dressed for trouble, complete with feathers in their hair and paint on their faces. But even through their masks, I could see that they were not full grown men. Boys. Juveniles. They appeared to be no more than a bunch of ruffians out looking for mischief. I took them to be from the tribe known as the Bannock, as this was their territory. But in this day and age, what with the Indians so uprooted and strewn asunder by the white man's Manifest Destiny, it was not uncommon for the tribes to comingle somewhat, in an effort at collaboration against the Caucasian onslaught. They could have been from any number of tribes.

They still did not advance, and neither did they whoop nor holler in that way one expected. They clomped round and round. The longer it went on, the more hopeful I felt that we were not in mortal danger. I stepped forward with my hands raised in the air as a sign of peace. I smiled. "Greetings, friends!"

They gathered in a bunch before us, their bows still poised to shoot us through with arrows.

"Do any of you know English?" I asked. "I regret to say that I do not speak your tongue."

They stared at me, their eyes flashing a wild mix of fear and excitement.

"We are traveling through your country here." I spread my arms to the surrounding hills. "And a fine piece of property it is. Quite spacious. We mean you no trouble, and would appreciate it if you would let us pass without incident."

At this, the biggest boy – the one I took to be the leader – hopped down from his horse's back and stepped close. He glared at me, leaning in so that I could feel his breath while he examined my face. He wrinkled his nose, and made a curious expression. Then, of a sudden, he thrust his hand between my legs and groped my stick and stones.

"Whaa!" I squealed, and bent forward. For this move greatly surprised me.

He then took a handful of my dress and lifted it out to the side, admiring its velvety sheen. At last he turned to his friends and said something I did not understand.

They all laughed.

They then turned their attention to Virtue. It struck me that they were somewhat in awe of her. She *was* quite extraordinary to behold, as if she had been lifted right from a Renaissance fresco. I suppose even these heathens could see that she was something of an angel. Some of the boys were shirtless, and it seemed to me that they all puffed their chests for Virtue's benefit. Yes, they *were* handsome lads, well muscled and quite healthy. And yes, I admit to feeling a jealous pang at their advantage of youth over my own aged and battered physique. The leader seemed especially smitten with Virtue and strutted like a bantam rooster so that she could observe the finery of his plumage.

"Most unchivalrous behavior," I murmured. "Befitting of a fop!"

The youngster heard my admonitions of his character and turned to me. Uncannily, he seemed to understand what I had said and took offense. He stepped close once more, this time drawing a long knife from his belt. He walked around me, flashing his blade so I could see.

The others all grinned expectantly.

Without meaning to, I gulped.

With no small degree of drama, he circled me twice more, and then stood at my backside, laying the cold blade against the nape of my neck. He slid it inside my collar, and then, with a long slow move, he ran the knife down the length of my right sleeve, letting it run out at the cuff. The sleeve peeled away from my arm and hung empty at my side. He repeated this with my left arm as well.

All the while, his partners sniggered and grinned.

I tried to smile. What else could I do? It was a strategy I had learned many years before, when I was a boy myself, and subject to a similar scorn of the bullyboys at my school. Although honestly, it had never come to the disarming result I had always hoped it would.

The boy stuck his knife once more to the back of my neck.

He held it there against my skin, moving it lightly up and down, up and down, shaving at the little hairs like some sort of dainty barber.

Finally, in a wink, he thrust the knife downward with a great ripping noise. I expected to feel my spine and liver spill out onto the ground. But they did not. Instead, my velvet gown dropped away from me, leaving me bare of torso.

I clutched the material at the waist to keep myself partially covered. But the boy gave me to know, by way of a growl and fierce tugging at my arms, that he preferred for me to let go of the dress. And so I did. It fell to the ground around my boots. There I stood, shucked like an ear of corn, exposed for all to see.

I covered myself with my hands.

Now those boys hooted and hollered in true hooligan fashion.

I looked apologetically to Virtue. She was still atop Genevieve, surrounded by wild Indian boys, but she did not seem afraid or appalled or the least bit embarrassed on my behalf. If anything, she was patient, tolerant, composed. I was sorry that I would now be murdered in front of her, probably skinned and pierced with arrows. Probably castrated. I was sorry for what she would most likely have to endure because I had failed to deliver her as I had promised to the gods. We had come so far, and gotten so close. But alas!

Another boy got down from his horse and pushed me to the ground so that I fell away from my dress. He then snatched it up and ran off with it to a little tree growing on the hill. He tied the sleeves spread wide, letting the velvet flap in the breeze. From where I was kneeling in the dirt, the dress looked like the hide of some queer animal. The boy ran back over to the group, drew his bow, and shot an arrow through the dress. Everyone whooped, and then they each did the same, filling the empty gown with a constellation of tiny holes that let in the daylight from behind.

When they were done with their target practice, they turned back to me. I was still on all fours. Someone shot an arrow into the ground between my hands. They all laughed when I flinched. Then one of the boys came over and jerked my arm, indicating that he would have me to stand. I struggled to my feet. The lad shouted in my face. His own face was painted to look like an owl. Large circles around each of his eyes. Something like a beak drawn over the bridge of his nose. He shouted at me once more, but I had no idea what he was saying.

"I am sorry." I shrugged.

He took an arrow and tapped its shaft hard against my chest, shouting nonsense.

I knew that this was it. I was done for.

Again, he slapped me hard on the breastbone with the arrow. Thwack!

I gritted my teeth against the pain.

I waited for him to do his worst.

But then the Owl Boy did something I was not expecting. He leaned forward, squinting at my chest.

"Oooh!" he said.

He lifted his hand slowly into the air between us, and then he touched his finger to my skin. It was a most bewildering moment. Transfixed, he traced the perimeter of my tattoo, going all around its edge, again and again, so lightly that, even with the anxiety of my predicament, it almost tickled.

I DECIDED TO TAKE a chance.

What, I figured, did I have to lose?

I licked my lips, cleared my throat, and said to the Owl Boy, "*Syatapis!*"

He let his finger come away from my skin and stared at me. His eyes grew so large they seemed to fill the exaggerated owl-eye circles drawn around them. I did not know if he was a stray Blackfoot, joined up with the Bannock or Utes. I did not even know if it was reasonable for those tribes to blend. But the word obviously meant something to him. He took a quick step away from me and turned to his fellows. With a solemn tone, he said something to the boyish chief.

The leader snorted, and dismissively jerked his chin. But Owl Boy persisted. He pointed at me and repeated what he had said, this time even more earnestly than before. The bigger boy appeared unsure. He grunted. He strode over and peered at my tattoo.

Owl Boy prattled on and on, trying, I surmised, to explain what a special creature I was. The leader listened, deliberating, while the others all leaned in behind him, trying to catch a glimpse of the mark on my chest. One of these boys called out to the leader. I heard him use the word *Syatapis*.

I took this as a good omen, and boldly I lifted my arm toward Virtue. "She, too, is *Syatapis*," I announced. "She is the princess of all *Syatapis*."

They all turned and regarded Virtue with wonder.

But the leader was not going to let it go at that. He needed to be sure. He needed to show himself as the boss. He studied me all up and down, looking, I supposed, for gills or fins or some other indication of my *Syatapis* heritage. Although I was naked and more defenseless than I would have preferred, I tried to stand tall, and show a character worthy of the noble underwater people I was professing to represent. I tried, that is to say, to look as much as I was possibly able to look like the brother of a turtle or a fish.

The boy chief examined my tattoo. He touched it. Then, straightening up, he touched his own chest over the place where he kept his heart. Lifting his other hand to his face, he laid a single finger at the corner of his eye. Gazing deeply into my own eyes, he slowly drew the tip of his finger down his cheek, as if marking the path of a teardrop. The motion took a long second to complete. When he was finished, he tipped his head at me and asked, quietly, "Heart tear?"

Now I do not know if he posed this question to me in English, or some language of the American Indian. The stress of the circumstances made it hard to distinguish. Either way, the essence of what he uttered connected in the deep well of sounds from which all we creatures draw to make our meanings known. I understood what he meant. And what is more, I understood that *he* understood something about *me* that I thought was a secret. A tremor flowed through me right then. It was one of those rare times when one being on this planet – no matter how different from us they might seem – connects with us on the level of the soul. It was like reading a poem at midnight. It was all that deep mystery stuff of life.

Moved by this familiarity, I lifted my hand and laid it flat against the boy's chest. He did not recoil, but stood stock-still. His heart beat a rhythm – ka-thump, ka-thump, ka-thump – against my palm. I thought to myself, When voices of children are heard on the green...

The boy thrust his chin upward, and stepped away toward his partners. He did not speak for a moment. But then he announced something to his band of would-be renegades. They all listened intently, shooting respectful glances at me and Virtue. The leader went to his horse and grabbed down a bundle. He unrolled it and presented me with a pair of buckskin leggings and a fine buckskin shirt. Another boy gave me an elk hide robe. Another gave me a cap lined with rabbit fur.

I slid into these with thankfulness. It was chilly there in that windswept setting, and I was eager to end my exposed and vulnerable state of being. I was pleased to find the new suit fit me very well.

With Virtue the lads were more timid. She was still sitting on Genevieve. The boys walked around her, trying to steal peeks at her without obviously lifting their eyes to hers. At last the leader took something from a bag hanging around his horse's neck – some charm or talisman – and walked over to the girl. The other boys parted as he stepped up beside Virtue. He said a few words of his language, and handed something to the young lady. She took it from him, and smiled.

And then it was over.

Quick as that they all hopped onto their horses and galloped back over the hill from where they had come.

Nonplussed, I held out my arms and admired my new clothes. My old velvet dress dangled like a shed skin from a tree branch.

I looked to where Virtue was waiting expectantly.

It was almost as if nothing at all had happened. Except that I was newly attired, it was almost as if we were right back in that moment before the hoodlums had arrived. I grew newly nervous when I remembered.

"Well," I laughed. "Where was I?"

I looked to the west, trying to gather my articulacy, endeavoring once again to find the words. But it was no good. Something had changed in the interim. I suppose seeing those Indian boys in all their youthful glory had intimidated me somehow. I guess when I had been made naked in front of all the world I had seen myself for the dilapidated lowlife that I truly was. I surely was no noble *Syatapis.* Anyhow, I lost my nerve to up and ask Virtue if she loved me. The thought that she might not was too dreadful to contemplate. I do not think I would have survived her rebuke.

"Well," I said, and spat out the metallic taste that had settled on my tongue. "Well, we are getting close now."

Without so much as glancing at Virtue, I climbed up onto Brownie's back once more, making that last push toward the legendary City of Rocks.

A SHARP BREEZE CUT down out of a birdless blue sky.

"Huh," I mumbled. "Well."

Puck, Brownie, Genevieve, myself, and Virtue all stood on a high hill gazing over the hallowed homeland of the Restructured Truth. At long last we had reached our destination.

I do not know exactly what I expected. I suppose one lets his imagination run amok. One conjures in his mind some sort of fairytale complete with bubbling waterfalls and bright colored rainbows. I was not necessarily thinking the place would be lined with streets of gold, or peopled with angels, but something close to it. Thurman's description of his nouveau Zion had inspired visions of Utopia. I had been eager to see it for myself. But now... I felt like a thirsty child who has just been handed a cupful of vinegar.

Well, I encouraged myself. The place has potential. Even Jericho had to start with that first stone placed upon a stone.

The naturally occurring landscape was impressive enough. A preponderance of lofty granite pinnacles shoved up out of the sage-cluttered valley and hillsides. Junipers were placed throughout like potted plants. It *did* look like some sort of primitive city, albeit one built by titans before time. But to my eyes, it was the human element that stained the scene. A sense of struggle and defensiveness pervaded. The place exuded an overall personality of distrust and desperation.

An area of about two hundred acres was enclosed within a wall. This barrier was made of stone and appeared to be a work in progress, with the intention being to build it high and formidable. Random piles of rock lay waiting to be placed into the barricade. A single arched gateway allowed entry into the compound, and two men with rifles were stationed on steeples above said ingress. (Was it a fort, a sheep pen, or a prison?) Inside was a collection of mud and stone houses, one of them quite large, what could pass for a palace in this part of the world. This was the Prophet's home, I figured – the place where he received his visions and penned his covenants. But most of the dwellings were built right into the natural rock hummocks. They looked like the warrens of rabbits and chipmunks. Wisps of smoke could be seen rising from the cracks in the stone rooflines.

A network of wooden ladders rose up the sides of the rock towers to what appeared to be nests for battlements. Rope bridges connected the ramparts, strung between the tower tops like spider web. I spied at least four canons poised for action upon these turrets. Armed men were watching out in all directions from the perches. It appeared the Restructured Truth needed considerable protection from the outside world.

A parcel of the enclosed acreage was reserved for gardens, and women and children were bent harvesting in these plots, pushing wheelbarrows of potatoes and squash. I thought to myself that the sisters Shadrach, Meshach, and Abednego would fit right in here. A flock of grimy white chickens pecked at the ground all around the workers' heels.

As far as I could see, the land was parched, with only a single thin stream winding through the heart of the settlement. It seemed hardly big enough to provide drinking water for the clan, let alone irrigation for the crops. Some Mormon miracle must surely be at work. A languid, oat-colored ox stood in the lower end of the stream where it trickled under the wall. The remainder of the stream's moisture was sucked dry by the dusty desert beyond the stronghold.

We stood there for the longest time.

None of us could make up our mind to go down.

I could not guess what Virtue was thinking.

I, personally, was a bit perplexed. I suppose I had believed all along that I was actually on a mission for God. I confess that I thought we would be greeted by fanfare and banners, singing and a banquet. Surely I was some sort of victorious champion who had outsmarted many a peril in my gallant delivery of the Holy Betrothed. I had even fancied that I might be offered a home in this dreamland, be granted high office, and even presented with a couple of wives for my trouble.

For it was well known that Mormons and their outgrowths were keen on polygamy. (Such has always been their appeal for lonesome bachelors like myself.) And I had figured if I could not have Virtue as my bride, I could at least start a small harem of my own. A quantity of feminine flesh, I consoled myself, might make up for any lack in quality.

But now…

"Well," I considered. "I suppose even Muhammad had to start somewhere."

I glanced sidelong at Virtue. She stood with Genevieve's head over her shoulder, absentmindedly stroking the mare's nose. The young lady was to be the Doyenne of this colony – the Queen Bee in the hive. That was something, I suppose. But even so, I could not help but think Virtue deserved better. Goodness sakes! The place had no water! And yet, who was I to offer her any option other than this one spread out before her?

Right then, we heard the distant blare of a shofar.

It seemed the sentinels had at last discovered us on this distant ridgeline, and were announcing to their coterie that intruders were afoot. At once, the place looked like a nest of panicked ants. Women and children dropped their potatoes and scurried toward their huts. Chickens scattered with a flurry of wings. The men all trained their rifles and canons on our little party.

"It appears they saw us," I said.

And that was when I saw Him.

At the front door of his big house.

The Prophet.

He alone was dressed in a white robe, as if he had been plucked straight out of an old Bible story. And he was tall. Even over the distance one could detect a certain demeanor, a *je ne sais quoi*. One felt himself being granted a vision. One felt himself brushing against something not quite of this world.

The Prophet turned and looked our way. Even from afar, I felt his gaze. A wave of goose pimples tightened my skin. I nodded, as if to say hello. The fellow was over half-mile away, but I swear he returned my nod. Uncanny. He looked to be an older brother of Jesus Christ himself.

A group of men congregated before the leader, shooting us glances and, I surmised, discussing a plan of action. After a minute, five of them marched off to some horses, mounted, and galloped out of the compound, turning up the slope in our direction.

I swallowed at a knot of nerves, and chewed at my lip.

"We will wait," I decided. "They can come to us."

I KNEW THAT THE Salt Lake Mormons often enlisted the help of the Utes, and two of the riders now coming our way appeared to be cut from that Indian ilk. Only one of the five wore the wrap-around beard so emblematical of the Restructured Truth. The remaining two, I surmised, must be out-for-hire gentiles, like myself, doing the dirty work for the greater glory of God. The pair appeared tough, savvy, and none too holy.

They all rode up and halted before us, their mounts breathing hard from the climb. I noticed that the two henchmen at once scanned our horses and my person, searching – I could read that look – for any sign of a weapon. They themselves wore pistols on their hips, and carried rifles in scabbards slung from their saddles. The Utes both carried shotguns over their laps. Except for his big hairy smile, the Truther remained unarmed.

Once they had assessed me, and decided I was not dangerous, all eyes went to Virtue. It was with no small degree of dismay that I noted a randy blush eclipsing the faces of the three white men. I knew that look. And I knew exactly what fantasy was playing out in each of their ignoble heads. To say the least, it was disappointing. I had expected better from this hallowed lot of Chosen Ones. Had they been devout Ablutionites, they would have quick skulked off to take a long, cold bath. But I sensed that a redemptive rinse was not the immediate subject on their minds.

I glanced at Virtue. She stood rigid, enduring their scrutiny.

"Salutations!" said the bearded one. He tipped his hat.

I nodded, doing my best to smile.

"I assume that you are Mister Rain."

"I am."

"I am Brother Junilay – adjunct to his Holiness."

"It is a pleasure," I said.

The man thrust his bushy chin in Virtue's direction. "And this, I presume, is our blessed bride."

"Virtue," I said. "Her given name is Virtue."

"Yes. Well. We have been eagerly awaiting your arrival."

Virtue tipped her head to the man, but she did not smile.

The fellow regarded her for a long moment, as if he were sizing up a filly, or perhaps a plate of fried eggs, running the tip of his tongue over the bristles on his lower lip. And then he turned to me. "We greatly appreciate your services, Mister Rain. I presume the merchandise – that is, the girl – is healthy and…" He scratched his ribs with a thumb. "…remains the essence of purity."

"You will find none more pure," I assured him.

"Good," he replied. "Good. Good." He turned to his white cohorts and shot them a look.

They both squirmed in their saddles, and returned his gesture with small nods.

The Indians waited behind them.

"Well, then," said the good Brother Junilay. "It seems you have completed your mission for us, Mister Rain. And now, without ado, there is nothing left but for us to take the young lady off your hands."

Everything was happening too fast for my taste. I did not like the idea of this being the end of it with Virtue. Would we even be given time for a proper goodbye? "Well," I said. "To be sure. The job is completed. It was quite a trip. And now I suppose we just need to make our swap."

The man looked at me, an eyebrow raised. "Swap, Mister Rain?"

It was the most pathetic piece of acting I had ever witnessed.

"Yes," I said. "I will now take my payment, and you will take the girl. As agreed."

Junilay put on a frown of consternation. "But, Mister Rain. I believe the agreement was that your payment would be paid to you upon your return to Independence." He spread his fingers sincerely over his chest. "That, at least, is how it was understood by us."

A knot began to twist in the pit of my solar plexus. "Oh no!" I said, and laughed good-naturedly. "There must be some sort of mistake. Brother Thurman clearly indicated that my payment would be handed to me by the Prophet Nehi himself when I delivered Virtue into his waiting arms."

"Hmmm!" said the bearded rascal. "Well, obviously communications with our eastern chapter have been misconstrued." He raised his palms and shrugged. "I suppose that is bound to happen from time to time, what with such a vast distance between us and them."

"I suppose," I said. "Nevertheless…"

Now there was no body of water anywhere of any size in any direction one could see, but somehow, right there in that vast desert expanse, I began to smell the unmistakable odor of fish.

"I'm sure it will all work out for you, Mister Rain. You have done a great service for the Restructured Truth. It will be noted in our history. Your name will be uttered for all the ages to come. Just find Brother Benjamin upon your return to Independence. He will have your money for you. Besides, there is nowhere to spend it out here anyway." He chuckled at this. "You can keep your horse. But now, I am sure the Prophet is eager to meet his new bride." He held his hand toward Virtue, indicating that she should mount Genevieve and prepare to go.

Virtue looked at me.

I looked at her.

"Yes," I said. "Yes. I am sure you are anxious to get the girl to her… to her… But we can clear up this matter right here and now. I have a copy of the contract somewhere." I patted my shirt with my palms. "Rain," I muttered, "where did you put that?"

"There is no need, sir. Just return to Independence for your fee."

"No," I said. "I am sure I have a signed copy here somewhere. Now what did I do with it?" I scratched my chin and stared at the ground, as if trying to remember.

Junilay sighed and shrugged to his men.

My mind was running like a deer.

"Girl!" I said, and snapped my fingers. "Come here! Help me look!"

I hated the expression on Virtue's face, but I knew I had to keep up the act. She paused, but then, trusting me, she stepped over to where I was standing by Brownie.

Out of the corner of my eye, I saw Junilay give his men a secret signal. They dismounted, and started my way.

I watched them without watching, keeping track of where they were in relation to my person. "Where did I put that paper, girl?"

Virtue stood beside me with her hands at her sides. She did not speak.

"Mister Rain," said Junilay. "There is no need."

I unlatched the strap on my saddlebag and reached inside, as if searching for the missing document. "It says right there on this paper… Payment in full. I am sure of it."

DELIVERING VIRTUE

The henchmen were close now. They had not drawn their pistols, but I suspected they were about to. I desperately groped inside the bag until, at last, my hand came in contact with what I was searching. I curled my fingers around it, took a big breath, and pulled it out with a howl of the likes uttered by a demon from the deepest pits of hell.

"Awooooh!"

I grabbed hold of Virtue, twisting her arm behind her back, holding her close to my front side, and pointing my Francote Pinfire revolver, Belgian made, at the pair of dragoons stalking my way.

"Halt!" I cried. "Do not take another step!"

THE HENCHMEN STOPPED IN their tracks and half squatted down, greatly shocked. They both moved their hands into position over their sidearms, fingers twitching, but did not make to draw their guns from out of their holsters. They were but a single rod before me, and my aim was too close for them to take a chance. The Utes sat up in their saddles and raised their shotguns part way to their shoulders. Junilay's eyes grew large. His horse pranced a quick nervous circle. The bearded man held up his arm as a signal for the Indians not to shoot.

An eternal moment passed where we all reconnoitered our positions.

Brother Junilay's complexion turned the sickly pallor of a cod's belly. He squeezed his arms into his sides and hunched up, as if to hold himself together. "Mister Rain," he quavered. "Mister Rain, what are you doing?"

"Hear me!" I cried. "Ye men of unrighteous conduct!"

The henchmen narrowed their eyes.

Junilay visibly shuddered.

"Verily, verily, I say unto you!" I cried this at the top of my voice, as volume somewhat added to my slim daring. I did not honestly know where I was going with my theatrical evangelism, but I hoped that some spirit would take me over and guide my tongue. "Verily!" I cried. "Verily and behold!"

The group waited before me.

Virtue pressed her shoulder blades against my chest. I held her wrist between my belly and the small of her back. Even in that heated moment, I could smell her sweet-as-flowers scent. It bolstered my courage.

"How dare ye!" I continued with my rant. "How dare ye suspend the workings of the Almighty! For *I* am the Blessed Deliverer, sent to do His bidding! Who be ye to darest interfere with the will of God?"

Junilay hemmed, and then started to speak, but I did not give him time to make an answer.

"For the prophecy hath declared my soul's earthly cask the right of passage through the wilderness. *I* am protected! *I* am the Chosen One! *Mine* are the hands that will deliver the Holy Betrothed unto the Prophet. The prophecy shall be fulfilled by the might of Didier Rain! So commandeth the voice of God! Amen!"

Junilay took ahold of his beard in one hand, fondling his whiskers while replaying my words in his head. He looked a bit dazed. He asked, "What would you have us to do, Mister Rain?"

"First, ye must cast down your arms." I waved my pistol at the two men before me. "Slowly."

The men glanced at one another, and then studied my weapon. Mine was not as impressive as their rather large revolvers, but it enjoyed the advantage of being already drawn and aimed. I hoped they were unable to tell that my gun was not loaded. They seemed to be weighing the situation, each one trying to decide which of them would be most likely to take a bullet if they pounced. They looked to be doing mathematical equations in their heads. I pointed my gun first at the heart muscle of one, then the other, back and forth like that, to keep them guessing.

"We had better do as the man says," advised Junilay.

"Slowly," I said. "One at a time." I thrust my gun barrel toward the chest of the one on the right. "You first. Reaching across with your left hand."

The man thought about this sequence, and then did as I said, holding the pistol daintily by the handle, and then tossing it gently into the dirt in front of him. I turned my pistol on the other man, and he repeated the procedure in more or less the same manner. I felt greatly relieved, but not necessarily out of trouble just yet.

"Now," I called. "You two back there. Crack those double barrels and kick out the shells onto the ground."

The Indians looked to Junilay, as if bored. Junilay bobbed his head. The Indians opened their guns and plucked the shells from their chambers, dropping them at their horses' feet.

"Now the guns," I commanded.

They dropped the shotguns to the ground.

I figured Junilay was no marksman, and so I decided that he should go to the empty horses, pull the rifles from their scabbards, and toss them away to the side. He did this at my orders, his hands shaking like leaves in a breeze. I felt certain he lacked the nerve to try anything too bold.

With all the men unarmed, I then narrated for them the story I would like to see played out for my benefit.

"You will now ride back down to the Prophet. All in a bunch, together. No stragglers. I will be watching from my perch on this Mount Pisgah. In one single hour, you, Brother Junilay, will return. You will be accompanied only by the Prophet Nehi."

Junilay looked doubtful at this, and I felt a need to reiterate.

"You and the good Prophet will return *alone*, and unarmed. You will bring me thirty thousand dollars in earthly currency. Gold or cash. It makes no difference."

"Mister Rain..."

I held up my pistol to silence the man. "As it is written!" I cried. "According to the writ of the Prophecy!"

Junilay sighed, and slowly nodded his blanched hairy face.

"Upon receiving my reward, I will graciously deliver Virtue into the arms of the Prophet. As agreed."

I quick went over in my head to think if I had forgotten anything important. I was rather nervous, and it would not have surprised me if I had. But I felt I had said enough.

"Now let me warn you," I concluded. "You do not know who you are dealing with here. I am not one to be taken lightly." It pained me to do so, even with my gun empty, but I turned the pistol so that its snout rested against the beautiful blond shock of hair draped over Virtue's temple.

She tensed, and arched her back.

I cocked the pistol for emphasis. "No heroics," I said. "No attempts at trickery. I assure you, gentlemen, you do not want to cross me. For hers will not be the first young girl's life I have taken for the sake of treachery."

The truth in what I said instilled a doomful weight to my words that surprised even me. It no doubt impressed Junilay and his contingent. He seemed quite earnest, and eager to be away from me and my apparent lunacy. But in truth, my little act struck me as thin and unconvincing. Had it been a horse, I might have shot it for lame. But it seemed to serve its purpose.

"Now go!" I commanded. "And sin no more!"

THEY TROTTED AWAY DOWN the hill, with Junilay glancing back over his shoulder.

I held Virtue a while longer, not realizing that I might possibly be hurting her arm with my maniac's grip. I leaned against her – for support truly – my chest against her back. I had grown weak in the knees, and she was so nice to hold onto. But then I gathered myself and, somewhat embarrassed by my behavior, I let go of her wrist.

She hastily stepped away from me, grabbing the lower part of her arm and rubbing it back to life.

"I am sorry," I said. "Are you all right?"

She glared at me, as if trying to read what I was up to, as if endeavoring to comprehend who I truly was. It pained me to undergo this critical character inspection from the one person in all the world for whom I cared. But I suppose I had it coming.

"I panicked," I explained. "I saw no other option. Please forgive my ungentlemanly behavior."

Apologetically, I held up my empty revolver and dropped it to the ground.

Virtue nodded doubtfully, still rubbing her wrist.

I wanted to explain myself further, to drop on my knees before her and pour out my heart. There suddenly seemed so much to say. But I felt there was some pressing business to attend to first. I needed to figure some things out quick. I needed to make sure the riders were doing as I had instructed. I stalked over so that I had a clear view of the slope leading down to the compound. Junilay and his thugs all galloped in a bunch, appearing to obey my request.

I picked up a loose shotgun and tossed it as far as I could into the sagebrush, uttering a sibilant growl. I performed the same act with a rifle. I could not say why I did this, as it served no good purpose in the conundrum at hand. Perhaps it was just for a bit of exercise to release some of my frustration.

The five riders turned their horses back through the gate and went directly to the big house. They all dismounted, but only Junilay went in through the front door. The others hastily went off to reconnoiter with some other men. The group looked our way more than once. Even from afar, I noted many a rifle barrel glinting in the sun.

"Oh, man," I moaned, and rubbed my face in my hands. I felt I had squarely kicked a beehive, and now the drones were all abuzz.

"Damn!"

I paced back and forth along the ridge, chewing at my thumbnail and doing some quick calculations. Anyway I turned it, nothing was adding up in my favor.

Virtue stood quietly near Genevieve.

I tried to imagine her down there in that weird settlement. I tried to see her as a part of that clan – ultimately its materfamilias. But all I could conjure in my busy mind was an unsavory image of her with the Prophet Nehi. I could not say. I suppose it was just pure boyish jealousy. But that vision was distasteful to me. It made me angry. It stirred in me a peculiar mixture of paternal protectiveness and a cuckold's ire. Most confusing. For I was neither her parent nor her spouse. But either way, I felt an overpowering reluctance to turn Virtue over to the Restructured Truth.

"Now, Rain," I told myself. "That decision is not rightly yours to make."

Nevertheless...

I looked at the sky. Cloudless. Blue. Maybe Paradise. Maybe not.

I strode over to Puck and Brownie. They were nervous too, quite agitated. "What do you think, boys?" I stroked their shoulders. I assessed their condition. Their legs were covered in scratches and scabs, and Puck's fetlock was swollen. Their ribs were showing through their mangy hides. The straps on Brownie's saddle and Puck's pack frame were buckled all the way to the last notch so as to more snugly accommodate their diminishing girth. They were both in sore need of a long rest.

"Well," I said. "Do you think you have it in you?"

Brownie did not hesitate, but blew an affirmative blast of air through his nostrils. Puck followed his example.

I felt privileged to be a comrade to such noble beasts. I felt myself somewhat reinforced by their selfless courage.

"Well," I said. "We will see how the events develop."

I turned to Virtue. She stood on the edge of the hill, alone now, gazing down at the City of Rocks. I surmised that she was considering her role in this scenario, and in the world at large. In so many ways, she had never seemed a part of this world to begin with. And yet, she was somehow, at the same time, the very life essence of the world itself. It was an impossible idea to explain. Like a dream. More felt than anything. And I did not have the leisure to work it out in my head right then. Although I secretly hoped I could someday find a way to express it in a simple poem. But that would have to wait.

I walked over and stood beside her.

She did not look my way, but I felt she was aware of my presence.

I pulled a deep gulp of air into my lungs, and then let it out. "Virtue," I said, feeling weak and inept.

Oh, where to begin?

"Virtue. Darling girl. It seems the circumstances are different than we imagined."

She did not speak.

I sighed. Then swallowed. "I have never been much of a man," I confessed. "I know that about myself. I have multiple failings. They have overwhelmed my good intentions more than once. And I regret to admit that I have defied every Thou Shalt Not from here to Sinai and Parnassus." I shook my head. "I do not suppose I can rightly expect much assistance from any of the available gods."

I peered at the commotion down in the valley. Something was happening, forces were gathering, strategies were being quickly planned. I knew we hadn't much time.

"But you, Virtue. You are good. You are innocent and blessed. I am sure that whatever you do, and wherever you go, you will be looked out for by the forces that be." I shrugged. "That is but my humble hunch."

Precious seconds were ticking away.

"I feel I have become better by knowing you," I continued. "I feel like it was a fortuitous occurrence that you and I should meet, and have had such occasion to know one another while traveling through the wilderness." My voice was thin, and somewhat quavering as I said all this. "I feel privileged to call you my friend."

Virtue did not apparently respond to my openness, and this disturbed me, as I suppose I hoped she felt somewhat the same about me. If she did, she did not say so at that time.

Down below, men were gathering, and horses. I found it hard to believe they would not at least make a pretense to follow my guidelines. I was sure that Virtue meant too much to them to ever dare a brash act leading to her harm. One felt that their entire earthly enterprise somehow depended upon her survival and participation. The Restructured Truth was surely destined to evaporate into the blue ether without Virtue. Still, they seemed to be gathering for an alternative plan than the one I had outlined. I figured that even if they had thirty thousand dollars to give, they would then hunt me down and take it back. What I was witness to now, I decided, was but an assembling of that hunting party.

"I will do as you ask, Virtue. I respect your decision, one way or another. You can go down there right now, with no more kerfuffle, and take your place in their grand scheme. I am sure you will be treated like a queen." I rubbed my neck, and nervously scratched at my buckskin collar. "I will just ride away." I turned and looked over my shoulder toward the northern horizon line.

"But," I said. "I want you to know, if you need my help... if you want me to take you out of here... I swear to you that I will use every bit of my strength and cunning to deliver you to safety." I bobbed my head, and held my fist over my chest. "You have my word."

The girl still refrained from looking my way.

I could not guess what she was thinking.

I watched her face in profile. Impassive. Perfect. Almost like a statue.

I had never been so thirsty.

I knew things were happening down below. It did not matter to me right then just what they were up to. I could not take my eyes from Virtue. I understood that this might well be the last image of her I would ever have in my possession, and I wanted to linger over it for as long as possible.

A chill breeze swept over the ridge.

From somewhere, even in that stark landscape, a lark trilled musically, almost hauntingly, from out of the distance.

I took that as my signal and was about to turn and go, when Virtue did something I was not expecting. She reached over and, without looking at me, she took hold of my hand, lacing her fingers in my own.

My heart flopped like a fish.

We stood like that for a long moment. Just me and her.

And then Virtue turned to me, gazing into my face with her damp blue eyes.

"All right, Rain," she said at last. "Take me away from here."

PART THREE

FLIGHT

TRUMPETS BLARED AND SOMEONE fired off a canon as we mounted our horses and sped away. It was a most impressive display of animosity, shaking me to my bones, and I felt it all directed toward me individually. For I had stolen their angel. A most egregious and unpardonable sin. One that I felt sure would lead to a torturous Old Testament rebuke if we were ever caught up.

We rode north at a full gallop.

Ours was the advantage of a half-mile head start at the top of a hill; theirs was the advantage of many men and fresh horses. As for conviction – that motivator so nebulous and powerful in such cases of righteous determination – we were both parties about the same. They were driven by the justification of the Restructured Truth; we were propelled by our revulsion to the same.

In a questionable move, not necessarily prudent, I decided not to take one of the available guns. A rifle might have been a handy card to have in the gamble we were now undertaking, but it was the principle of such an act that caused me to abandon my good sense. I figured that in the end, I would want it to be as I had agreed back in Independence. That is how I would prefer the story to be retold. Perhaps I was already preparing for my impending martyrdom. It was admittedly a bit late in the journey to be so admirable, but it turns out that even the lowliest beast can rise to scruples when pressed. And maybe, just maybe, some god might look down on me and see this decision as noble, therefore providing us with safe passage. I could only hope. It was, I suppose, a matter of faith.

Brownie, Puck, and Genevieve seemed to understand quite clearly our predicament. They ran fast and hard. I noticed a slight limp in Puck's stride, but he muscled onward and did not let it slow him down.

The plain was wide and barren north of the City of Rocks. The hills flattened out and the expanse stretched before us for miles.

Peering back over my shoulder, I could see the faint cloud of dust rising from the pack of Jack Mormons hounding our trail. I figured there was about twenty of them. Like us, they were running at top speed. For the first hour, the distance between our two groups seemed to be staying about the same. But as the afternoon progressed, I sensed that the intervening space was diminishing. Our horses were doing their best. They were greatly lathered and heaving with labored breaths. One could feel their determination. Still, I figured we had but one desperate chance to pull ahead. And even then I could not make a guarantee.

On and on we dashed.

I had been in this part of the world before, during one of my previous deliveries, and I was hoping now that my memory was correct in regards to its topography. I spied what I believed to be the butte I was looking for, and we angled toward it. We were drawing close to our moment of truth.

One could see a cleft in the landscape up ahead. I knew this to be the Snake River – a wide and powerful band of churning hydrology. My hope was that we would come to the river's edge at a fording place that was right at that teetering point between possible and not. My hope was that we could cross over and survive, but that the place at which we did so would be too intimidating for our chasers to take the risk. I was counting on my memory not to let me down.

"Well," I said, as we came to the river. "At least it is not so wide as I recalled."

We paused on the waterway's high bank.

It was true that the river was narrower here, but it seemed that that very narrowness was what made it such a formidable piece of turbulence. A large volume of water was being constricted into a too narrow channel, and this resulted in a most tumultuous and rollicking width of whitewater. Tall waves raised up and collapsed beneath their own frothy weight. The noise of it was incredible. It did not appear passable.

I peered downstream and up. I glanced back behind. The evening was coming on, the light was growing dim, but I could see that the riders were close now. Not more than a quarter mile away. I quick figured up how much lead we would require to work our way downriver to a better crossing. But the bank was thick with willows and runneled terrain and I knew that this would cost us too many precious minutes. They would surely be on us in no time.

"Virtue," I hollered. "It is not too late. You can go to them if you want. They will not blame you for our attempted escape." I looked at the water. "I can take my own chances."

She looked at me for only the slimmest part of a second, just enough to convey all the insult and incredulity she felt at my suggestion. Then, in a snap, she kicked Genevieve in the ribs, urging the mare to leap into the mighty Snake River.

What could I do but follow?

THE RIVER WAS MORBIDLY cold and it squeezed me like a fist as I sank down into its watery clutches.

We will now drown, I calmly assured myself.

There seemed no way around it.

I saw a flash of Virtue's blond head in front of me. She was there, and then she was not. The waves between us rose and fell away and then rose up again.

I slid from Brownie's back on the downstream side and held onto the saddle horn, swinging and bouncing along his flank while trying to keep myself away from his frantically churning legs. I spied Puck a ways upstream. The trunks on his sawbuck seemed to buoy him up. A wild and determined look shined in his wide open eye.

I went under the water, a roar in my ears.

And then I was up.

Back and forth.

Instinct told me when to hold my breath, but after a while of up and down in the rapids, my timing was thrown off and I gulped a big swallow of water. Right then I went back down under. There was no way to spit out, and there was no way to take a breath. It was a most panicky sensation, ultimately resulting in an inhalation of water into my chest. When my head finally did bob to the surface, I puked up out of my lungs, swallowed a short breath, and became submerged once again. My grip slipped from the saddle and I was free floating in the river, unattached to Brownie. Somehow, even in the throes of it, I knew that all hope was lost if I did not keep hold of my horse. I could never swim out of this raging cataract of my own. I groped wildly in the spume toward Brownie. But nothing.

Nothing.

All is done, I thought. It is finished.

Then my fingers happened into the long hairs of Brownie's tail. I pulled myself toward my horse's rear end, taking hold if his tail in both hands, rolling onto my back, dragging along behind as he kicked through the torrent toward the far bank. I concentrated on opportunities to breathe.

After a time, the ride became almost peaceful. The river itself was no less wild, the waves no less large and cold and threatening, but a complacency overwhelmed me. Time seemed to go away. Nothing at all seemed to matter. I could hold onto Brownie, or just as soon not. It did not seem of much importance one way or the other. What would be so bad about letting oneself go? It was only death. People do it every day. A short struggle, and then it would be finished. Oblivion would be mine. That did not sound so bad.

But then I recalled my promise to Virtue.

There was still a chance that she was not dead.

I held on, doing my best to stay alive.

At last, I felt my heels and buttocks banging along the rocks. The water grew shallow. Brownie heaved his body out of the river, dragging me to where I dropped into a sand-bottomed eddy. I lay there, stunned, choking, floating on my back and looking up into the sky.

I was surprised to be gazing at the moon.

It floated in the rosy evening light.

So lovely!

"Virtue!" I coughed. "Virtue!"

I sloshed and staggered until I found my feet. My legs were not obeying my requests, and I fell twice before I could take command of my body. I knelt on the shore, spewing greenish water onto my knees, taking stock.

Brownie was there in front of me. He was accounted for.

I gazed upstream. Puck was only just now crawling out onto dry ground. He limped up into some willows and turned to look our way.

I turned and glanced along the downstream bank. Virtue was there, half bent over, wringing the water from her dress. She appeared to be in one piece.

I stood and waved to the girl. "Ha!" I called.

She looked at me and waved a hand.

A ways further down the shore, I could see Genevieve standing near a naked poplar tree. Her head was going up and down, and it occurred to me that her reins were tangled in the brush. I moved to go help her out.

"Go to Puck and Brownie," I told Virtue, as I passed. "I will fetch Genevieve."

The rocks were slippery and I was battered from my swim. I stumbled my way to the mare. She stood waiting. She had given up freeing herself on her own, and was waiting for my assistance. I leaned with a hand against the trunk of the poplar. Crunchy leaves littered the ground. Genevieve's reins were all wrapped around a snarl of driftwood that had lodged into the tree's exposed roots.

"Hold on, girl," I soothed. "Whoa. Be still."

I placed my hand on her neck, stroking it reassuringly, and then I squatted down, endeavoring to loosen the knot of leather straps.

"You have a genuine mare's nest here," I joked, trying to calm her nerves.

She was breathing hard, her head held low, her eyes glazed with weariness.

The wet leather had synched up tightly with her struggles and I had quite a time getting them to come apart. My hands were still shaking from the rush of adrenaline that had swept through my body during our swim. I seemed to be cursed with ten thumbs. Finally, the reins were free and I stood next to the horse.

"There we are," I said. "Let us go." I then turned to lead her back to the others.

To my great surprise, the poplar trunk exploded near my head, large chunks of bark spraying along my cheek. I winced and nearly fell. Then, even over the roar of the river, I heard the small pop of a rifle shot. I glared across the river. We had been washed downstream about a half mile from where we started, and our pursuers had finally worked their way down so that they were even to us. They were strung out along the far shore. I could just make out their ghostly shapes working along in the evening light.

One of them was on his knee, a rifle aimed my way. It took me a moment to comprehend the consequences of his posture. I suppose I was still somewhat dazed from my swim. I realized that I was far from Virtue. They would not take a chance at hurting her, but the distance between us at the moment was so great that there was no danger of that happening.

A puff of smoke bloomed from the man's rifle barrel.

He jerked with the repercussion.

And then of a sudden, Genevieve screamed.

Followed directly by the sound of the shot.

The reins jerked out of my hand and the mare's hindquarters dropped to the ground. At once I saw where the bullet had torn through the top of her back, just behind her saddle, severing her spine. Blood and bone chips rained out over the leaves. She staggered, pulling herself forward a few steps with her front legs, but then she pitched over into the river.

It was most horrific to witness.

I bent forward, my hands helplessly reaching toward her.

Her legs were thrashing madly in the shallows, but this only served to move her into the deeper water. At last she was caught in the swifter current. Her head raised far up out of the waves, and then she submerged for good into the black churning water.

I stood there with my mouth hanging open, stunned.

Until another bullet exploded in the rocks at my feet.

I lurched up the bank, scrambling on my hands and knees into the willows.

Yet another bullet tore through the branches past my ear – thwiiiit!

Then many bullets zipped through the willows all around me. It seemed a small army was trying to fill me up with holes. I heard the shots over the roar of the river – Pam! Pam-pam! Pam!

I wiggled like a snake on my belly, squirming over a rise in the embankment and then back down into a shallow dish of earth on the other side. The bullets kept coming, thunking into the sand and rocks in the berm. This shallow channel formed a ditch-like trough and I crawled upstream within its protection. Although the shots continued, I sensed no more bullets were hitting anywhere near me, and I figured they had not seen me make my move and were still shooting at the place I had been. I wondered what Virtue and the horses were up to.

It was foolish to risk showing myself, but I felt a need to see what our enemies were doing. I carefully lifted my head from behind a bunch of grass, just enough to peek through a crack in the willow stalks.

Some of the men were standing knee deep in the river, their horses beside them. They seemed to be testing the waters. The waves rose up menacingly between our side and theirs. If anything, this was a worse place to cross than where we had entered the river ourselves.

"Good!"

The men were hollering to one another, gesturing with their arms, trying to come up with a plan of action. Their shouts sometimes rose up like bird chirps over the rumble of the river. The light was going fast now, and they were but silhouettes. None of them were willing to dare cross the river at this particular point. Some of them were gathering on the high bank. They conferred, and then headed downriver, searching, I assumed, for a gentler ford.

I heard Brownie and Puck's hoof beats somewhere through the brush inland from the river. Then they stopped.

"Rain!" It was Virtue calling. "Rain, are you there?"

"Here!" I called. "Stay there! I will come to you."

Squatting down and bent over, I scampered through the willows and small trees. Soon there was enough brush between me and the river so that I was out of sight of the riflemen. I stood in a narrow clearing. Virtue and the horses stepped out of the trees.

"Are we all of a piece?" I asked.

Virtue nodded, and then looked past me into the willows.

"Genevieve is gone," I said. "I am sorry. She is shot."

All three of my companions were dispirited by this news.

I looked back over my shoulder in the direction of the river. "She was a good friend," I consoled. I turned back to Virtue. "But now we must go."

I quickly knelt in the sand at Puck's feet and inspected his fetlock. It was swollen to twice its normal size, and tender to the touch. I cursed internally, but did not let him know my anguish. I stood and stroked his neck. "It is all right, boy. You will be fine."

I climbed onto Brownie, and then turned to Virtue. "We must double up," I said, and reached a hand down to the girl.

She took hold of my arm and then, with a lift and hop, she swung up onto Brownie's back so that she was astride the saddle behind me. She wrapped her arms around my middle.

"Okeydoke?" I asked.

She gave me a squeeze.

THE MOST DEVOUT HOURS of my life were those spent riding through the primordial blue moonlight with Virtue. We could have been on the moon itself, so otherworldly was that sterile landscape, so preternatural was that velvety night.

Brownie slid into a rhythmic canter, steady and pressing, pressing forward. The gentle rocking of his body lulled me into a trance-like state. We felt to be fairly floating over the earth. Virtue's cheek rested on my shoulder. She held herself tight against me. The air was raw and cold, our clothes still damp from our swim, but a warmth pervaded my being. In spite of our calamitous circumstances, a contentment inundated my soul. Quite inexplicably, I found myself happier than I had ever been.

But then came the dawn.

It was somewhat like being yanked from out a pleasant dream.

Puck was doing poorly. By end of night, Brownie had slowed his own stride to accommodate his partner's lagging pace. I allowed this for a time, but soon it became apparent that Puck was costing us our valuable lead.

"Hold up," I called. "Let us take a short rest."

I let Virtue down from Brownie's back, and then hopped down myself, stepping close to Puck and laying my hand along his sweat-slicked shoulder. Puck stood on three legs, holding his fourth leg bent without weighting it.

"Puck old boy, let me take a look at that sore joint."

I knelt on the frosty ground and examined the horse's leg. It was bad. Twisted and puffed-up. One could only guess what was going on inside that knee bone, but I figured the apparatus was torn pretty bad. With our desperate push we had quite possibly damaged it beyond repair. I bowed my head and rubbed my eyes. I stood.

"Well," I said. "I do not think you need to be carrying a load."

Unstrapping the trunks, I lifted them down from the sawbuck, setting them side-by-side in the dirt. "Virtue, will you please take the minimum of what you need from the trunks, and then roll it up in a blanket that we can easily carry it?"

She moved to do as I bid.

I then removed the empty sawbuck and blanket padding from Puck's back, propping it on a rock, and then I moved to his head. I laid my forehead against his cheek, stroking his neck. I had added up the situation a number of times in the last hour, but it did not make sense that we all should die for the sake of only one of us. And yet, I felt like Mister Iscariot himself for what I was about to do. I removed Puck's halter, pulling it over his ears and tossing it to the side.

"Here is what we are dealt, Puck."

He was still breathing heavily. He was beyond weary. But he held up his head, his spirited and puckish manner revealing itself to the end.

"You are not fit to run with us, and run we must. We will leave you here for now, unburdened, in the manner of a wild horse who is free to roam." I bit my lip. I squinted into the distance from where we had come. It was very small, barely more than the thinnest black line on the horizon, but I could see the band of our pursuing riders. They were some miles behind, but had not given up on our trail.

"I do not think they will pay you any attention. They are after us, not you. And so I suggest that you work your way west." I pointed in that direction. "There are some pleasant valleys yonder, grassy and with clear streams running down out of the mountains. It is a veritable paradise for horses. Perhaps you will meet up with some kindly Indians who will take you in with their own. At any rate, a new life awaits."

I was having a hard time keeping the cheery tenor in my voice, as my throat was constricting with emotion.

"You... Puck, you have been a noble friend. I could not have asked for better. You should be proud of what you have accomplished."

I patted him on the nose, but said nothing more. It seemed best that way. I walked away and climbed up onto Brownie's back, taking the rolled blanket from Virtue and slinging it across my lap so that it hung over both sides of the saddle.

Virtue went to Puck. She took his neck in her arms and whispered into his ear. She held him like that for a long moment. The horse seemed to grow calm with her attentions. And then she came and climbed up behind me.

Brownie whinnied farewell to his good friend.

Then we rode away.

Simple as that.

I could feel Puck's eyes watching us as we galloped over the rise. It was not pleasant.

After some time, Brownie's ears pricked up. Then, very small, almost inaudibly, I heard a rifle's report carrying through the crisp morning air.

One assumed they had shot Puck dead.

BUT FOR HIS LACK of wings, Brownie was an out-and-out Pegasus.

I had never known an animal to have such charisma and stamina, such vigor and grit. Without Puck to slow us down, Brownie was able to run at his top traveling speed. The Mormon hounds on our heels must have been quite confounded. How could a horse burdened with two riders maintain such a momentum? They could not close the gap. Surely Brownie was something special – an agent of the gods if ever there was one.

We continued by our northward route.

Virtue held tight to my waist.

On through another moonlit night, and into another day.

We entered up a long drainage into the mountains. Pines clung to the shaded sides of the hills, the slopes becoming evermore forested the farther we traveled, and higher. The air grew rancorous cold. Clouds began to build over the highlands, dark and foreboding. A harsh breeze gusted over the ridgelines.

Westron Wynde, when wilt thou blow...

It elicited ice tears from my eyeballs.

I snugged my elk skin robe up tight around my throat, and hunched myself up against the cold. It felt good to have Virtue hugging me tight.

Although Brownie was tough, I was less so. Some sleep would have been nice, and some food, but there was no way to have any of either while riding, and no leisure to stop for a rest. A few snowflakes began to spit out of the roiling sky. For the first time since we began our journey, I found myself praying for an all out snowstorm. Only something so desperate as an icy tempest could intimidate our pursuers. It would offer us a new challenge, but we needed the snow to cover our tracks.

At last we came to the high pass I had been searching for.

I gazed back down the valley behind us, but could not see the riders. Still, I knew they were there. Somewhere coming through the trees up that undulating basin, following our trail, sniffing us out like prey. Virtue was too important for them to give up on their chase just yet.

In the other direction – north – lay a wide valley. A thin river wound through the dead brown grass. On the western side of this valley, rising above the forests, stood a jagged range of mountains. They appeared almost gothic in character, so cathedral-like were their spires and tracery, so cloistered their innermost sanctums. It looked to be some sort of primitive kingdom. Independent and aloof. The tops of the peaks snagged and tore like goat horns at the blue-black bellies of the clouds.

"Just a ways more," I told my friends, and placed my hand over Virtue's where it was pressed against my belly. "These are the Sawtooth Mountains."

WE RACED ACROSS THE valley and climbed above tree line, entering into those ragged heights.

Clouds descended around us like curtains.

Snow began to fall.

Good, I thought. They cannot see us now.

Our tracks were covering almost as soon as we lifted our feet.

Abandon all hope ye who enter here.

The place was severe and forbidding – a world apart – one made of naught but stone and snow and air.

They will not dare to follow.

We seemed to be traveling within the protection of a large closed room, one made up of white walls and a ceiling. We continued on, more or less blindly, following some invisible path into the heart of this most austere wilderness. We rode Brownie for a ways more, but the terrain became too treacherous, even for such a docile beast, and Virtue and I dropped from his back and walked of our own power. Brownie did his best to stay with us.

The granite boulders were heaped up, in some places as large as small houses, and we picked and wound our way through the labyrinth. The sloping rocks were slick with the snow. We carefully scrambled over the boulders, oftentimes using our hands. But Brownie was an animal built for the open plains. It was hard for him to find good footing. When we came to a steep wall of stone, it became apparent that this was the end of his journey. I led him to the side as, once again, I prepared to say goodbye to one of the best friends I had ever known.

"Well, boy." I brushed the ice crystals from his mane, and removed his bridle. "You have certainly done your part in this endeavor." I removed his saddle and the rolled up the blanket containing Virtue's kit. I rubbed my hands all over his steaming back, wiping it clean of the wet snow. Of course, the falling snow began to cover his backside once again. I laid my hand on his neck and looked into his brown eye. There were snowflakes on his lashes. My own reflection was there, all abulge and shrouded in white.

"You have friends here," I told him, and gestured to the space all around us. "Do you see them?"

Since we had arrived, we had been watched by the silent white goats who lived in these mountains. Their coal black horns and eyes floated before us in the ghostly fog. One could hear their breath on the still air.

"I am sure they will take care of you."

I could not think what was left to say.

There seemed so much to say, and nothing.

Brownie nuzzled my arm with his nose. He seemed content.

"Anyway, friend," I said at last. "Have a good rest." I grinned and patted his neck. "Who can say? Perhaps we will meet again in paradise."

I slung the blanket roll over my shoulder and stepped away, leaving Virtue to make her own goodbyes.

When she was finished, Virtue and I climbed up the wall and continued on.

ON AND ON WE walked, somnolently, as if through a long entrance to a dream.

Virtue led the way.

She floated like a shadow before me.

Our footfalls became muffled as we shuffled along in the deepening snow.

One sensed the stony steeples teetering in the clouds above us; bluebirds perched like angels on their tippy-top points.

I found my thoughts drifting off and away to all the languages of the world, and to all the truths. I wondered about all the people in America – both the young and the old – the Mormons and gentiles and the Indians, too – with all of their thirsts and hungers. Then I imagined every poem ever written and joined end on end to make one eternal and joyous elegy for all the creatures through all the ages. I almost believed I could feel that poem living inside of me now. Like Delight's cooing voice. Like Turtle Dove's song. Like the Prophet's dreams. Like the Word of Words.

These were nonsense thoughts, to be sure.

Fluttering butterflies.

Wild flowers.

Shooting stars.

All but impossible to gather.

Gather ye rosebuds while ye may…

But such were my weary musings.

Until at last we reached a tiny stream.

❦

I knew this stream. From somewhere. In a sweeter time. I had been here before; of this I was certain. This was the stream that fed all the others. Surely this was the source of the seas.

It tumbled over the boulders, threading a wet black vein along its icy ripples. Pillows of snow mounded along its banks. Yellow and purple flowers slept there beneath their blanket of cold, waiting for the brief mountain springtide.

Virtue took me up this stream, delivering me to the pool.

"Here we are," she said.

"Yes."

The little pond was wide and calm and hemmed with snow-covered boulders. Snowflakes the size of small birds slanted into its black surface.

Virtue lifted the blanket roll from my shoulder and brushed it free of snow. She smiled at me. "I will go over there now," she said, lifting her chin. "You wait here."

I nodded dumbly, only half comprehending her words.

She stepped away into the fog.

I tipped my face to the sky. Snowflakes washed my cheeks. They dashed against my chest.

The world itself is the poem, I thought. And we are but its couplets.

I stood like that for a time, in something resembling an attitude of prayer.

"How do I look?" asked Virtue.

When I lowered my gaze, I was greatly pleased to see Virtue standing before me. The snowflakes bejeweled her blond hair. Her blue eyes flashed with happiness. She wore the wedding dress – as pure and white as the surrounding snow.

"You are truly beautiful."

This pleased her. She bowed her head shyly, holding an arm out to the side and admiring its fabric and cut.

I thought of my mother, of her gentle ways.

But then Virtue turned solemn, and gazed once more into my face. "What will you do?" she asked.

"Oh," I answered. "I do not rightly know." I looked at my hands. "But I have heard it said that the islands of the southern seas are a nice corner of the earth to visit. They are rumored to speak a language down there, one made up entirely of soft sounds." I considered this. "Perhaps I will find passage on a boat, and work my way across the ocean." I nodded at this idea, and sheepishly grinned. "It is surely a boyish notion," I said, "and probably not reasonable in this terrestrial sphere, but a land without the hard edge of consonants seems to me like a veritable paradise."

She smiled at my innocence. And then she stepped forward. She took my hand, placing a small stone in my palm, and then closing my fingers over its smoothness. She laid her fingers on my chest, over my tattoo. "Thank you, Rain," she said, "for delivering me."

A sizeable knot had formed in my throat right then, and I could but nod.

And then she turned away.

She walked to the edge of the pool.

She stepped into the water.

She waded out into its middle.

While I watched without moving.

She sank away into the black water, her white dress fading into the depths, a ring of ripples spreading out and then melting away.

The falling snow ticked and hissed as it crashed down to the earth like so many falling stars.

There was no other sound but my own breath, and my thumping heart.

I stood there, full of longing, watching for some sign of her to return. But it was no good. Such angels do not show themselves to us every day. Such miracles are too often hidden beneath the surface of our banal existence. I knew this to be true from my own experiences. On this earthly journey, such would have to suffice as my truth.

I stepped to the edge of the pool, crouching at its bank, and dipped my empty hand into the water like a cup.

I drank of that water.

No wine compared to its sweetness.

No kiss.

I stood, peering down at the blue teardrop stone in my hand, turning it over in my fingers. I tossed it out over the water – Plunk!

And then, before that little stone ever reached bottom, I turned away, heading in the direction I felt to be west.

I walked and walked.

Alone.

And as I dropped down out of the mountains,
the snow
turned into
rain.

Other titles by Brian Kindall:

Magical Middle-Grade Fiction:

BLUE SKY
PEARL

DELIVERING VIRTUE, BLUE SKY, and PEARL are available in ebook
format at major online retailers.

For further reading visit www.briankindall.com where you will find
resource materials for each book and Brian Kindall's Author Blog.

We ask you to please share your thoughts and opinion of DELIVERING
VIRTUE with other readers by writing a review at your favorite
retailer.

Thank you for reading!

CPSIA information can be obtained at www.ICGtesting.com
Printed in the USA
LVOW07s2235070916

503668LV00005B/261/P

9 780990 932864